THE NEXUS LETTERS

‘You have her well trained, Nick,’ George said to me, ‘but how does she respond to punishment? I’d imagine her skin colours beautifully.’

‘Why don’t you find out?’ I replied, knowing how humiliating it must be for Sara to be discussed as though she was not in the room.

‘I’d love to,’ George said, unbuckling his belt and removing it from the loops in his trousers. Coiling the buckle end around his hand, he flexed the thick leather thoughtfully as he looked at Sara.

‘Open your legs wider, slut,’ he ordered, and she did as she was told without flinching, though she must have been aware that we were now presented with a breathtaking view. The next thing I heard was a whistling as the belt flew through the air, to land with a loud crack across the cheeks of her bum. Sara yelped, but held her position, and George smiled at me, acknowledging that I had taught her well.

A NEXUS CLASSIC

THE NEXUS LETTERS

True Confessions of Bizarre Sex

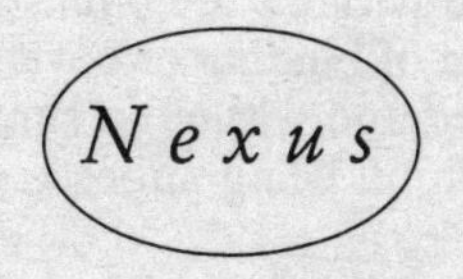

This book is a work of fiction.
In real life, make sure you practise safe, sane and consensual sex.

This Nexus Classic edition 2005

First published in 2001 by
Nexus
Thames Wharf Studios
Rainville Road
London W6 9HA

www.nexus-books.co.uk

Typeset by TW Typesetting, Plymouth, Devon

Printed and bound by Clays Ltd, St Ives PLC

ISBN 0 352 33955 1

CONTENTS

The Ties that Bind

TIGHT FIT

When my boyfriend Carl and I went on holiday to Amsterdam, we used it as the opportunity to act out one of my long-standing fantasies. On our first night there, we headed straight for the red-light district and found a sex shop which had the biggest range of toys and accessories either of us had ever seen. We knew exactly what we wanted to buy: fur-lined wrist and ankle cuffs, and a dildo of almost freakish proportions. It was black, a good twelve inches long and as thick round as my forearm. My fantasy has always been to be tied up and forced to take an object of this size inside me, and tonight we were going to make that fantasy come true.

Back in our hotel room, Carl stripped the covers off the bed, then encouraged me to lie down beside him. We spent a long time kissing and gradually taking off each other's clothes. Soon, Carl was paying attention to my tits, licking and sucking my little brown nipples, while his hand explored the folds of my pussy. I was going to have to be very wet and ready to take that monster dildo, and Carl knows the best way to achieve that. He laid me back on the bed and moved so that his head was between my legs. For the next half an hour he concentrated on exciting me with his lips and tongue, until my cunt was dripping. Then he went to fetch the cuffs, quickly securing me to the bed, spread out like a star. I knew now that I would not be able to back out, and that soon I was going to be feeling that dildo inside me.

Carl began to work on me with his fingers. I was already so wet that he could slide two fingers into me without any difficulty, and he quickly added a third and then a fourth, while his thumb gently teased the entrance to my arse. In that moment, I knew that if he wanted to, he could get his hand inside me to the knuckles, and the thought turned me on even more.

Soon I was begging him to use the dildo on me, and he took it out of its box and presented it to my lips for me to suck. I could barely get my lips round the end, and so I used my tongue to lave its length, my saliva soon glistening on the black plastic.

At last, Carl pulled the dildo away from my mouth and pressed it to the opening of my cunt. As he pushed, I began to fear that this thing was just too big for me to take, and that it would split me in two if I tried. But then my pussy parted wide enough to allow the end to slip inside me, and I realised my fantasy had finally started to come true.

I can't tell you how long it took for Carl to slide that obscenely fat sex toy into me. I could feel my sex lips being stretched painfully wide as inch after inch of the dildo pushed the walls of my cunt apart, but the pain was tempered with a perverse pleasure at being able to accommodate something of such outrageous proportions. At last the tip of the dildo nudged against the neck of my womb, and I knew that my vagina was completely stuffed with rigid, unforgiving plastic. No man had ever filled me so full, and I could see a look of admiration and lust on

Carl's face, coupled with the humiliating knowledge that he could not satisfy me in the way this dildo could. He had secured me so I was facing the bedroom mirror, and I looked at my reflection, with my pussy full to bursting point, the lips taut and shiny around the dildo.

Slowly, he began to ease the phallus in and out of me. Secured as I was, I could do nothing to prevent the speed or intensity of his movements, and I knew that when I had an orgasm, it would be on his terms. It was almost as though he was punishing me for wanting that huge, fake cock inside me – a cock that was so much bigger than his own.

I moaned and gasped as he tormented me with the dildo, begging him to let me come. It was hot in that little bedroom, and I could feel sweat trickling down between my breasts as I writhed in my bonds, trying to get him to stimulate me in the ways that would bring on my climax.

At last, he reached down and ran his fingernail lightly over my clit. My nerve-endings were so sensitised, that was all it took, and my body exploded in orgasm, bucking and shuddering on the bed.

Carl withdrew the dildo from my aching pussy, and presented it to my lips, making me lick it clean of my juices. I was sore and exhausted, but I felt utterly satisfied. Perhaps one day I will get the chance to use that huge dildo on Carl!

Julie R.,
York

BIRTHDAY BONDAGE

When my husband asked me what I wanted for my birthday, I think my answer came as a surprise. Instead of asking for a piece of jewellery or a new dress, I told him that I wanted to be tied up and fucked by several men. More than that, I didn't want to know who was actually fucking me: they could be friends, they could be strangers, but I wanted to be blindfolded throughout the whole event, so that I could experience the sensation of being pleasured by an unknown number of anonymous bodies.

David agreed to this, as we have often invited other men to have sex with us, and he loves to watch me writhing on a big cock, or sucking another man's dick while he ploughs my cunt from behind. I could also see that the idea of me being restrained while I was fucked was something of a turn-on to him, and I was really looking forward to my birthday treat.

Come the day itself, David and I shared a bottle of wine, and then he led me upstairs to the bedroom. I stripped down to my stockings and suspenders, and then he used fur-lined cuffs to fasten my wrists and ankles to the bed, spreading me out so I was open and vulnerable. Then he took a black silk scarf and tied it securely over my eyes, blocking out the light. The next thing I heard was his footsteps leaving the room.

I don't know how long I lay there, wondering what was about to happen; with the blindfold in place, it was impossible to keep track of time. The anticipation was making me wet, my pussy gently pulsing and moistening as I waited. Then I heard footsteps on the stairs, and I strained my ears to see if I could make out how many men might be coming to join me.

Suddenly, I felt hands caressing my tits, gently at first, but then squeezing with more pressure, turning my nipples into two hard peaks. The hands were replaced by a mouth; I felt a rasp of stubble as teeth nipped at the tender buds, and realised this was not my clean-shaven David. My excitement grew as a hand snaked between my legs. Was this the same man, or someone else entirely? I had no way of knowing. Perhaps David wasn't even in the room, though I thought this unlikely as he wouid want to watch every moment of what was being done to me.

A cock was presented to my lips, and I began to suck on it, recognising the clean, salty tang of my husband's dick. As my tongue flicked over the bulbous head, the hand between my thighs probed more deeply, fingers parting my cunt lips and thrusting without ceremony deep into my wet sheath. David groaned and came deep in the back of my throat. As he withdrew his wilting cock, it was replaced by another. A mouth was still busy sucking my tits, three fingers were pumping in and out of my sex and now I was beginning to get confused.

The fingers were pulled from my cunt and now they were playing with my arsehole. I groaned around the cock that filled my mouth as a finger slipped into my tight anal passage. I writhed in my bonds, my body being overwhelmed by the sensations that were rushing through me. When a mouth settled on my clit and began to nibble it gently, I shrieked and came, thrusting my mound up towards the unknown lips that were giving me so much pleasure.

For the next couple of hours, it seemed as though my body was constantly at the mercy of hands, mouths and cocks. I was fucked so many times I lost count, and when I was not sucking a hard cock, I was being urged to lick a limp one back to full erection. One of the men David had found had the biggest cock I've ever encountered, and though I never actually got to see it, I had the sheer joy of this monster stretching my cunt to its absolute limit. At one point, I had someone squatting over me, wanking his cock between my big, firm tits. When he came, his spunk splattered over my face and hair, dribbling down into my mouth.

By the time the men were finally satisfied, my cunt was swollen and sore, and I was so full of come it was oozing out of me and down the crack of my arse on to the bedsheets. Spunk matted my hair to my cheeks where I had thrashed against the pillows in my excitement, and I was sure the fingers that had groped my tits had left bruises on my flesh. I had loved every moment of it, and I still had no idea exactly how many men had fucked me. David has kept silent on that point, and I hope he continues to do so. I look at all his friends speculatively now, wondering if I have sucked their cocks, or taken them deep inside my pussy, and the thought that I may well have done brings all the excitement of that unforgettable evening flooding back.

Fern L.,
Halifax

A QUESTION OF TRUST

'Do you trust me?' he asked. It was a strange question, given that I had already allowed him to strip me naked and chain my arms together over my head, but there was only one answer I could give. I trusted him utterly and without question. In the few short months we had been together, I had trusted him to gradually enslave me, to take me down the path towards complete submission and to push me past limits I had sworn I would never go beyond. I had learnt to come while I was being beaten, taking pleasure in the pain he inflicted on me and begging for more, and I wore silver rings through both my nipples and my clitoral hood, rings which had been placed there at his desire. I had already been hanging in my chains for the best part of an hour while he had paddled my arse and the backs of my thighs until they were red and sore, and I was willing to suffer whatever indignities he might wish to inflict on me.

Yet even though I trusted him implicitly not to hurt me, I could not hide a shiver of fear as he drew out the item he had been hiding from behind his back. It was a hunting knife, which he drew from its leather case, its blade gleaming in the half-light of this little stone-walled room. No doubt he had picked it up on one of his business trips to the States, which was where he found many of the little toys and implements he had used on me in his dungeon.

He touched the edge of the blade to his finger, as though testing its sharpness. This would be the ultimate test of my trust and love for him, and as he pressed the flat of the knife against the flesh of my breasts, I flinched away from him.

'Relax,' he told me. 'It's nothing to be afraid of, little one.' Gently, he played the blade over my breasts and down my flat stomach, moving closer to my pussy. I was breathing shallowly, my breasts heaving and sweat glistening on my tautly stretched body. I had to believe that he would not hurt me, and I did my best to stay completely still as the tip of the blade moved between my swollen pussy lips, to catch in the ring that protruded from my labia. He tugged firmly, the pressure as the ring pulled at that delicate nub of flesh agonisingly sweet. He had not allowed me to come yet; every time I had come close to the moment of crisis, he had pulled back, and now I was desperate for relief, having been denied it so often. As he pressed the flat of the cold blade against my overheating sex flesh, I begged him to let me come.

I wanted him inside me as the knife played over my skin. I wanted him to mark me with the blade, so that everyone would see it and know that I was his. At this moment, I would do anything for him, and let him do anything to me. He moved the knife up so that it was resting against my throat. I swallowed hard but my fear had gone, and I trusted him to bring me only pleasure.

As though sensing I had passed the test, he thrust the knife back into its sheath and let it fall to the floor. The next thing I felt was his hard cock sliding into my wet cunt, claiming me as his. As I hung there, my toes making the barest contact with the floor, he thrust up into me hard, the pressure of his pubic bone against mine stimulating my sensitised clit. This time I had his permission to come, and I did, calling his name and screaming out how much I loved him. Of course I trust him; no one else understands me like him, and no one else would ever be allowed to do the things to me that he does.

Abigail M.,
London

WAXING CLEVER

There is nothing finer than taking someone who loves and trusts you, and pushing them to the absolute limit of what they will do for you. I am happy to say that in Callum, I have found someone who will obey me utterly, and loves nothing better than to kneel at my feet, his hands bound behind his back, worshipping me in whatever way I desire.

Callum enjoys being subservient to me, but he does not like pain, and I recently decided to have some fun with him, to see just how much he would be willing to accept. I secured him to the bed with lengths of bondage tape, making sure that his movements were severely restricted, then I used my fingers, greased up with a little massage oil perfumed with jasmine and ylang ylang, to bring his cock to full erection. I do love his cock – it may only be a little over five inches long, but it is satisfyingly thick and can stay hard for hours on end – and there is nothing nicer than to pull the velvet sheath of his foreskin back and forth over the head until the whole length points skyward. When I was satisfied that he was as hard as possible, I went to fetch the little treats I had in store for him.

Often, I will blindfold him before I begin to torment his bound body, but today I wanted him to see exactly what was about to happen. His eyes widened in fear at the sight of the first toy I brandished in front of him. It was a bunch of nettles, which I had picked from the wood at the bottom of our garden only half an hour earlier. I waved them in my leather-gloved hand as he moaned and begged me not to use them on him. I smiled ruthlessly.

'It's nice to appreciate the benefits of nature,' I told him. 'Just relax . . .'

As I spoke, I brushed the nettles lightly over his nipples. Immediately, his pale, freckly Celtic skin began to flush a mottled red, and the little hairs around his areolae stood up stiffly.

'Please, no more, Mistress,' he whimpered.

'But we've only just started,' I told him, and brushed the nettles over the wet head of his cock, so lightly that at first it barely registered with him. Then he must have felt the stinging pain, and he groaned. When I took the dark green leaves more tightly in my gloved fist and wrapped them around the veiny shaft of his penis, rubbing them up and down, his eyes rolled in his head and his manhood jerked so convulsively that I thought he was about to come then and there.

'It stings . . .' he complained, almost choking on the words.

'Yes, but you love it, don't you?' I said. 'Or at least, your cock does.'

I gestured towards his twitching member. Despite the apparent discomfort he was in, his erection had not wavered in strength; if anything, it was even harder than when I had begun to torment it. But how would it react when I turned to stage two of my wicked little plan?

When I tossed the nettles casually into the waste paper basket, Callum breathed a little sigh of relief. It was short-lived, as he watched me take the candle I had also brought with me. Striking a match, I lit it and let it burn for a moment, until a little pool of wax had begun to form around the wick.

Callum, realising exactly what I had in mind, went crazy. He began to shake in his bonds, knowing he was powerless to free himself but seeming almost desperate to do so. There is a little word that is kept secret between the two of us, which he can use at any time to call a halt to proceedings, and I waited for him to utter it. As I might have known he would, however, he remained silent.

I bent over him, giving him a good view down my top to where my big breasts nestled in my bra. He licked his lips at the sight of the creamy globes, pressed together to form a deep, inviting cleavage.

'If you're still erect by the time I've finished, you can fuck them,' I told him. I know he loves nothing better than to come between my tits, and it seemed a suitable reward for what he was about to undergo.

He nodded his assent, his eyes torn between the glimpses he was getting of my tits and the sight of the candle flame flickering on the bedside cabinet. When I reached for the candle, he groaned and his cock twitched again. I held it over his chest, a good distance away, and tilted it towards him. A fat drop of wax formed at its tip, then dropped on to his skin. He let out a little yelp as the wax rapidly cooled and hardened. I scraped the blob away, intrigued; beneath it, his skin was reddened, but not burnt.

Satisfied with my handiwork, I let another drop fall, this time on to his nipple, and he gave a little shriek.

'You really are a little wimp, aren't you?' I said. 'If you're squealing like a girl when it touches your nipples, what are you going to do when it touches this –'

With that, I let a couple of blobs of molten wax land on the shaft of his cock in quick succession.

'Please, Mistress, no more,' Callum begged, but he was still fully erect and seemed to be riding the sudden flashes of pain.

When I had tied him up, I had made sure that his spread legs were bent at the knees. In this position, I had access to his arsehole, as well as his cock, and as he gibbered and pleaded with me to show some mercy, I let a trail of wax dribble down the sensitive skin of his perineum, all the way down to the puckered entrance to his arse. Tears had formed in his eyes and he was biting his lip, but he had still not said our code word.

At last, I decided he had had enough. I picked off the hardened wax from the shaft of his penis with my fingernails, and scraped it away from where it had matted his pubes, then I pulled off my top and unfastened my bra, letting my tits fall free. They are so big that I can actually lift them to my mouth and lick my nipples, which I did while he watched avidly.

As I bent over him, unfastening the tape which bound his wrists and ankles to the bed, he raised his head, trying to take one of my nipples between his lips, but I slapped him away.

'Don't be greedy,' I told him, even though my cunt was getting damp at the thought of Callum's mouth suckling me. I moved down the bed and pushed my breasts together around his straining erection, urging him to thrust his hips upward. I lowered my head, so that as the tip of his cock emerged from the valley of my cleavage, I could give it a little lick, like it was a warm, salty lollipop. It only took a few strokes before Callum groaned and announced that he was coming. I opened my mouth wide and took every drop of his salty seed down my throat with relish.

It proves you don't need to spend a fortune on expensive equipment to keep a submissive in line; all you need is some imagination and, if you're feeling particularly kind, some dock leaves to soothe away the sting.

Renee G.,
Manchester

ANAL INTRUDER

My boyfriend Roy and I love role-playing games, particularly ones which enable us to indulge our joint passion for bondage. One of our favourites is when he pretends to be a burglar who breaks into our flat, and I am the woman who discovers him going through my possessions, looking for something to steal.

When I see what he is doing, I threaten to call the police, but Roy quickly moves to overpower me. I put up a mock struggle, but he is a big bloke who works out in the gym on a regular basis, so he is much too strong for me. He pushes me down on to one of our wooden-backed dining chairs, and uses one of my stockings to tie my hands together behind me. To make sure I am securely fastened and cannot move to raise the alarm, he uses more stockings to tie my legs to the legs of the chair. When we play this game, I am usually wearing nothing more than a semi-transparent nightie, which shows the dark points of my nipples and my pubic bush through the thin fabric. Roy will also push the nightie up round my waist when he ties me in place and, with my legs spread apart, this means my wispy blonde pussy is on display. Of course, I am protesting about the intrusion, and he tells me that if I don't shut up, it will be the worse for me. As he speaks, he runs his hand over the swell of my breasts and down between my legs. I can't stop myself from moaning, and he laughs, telling me I'm just a wanton little slut who deserves everything she is going to get. Roy really looks the part, with his shaven head and big, bulging muscles, and I'm frightened and excited by the situation, even though I know he would never seriously lay a finger on me.

I carry on making a noise, telling him he can't treat me this way, and that if I scream loudly enough, someone in one of the neighbouring flats will hear me and come to investigate. He says he has the solution to this, and uses a handkerchief which he pulls from his pocket to gag me. Being treated in this way is really making my juices flow, and I want to move on to the next part of the game, which is where the 'burglar' decides to fuck me before making his exit, but I am at Roy's mercy. He can string proceedings out for ages if he wants to; often, he will spend a long time playing with my nipples and exposed quim, until I am panting through my makeshift gag and desperate for him to enter me with his big, hard cock. On one occasion, he actually ripped my nightie right down the front before mauling my naked tits with his leather-gloved hands, and this display of casual strength nearly had me coming before he had even touched my pussy.

At last, he announces that it is time for him to go, but before he does, he wants to leave me something to remember him by. He unties me from the chair, but as I vainly try to rub the life back into my aching wrists, he shoves me down on to the settee, and, with his knee in the small of my back to keep me in place, he ties my wrists behind me once more.

He warns me to stay where I am and not look round as he takes something down from the mantelpiece. I hear the sound of his zip coming down, and then a soft, squelching sound. Not caring that I am disobeying his orders, I turn my head and see that he is stropping his erection with liberal amounts of my honeysuckle-scented hand cream. As my cunt is running like a river from the stimulation I have already received, I know I do not need any more lubrication if he is going to enter me there, and realise he has another target in mind. That realisation is confirmed when he roughly kicks my legs apart and starts smearing more of the hand cream into my anal hole. I start to protest again, telling him that no one has ever had me there and that I don't want him to be the first. Of course, he ignores me, and the next thing I feel is the head of his cock nudging at my greased anus. Relaxing my ring, I give up any resistance – after all, I have been looking forward to this moment since we first started – and let him slowly ease his way into my tightest passage. The excitement the game has created in both of us means that our fuck is fast and frantic, and soon he is pulling out of my arse to spray his hot come over its upturned cheeks.

A couple of weeks ago, Roy started a new job as a security guard. His uniform has given us the opportunity to play some games where I am the one who is on the wrong side of the law, but that is a story for another time.

Julia K.,
Bradford

Spanking Good Times

A SACKABLE OFFENCE

When my new secretary started work, I knew she was going to be trouble. Karen was in her late teens, with long, blonde hair, a curvy body and long, slim legs. She was an immediate hit with the blokes in the office. Not that I was jealous, but she spent more time on flirting with them by the coffee machine than she did typing up my correspondence or filing paperwork. That was annoying in itself, but I also had the feeling she was doing some petty pilfering, too. No money ever went missing, just little things like staplers and scissors. I was certain she was taking them, as the problem coincided with her joining the firm, but I had no way of proving it. So I decided to set a trap for her.

One lunchtime, I made a great show of leaving some books of luncheon vouchers on my desk, which were supposed to be handed round with the pay slips, then I slipped my coat on and told Karen I was popping out for five minutes to get a sandwich. But I didn't leave the office. Instead, I waited round the corner, counted to thirty, and walked back into my office just in time to see Karen slipping the vouchers into her handbag.

Even though she knew she had been caught red-handed, she still tried to brazen her way out of the situation.

'You think you're so clever, don't you?' she said cockily. 'Well, it's your word against mine.'

'But I know who's more likely to be believed,' I replied.

'So what are you going to do – fire me?' she asked, knowing I would be completely within my rights to do so.

I shook my head. 'I want to teach you a lesson. You don't seem to have learnt that stealing is wrong, and I am going to make up for that gap in your education. And the only way I can do that is by punishing you.'

'You must be joking,' she said, but something of the cockiness had gone from her voice.

I picked up the thick, clear plastic ruler that was lying on my desk. 'I've never been more serious,' I told her. 'Now, bend over the desk.'

She stared at me, open-mouthed. 'Of course, I could always call the security guard and have you escorted from the building,' I told her.

Perhaps realising she had no other option, she turned and bent over as I had asked, gripping the edge of the desk with suddenly shaking fingers.

'Spread your legs,' I told her, and again she obeyed.

Revelling in the sudden rush of power I felt, I went to stand behind her, and caught hold of the hem of her short, black skirt. 'Hey, what are you doing?' she protested, as I rucked the skirt up around her waist. Beneath it, she wore a pair of plain white cotton knickers that stretched tautly across her round bum cheeks. It was a tempting target, and I knew I was going to give it something it had deserved for a long time.

I measured my swing, giving the ruler a little tap against her backside, and then I let fly. The ruler landed with a satisfying slap across her bum, and she yelped in anguish and stood up, rubbing the tender spot. 'Get back in place,' I told her, 'or I'll double your punishment.'

I laid half a dozen stinging blows on her bum in rapid succession. She was making small moaning noises, but she didn't try to rise from her bent-over position again. When I stopped, she must have thought that was it. She didn't realise that I had only just started.

I hooked my fingers in the waistband of her knickers and began to pull them down. She started to protest, but I think she was beginning to realise just who had the power in this situation, and so she stood meekly and let me tug her knickers down until they were around her knees. I could see the results of my handiwork so far; her bum was mottled red, and as I brushed my palm over it lightly I could feel the heat rising from what must have been sore flesh.

'We'll finish with a few without your panties,' I told her. 'Just to make sure you've really learnt your lesson.'

Karen whimpered in fear, but I was enjoying myself now. This time, the ruler landed on bare flesh, and I could see the red line which sprang up as a result. I knew it would form into a thick, solid weal which would make sitting down difficult for a day or so, and I rapidly followed it with a second and a third. In all, I put six stripes on her bum, by which time she was crying openly, her hair sticking to her cheeks and her previous cocky composure completely shattered.

Finally, I allowed her to pull up her knickers, rearrange her clothing and get out of the office. That night, I lay in bed, fingering myself to a powerful orgasm as I replayed Karen's punishment in my head. I'd half expected to find a letter of resignation on my desk the following morning. It wasn't, although the episode was never referred to again. When she did move on, however, I made sure to give her a reference which was as glowing as her backside had once been.

Rita J.,
Colchester

SPECIAL CONDITIONS

I have been looking for somewhere to rent, having recently split up from my boyfriend, but it has been hard to find something to suit my limited means. When I saw a postcard in the local newsagent's window advertising a room to rent at a price that seemed almost ridiculously cheap, I rang to make an appointment to view it, though I expected the room to have gone already. Instead, I was told by the flat's owner, Marcus, that there were special conditions attached to the rental of the room, which was why there had, as yet, been no takers. I asked what these conditions were, and he said he couldn't tell me over the phone. Intrigued, I made an appointment to view the flat the following evening after work.

The place, when I saw it, was beautiful. A lot of men can be very untidy – in fact, one of the reasons why my boyfriend and I went our separate ways was because I was sick of always having to clear up after him – but Marcus was incredibly neat. All his books and CDs were filed in alphabetical order, the pot plants on his balcony looked healthy and well cared for and the kitchen and bathroom were spotless. The spare room was not particularly big, and it only had a single bed, but I was not planning to have any male company for a while. I told Marcus it was just what I was looking for, and then I asked him what the 'special conditions' he had mentioned were.

To my utter surprise, he told me that he had been at public school, and had learnt there the values of neatness and order. He had been a prefect and, as such, he had been responsible for keeping discipline. At his school, untidiness had been a grave offence, and one which was punishable with a caning. Anyone who rented out his spare room would have to keep the place clean and neat, or suffer the consequences – by which he meant that they would have to agree to be caned by him.

I told him I didn't think that sounded too bad, at which he asked me whether I had ever been caned. I told him I had gone to an ordinary comprehensive, where the worst punishment anyone ever got was an hour's detention after school. He then said that a caning was not something to be taken lightly, and suggested that I experience one for myself, then and there. At this point, I suppose, the sensible thing would have been to have backed out and find another place to rent; this, I assume, is what had happened with the other people who had come to view the place. However, I had really fallen in love with that flat, the rent was a steal and after all, I told myself, corporal punishment could not be that bad, could it? Add to that the fact I found Marcus, with his floppy fair hair and almost hypnotic charm, rather attractive, and I had all the reasons I needed to comply with his bizarre desires.

I told Marcus that I accepted his somewhat unorthodox terms, and he told me to prepare myself while he went to fetch the cane. I was to remove my skirt, then bend over the big, leather armchair that dominated the flat's living room. When I baulked at the first part of this, he explained that the punishment was to consist of three strokes of the cane with my panties on, and three with them off, and that if I objected, I was free to leave at any time. Determined to see things through, I reached for the zip of my skirt, and let it fall to the floor.

When Marcus came back into the room, I was in the position he had specified. As I looked over at him, I saw he was carrying a stout, crook-handled cane – the type I have always thought of as a 'school' cane. 'Very nice,' he said, and I realised he was referring to the sight of my plump bottom in its navy-blue cotton knickers. I shivered with a mixture of pride and nervous anticipation.

'Now, I want you to count each stroke and thank me for it,' he told me. I nodded to show that I understood, gripping the leather arm of the chair tightly as I waited for my punishment to begin. There was a long, long moment when nothing happened, then I heard the cane whistling in the air, followed a split second later by a searing, burning pain like nothing I had ever known. It really felt as though I had been ripped in two, and I could not help jumping up and rubbing my wounded bum. As I fought to regain my senses, I remembered that I had to thank Marcus for what he had just done to me.

'One . . . thank you,' I croaked, wondering how I could take one more stroke, let alone another five. And three of those would be on my bare bum, without even the minimal protection my thin panties offered. In theory, I could still back out and walk away, but I had come too far down the path to turn back now. I straightened up, and prepared for the next blow.

This one came lower than the first, and parallel to it. It was just as painful, and I cried out as it landed.

Marcus said nothing, and there was a catch in my voice as I thanked him. The third stroke was lower still, perilously close to the tender crease where my buttocks met my thighs, and by now I was in tears. When I felt Marcus take hold of the waistband of my panties and haul them down to the tops of my thighs, I shuddered. How would I stand the pain of the cane on my naked flesh?

Marcus's fingers stroked lazily over the tramlines he had raised on my backside. 'It's such a beautiful sight when a virgin bum takes the cane for the first time,' he murmured, and I shivered despite myself as his hand moved lower, hoping that he would brush my now surprisingly needy pussy. I knew that in my bent-over position I was offering him a tempting view of my sex and even my bum hole, and I hoped they might be enough to distract him from his punishing task for a moment. But he could not be swayed from his purpose, as I became aware that he was raising the cane again.

This time, that thick, unforgiving length of rattan landed solidly across my bare bum cheeks and I shrieked out loud with the agony of it. I wondered if the neighbours were in and, if so, whether they could hear the anguished cries that were issuing from my mouth. Marcus allowed just enough time for the sharp pain to dull to a persistent throb before giving me the fifth stroke, and by now I was begging him to end my ordeal.

He had one last trick up his sleeve for the sixth and final stroke, and that was when I realised just how skilled he was at giving a caning, and how much sadistic pleasure he took in it. The cane was placed so it criss-crossed the welts which already marked my flesh; if I had seen my reflection at that moment, I would have noticed a strong resemblance to a five-barred gate.

I made to stand up and pull my panties back in place, uncomfortable though that would have been, but Marcus told me to stay where I was.

'You took that so well,' he told me, even though I felt like a snivelling wreck and my bottom was a steadily throbbing ball of pain. 'Wait there for a moment. I'll be back.'

He disappeared into the bathroom, and when he came out, he was carrying a tub of cold cream. Almost lovingly, he smoothed the cream over my tortured cheeks, the coolness of the cream taking some of the heat out of my skin. This time, his hand did work its way into my cleft, and when his cream-coated fingers settled on my clit and began to rub, the discomfort I was feeling began to change into something sweeter and far more pleasurable. Marcus knew what he was doing, and my climax was swift and sudden, leaving me shuddering as I clutched on to the armchair.

That was six months ago, and I have been renting Marcus's spare room ever since. I have only once been untidy enough to merit a caning, and he has never been able to work out whether I really did let a pan of milk spill over on to the stove by accident, or whether I did it because I knew it would give him a reason to bring me to the heights of pleasure and pain with his cane and his skilful fingers.

Jackie M.,
Surrey

PERSONAL SERVICES

You can call me naive, but when I first contacted Geoffrey and Maria, it was because I thought they were offering fitness instruction. I had never quite got my figure back after having my first child, and I was too self-conscious to go to the gym, so the idea of having someone who would come round to my house and put me through a workout was a highly appealing one. I had asked round and got a couple of recommendations, but everyone I tried seemed to have a full schedule of clients. Then I saw the advert Geoffrey and Maria had placed on their Internet site, offering 'personal training', and decided to give them a try. I was really looking for a female instructor, but after contacting the couple it soon became obvious they came as a package, and that what they were offering was a workout of a completely different kind to the one I was expecting.

They told me several people had made the same mistake as I had, though their advertisement was so ambiguously worded that I was not surprised by this, and they said their intention was not to offend anyone. I could have declined the suggestion that I meet them and continued my search for an orthodox personal trainer, but there has always been an adventurous side to my sexual nature, and the idea of being disciplined by a dominant couple was a strangely exciting one. My husband is a strict lights-out, missionary position kind of bloke, and when I had once confessed to him that I had a fantasy in which he caned me for being a naughty girl, his reaction had been one of such horror and disgust that I had never mentioned it again.

I arranged that I would visit Geoffrey and Maria in their detached house in a posh part of town. They were a respectable-looking couple in their late forties. He was tall and well-built with the stern air of a Victorian schoolmaster, and she had a head of iron-grey hair which she wore in an elegant chignon. They looked me up and down as I stood on their doorstep, making me feel much younger than my twenty-five years, and I wondered for a moment whether I was doing the right thing. Then they asked me to come inside, and I realised I must have passed the first test.

We had a cup of tea in their stylishly decorated lounge and made small talk. I began to relax in their presence, until I had almost forgotten the reason for my visit. Then, abruptly, the tone of the conversation changed.

'Go into the cloakroom and change, please, Ruth,' said Geoffrey. 'We will see you back here in five minutes.'

I had brought the clothing they had requested in a small holdall. It was my old games kit from school, which I had kept for some sentimental reason, but had not worn for the best part of a decade. As I squeezed into it, I realised how much my body had changed over the intervening years. I had been a late developer, and now the white Aertex top strained across my big, braless breasts, and the pleated skirt, short to begin with, barely covered the cheeks of my bum. I was wearing bottle green knickers to match the skirt, and white plimsolls which I had been ordered to clean before I came. The plimsolls still fitted reasonably well, but everything else was uncomfortably tight. With my brown hair fastened in two bunches and tied with green ribbon, I felt slightly ridiculous, and realised that by agreeing to dress in this manner I had already handed the balance of power to Geoffrey and Maria.

I was surprised to see that Maria had changed into a navy blue tracksuit which looked slightly old-fashioned, reminding me of the one my games mistress had always worn. The easy chairs had been pushed back, and the coffee table had been placed against one wall, leaving a large, empty space in the middle of the lounge. I stood self-consciously in that space, knowing what was to come.

'Just a few physical jerks, Ruth,' said Maria. 'We'll do some star jumps first.'

I did as she asked, jumping on the spot and flinging my arms and legs wide. My breasts were jiggling as I moved, and the fabric of my top was rubbing against my nipples, causing them to get hard. I could see Geoffrey staring at them with undisguised interest, and smiled to myself at the thought that I was turning him on.

After about twenty star jumps, I was beginning to sweat slightly. It was a while since I had done any serious physical exercise, and I was coming to realise I was not as fit as I thought I was.

'Now some running on the spot, please, Ruth,' Maria said. She urged me on, faster and faster, until I was puffing and panting. Big patches of sweat were appearing under my arms, and the tight fabric of my top was chafing me viciously.

Geoffrey must have seen me wincing, because he said, 'I think Ruth is a little uncomfortable in that shirt. I think it might be better for her if she took it off.'

Both Geoffrey and Maria knew that I had nothing on under the top, because their instructions as to how I should dress had been very specific on that point. I hesitated for a moment then, seeing Ruth's impatient look, I lifted the hem of the top and pulled it off over my head. Now I felt even more vulnerable, with my heavy breasts with their pale pink nipples exposed.

Maria told me to get down on the floor and do some sit-ups. Muscles I had forgotten I possessed groaned as I worked them for the first time in years, and all the time I was aware of Geoffrey's hungry eyes studying my heaving tits. Having him as a silent and appreciative spectator was both adding to my humiliation and making me more excited at what I was being forced to do.

At last, Maria ordered me to bend over and touch my toes. I went into the required position, grasping my ankles as I was bid, and knew at this moment my punishment was about to begin.

'Ten strokes with the paddle, I think,' Maria told me. She went over to what appeared to be a wooden drinks cabinet. As the door opened, instead of the bottles of spirits I was expecting, I caught a brief glimpse of a rack of canes and other instruments of discipline. She took a stiff rubber paddle from the cabinet, and slapped it against her palm thoughtfully.

'Don't worry,' she said, 'we always use this on beginners. It hurts less than the cane or the tawse, and if your husband should happen to see your bum in the next couple of days, you can explain away the bruising by saying you slipped on the stairs.'

So there was going to be bruising, even with the protection of my sensible school knickers. I shuddered with a mixture of fear and anticipation as Maria flipped my skirt up out of the way, revealing the cheeks of my bottom.

When the first blow fell, it did so without warning. The heavy pressure of the paddle was like nothing I had expected, and I yelped in surprise.

'Geoffrey, I think Ruth needs something to take her mind off the punishment,' Maria said. The next thing I felt were Geoffrey's surprisingly soft hands on my hanging tits, his fingers and thumbs rolling my nipples into small, tight balls of sensation.

Between them, they gave me a mixture of pleasure and pain, the feelings Geoffrey created in my tits a counterpoint to the dull, continual throbbing in my backside. It was like nothing I had known. I wanted it to stop; I wanted it to carry on until I reached the peak of ecstasy towards which I was slowly climbing. I was barely aware of the moment when Maria caught hold of my knickers and pulled them down around the tops of my thighs. The last four strokes of the paddle fell on my unprotected bum cheeks in swift succession, causing me to sob and snivel as Geoffrey's caresses of my nipples changed to pinches which bordered on pain.

And then I felt Maria touch my clit for long enough to have me bucking in orgasm as Geoffrey held me steady in his arms.

'Well done,' was all Maria said, and then she sent me to the cloakroom to change back into my normal clothes before making my way home.

That session with Geoffrey and Maria was a one-off, but it helped me to explore my fantasies in a way I had never thought possible until that day. I now have a legitimate personal trainer, who is helping me get back in shape; his name is John and he is very cute. Perhaps one day I might ask him to punish me if I fail to do the required number of stomach curls, just to see how he reacts . . .

Ruth J.,
Leicester

TIME TO BE PUNISHED

When Trudie was forty minutes late turning up to go out with me, I decided this would be the last time she would behave in such a discourteous fashion. We had been seeing each other for nearly three months, and from the first evening, when she had left me standing outside a cinema for twenty-five minutes, anxiously wondering whether I had been stood up, it had become apparent that punctuality was not her strong point. I, on the other hand, was brought up to believe that it was rude to keep someone else waiting, unless there was a very good excuse, and while another man might have overlooked this one flaw in the character of someone who was pretty, intelligent, kind and had the sort of body which makes other women jealous, I was not prepared to tolerate it.

We had arranged that Trudie would arrive at my house by seven o'clock at the latest, so that we could be at the restaurant by eight. She had promised me faithfully she would be on time, but as seven came and went, without any sign of her, I realised I had been stupid to believe that promise.

When she finally did ring the doorbell, I was sitting with a glass of whisky, pondering how best to teach her the lesson she so badly needed. I went to open the door and she breezed in without a word of apology.

'You realise I've had to ring and cancel the table, don't you?' I said.

'But I was looking forward to dinner,' Trudie replied. 'I haven't eaten since breakfast and I'm starving.'

'Well, how was I to know what time you would turn up?' I retorted. 'If you knew you were going to be running late, you could at least have called to let me know.'

'I'm sorry, Peter, it won't happen again,' she said.

'I wish I could believe that,' I replied. 'There's only one way to make sure it doesn't, and I should have done this a long time ago. I'm afraid I'm going to have to spank some manners into you. I want you over my knee, now.'

'What?' Trudie exclaimed. 'You're kidding, aren't you?'

I shook my head. 'I've never been more serious.' I caught hold of her by the arm and dragged her, protesting, to the armchair where I had been sitting nursing my drink while I waited for her to arrive. Trudie is only a little over five feet tall and barely weighs anything, so it was easy to haul her on to my lap. She struggled and tried to break free of my grip but, as I had told her, I was serious in my intent, and that lent me the strength to hold her in place.

She was wearing a short black dress with a flared skirt, and when I flipped the hem of that skirt out of the way to give me access to her backside, I almost laughed at my luck and her misfortune. The underwear she had chosen – a skimpy white lace G-string and black hold-up stockings – had obviously been intended to turn me on when we got back from dinner. I have to confess they were doing their job now, my cock beginning to rise from its dormant state as I took in the delicious sight of her full, creamy arse cheeks, with the little strip of lace disappearing between them to divide her sex, but I knew those skimpy panties would offer her no protection when I began to spank her. For all the area they covered, she might as well have been naked from the waist down.

'Forty minutes, wasn't it?' I said casually.

'What do you mean?' she asked.

'You were forty minutes late, I believe. I think forty spanks will help to bring the point home to you.'

I let her wait for a long moment, giving her time to mull over the implications of what I had just told her, before bringing my open palm down sharply on her buttock. She gave a little anguished cry, as if surprised by the force of the blow, though in truth I had not actually hit her that hard, and I think her reaction was more one of indignation that, as a grown woman, she was being treated this way.

After that little loosener, I really began to spank her in earnest, my palm landing rapidly and methodically over every inch of exposed flesh. I watched the white handprint form on her skin, before the blood flowed in to turn it red. Soon what had been pale flesh was a vibrant crimson, and Trudie was wriggling and squirming on my lap, trying to get away from the relentless onslaught. Her frantic movements were stimulating my cock, causing it to stiffen uncomfortably in the confines of my trousers.

As I carried on slapping her bottom, she began to cry, softly at first, but soon fat teardrops were rolling down her cheeks to land on the carpet. Her carefully applied mascara was running, and tendrils of her long, black hair were sticking to her wet cheeks. She looked wretched and humiliated, and I found that even more of a turn-on.

I ran an experimental finger over the taut gusset of her G-string, registering the damp feel of the fabric. When I slipped that finger under the lace to touch her pussy flesh, she moaned and thrust her pelvis back at me like a bitch in heat, wanting me to touch her more forcefully.

I pulled my hand away, smiling at her groan of frustration, and gave her the last five spanks. These were the hardest of all, and I had her squealing in pain as my hand landed with real venom on her tormented bum cheeks. Then, without ceremony, I pushed her off my lap and watched as she landed in a snivelling, dishevelled heap on the floor.

'Strip,' I told her. 'I want you naked by the time I've got my cock out, or I may just have to add a couple more to the forty I've just given you.'

She scrabbled to pull off her dress with none of the cocky defiance she had shown when I first announced her punishment. Trudie has small, perfect breasts which do not need a bra, and so all she had to remove was her sodden G-string. I took a moment to savour the sight of her beautiful body, clad only in the hold-up stockings, then I presented my now fully erect penis to her mouth and ordered her to suck. I was so excited, I almost came the moment her full, wet lips closed around my swollen glans, but I held back, not wanting it to be over so soon.

After a couple of minutes of the most exquisite suction, I ordered her to lie on her back and part her legs widely. I put the head of my cock at the entrance to her vagina and thrust home, feeling her tight, ribbed walls clinging possessively to my shaft, as if afraid I would withdraw it from them. I drove into her hard and fast, making her body slide back and forth on the carpet, knowing how this would be causing the rough fibres to scrape against her sore bum cheeks. She was gasping and crying as my hips gave a last convulsion and my come jetted up into her cunt. Then she gave a shuddering moan and I knew that she, too, was coming.

Since that evening, Trudie has usually been on time for our dates. When she's late, however, we both know why, and I relish the chance to punish that glorious little bum whenever it arises.

Peter B.,
Northampton

The Top and Bottom of It

A PRIVATE FUNCTION

My boyfriend Carl and I have just been to our first private SM party, and I wanted to tell you all about it. We have been going to fetish clubs for a couple of years now, and recently we were invited to a couples-only party at a big country house just outside Leicester. Carl has always been the dominant one in our relationship, and I am his submissive slave, an arrangement which suits us both.

We arrived feeling nervous and excited about what was going to happen. We had both dressed for the occasion. Carl was in tight leather trousers and heavy boots with lots of buckles, and a black fishnet top that showed off the ring in his left nipple. I was in six-inch stilettoes and fishnet stockings attached to a PVC suspender belt, together with a PVC bra that left my pierced nipples uncovered. I had not been allowed the luxury of panties. My pussy had been shaved for the occasion, and a small brass padlock had been attached to the rings in my labia.

Carl was led into one room where he could socialise and drink with the other doms, while I was taken into another room, where the slaves, both male and female, were chained to the wall and left until each one would be taken into the room where all the action was about to occur. The idea was that we would all be put through our paces in turn, so that the doms could see how well trained and obedient we were. I knew how humiliating it would be to have Carl punish me in front of everyone else, and there was always the chance that some other master or mistress would want to punish me, too. The thought of this was terrifying, and yet at the same time I could feel myself starting to get wet, my sex lips pushing against the restraints of the little padlock in anticipation of the pain and pleasure to come.

I was the third slave to be taken into the main room. There must have been a dozen people in there, and I glanced round nervously at the expectant audience. As I passed the leather- and rubber-clad doms, I could hear crude comments about the size of my breasts, which are small but very pert, and my shaven pussy, and remarks were made as to how much punishment I might be able to accept.

My hands, which had been cuffed together while I waited, were released, and I was bent over a padded whipping stool in the middle of the room by Carl. My wrists were then fastened securely to the far side of the stool, the padlock was unfastened and my legs were spread widely apart and held in place with a spreader bar. In this position, I knew that I was completely open and vulnerable, and that anyone behind me would have a good view of my moist pink sex and puckered rosebud. The audience were crowding round more closely, ready to see how well I had been trained, and the thought of being looked at so intimately only served to make me even wetter.

Carl walked in front of me, and I could see that he was holding a riding crop. This is my least favourite instrument of discipline because it's the one that hurts the most, and I knew that Carl really meant to test me. He used the end of the crop to tease my nipples, bringing them to full hardness, and I moaned softly.

Then the punishment began. Carl moved behind me, and tapped my bottom gently with the crop, measuring the distance of his swing. The crop whistled through the air, then landed square across my bum cheeks. It felt as though I had been ripped in two, and I yelled and bucked in my bonds, but I was restrained so securely that I could barely move.

Carl gave me a moment to recover from the shock of that blow, and then he followed up with a second, parallel to the first. Another line of fire sprang up on my abused flesh, and I pleaded with him not to hit me again. He was oblivious to my pleas, as he never lets me take fewer than six strokes in a session, and I knew I still had at least another four to endure.

Again and again the crop fell, welting my skin. Carl was careful to place the strokes so that each one covered a new area, gradually moving lower until he caught the fleshy underhang of my bum, dangerously close to my vulnerable pussy lips. I shrieked as the pain of the stroke hit home, but the agony was now answered with a sweet echo of pleasure, and despite the extremity of my position, I was beginning to feel the need to come.

Satisfied that he had punished me enough, Carl now decided it was time to reward me, but he told me I would have to beg for my pleasure. In front of everyone there, I had to tell him I wanted to have my cunt and bum fingered. He told me only sluts took pleasure in what had just been done to me, and I admitted that I was a slut. I was his slut, and I would do anything he wanted, with anyone he wanted, as long as he would make me come.

At that, he dropped the crop, and began to run his hands over my well-striped bottom. His fingers moved lower, down into my juicy crease. He circled my clitoris with his thumb for a moment, causing me to groan with pleasure, then he inserted first one, then two fingers into my cunt, thrusting them slowly in and out. Restrained as I was, I could do very little to direct my own pleasure, but Carl knows exactly what to do to make me come. He was stringing it out for the benefit of the watching crowd, gradually stretching me further by adding more fingers. Eventually, he had four fingers in my cunt and his thumb in my bum hole, and I was crying out as his pistoning hand took me closer to the brink. When one of the watching mistresses reached out a hand and tugged cruelly on one of my nipple rings, that was it: I howled my pleasure, my body spasming and my muscles clenching around Carl's fingers. The sheer humiliation of being made to come in front of so many people made it one of the most intense orgasms I had ever had.

I spent the rest of the evening back in my chains, my sore bum pressed uncomfortably against the cold wall and my labia padlocked together once more, while the other slaves were punished in a variety of ways. Carl told me about some of the things that are in store for me next time we go to one of these parties, and I know my limits will be tested even further. I can't wait.

Angie L.,
Leicester

THE BEAUTY TRAP

I would like to tell you about my regular visits to my mistress. She is my goddess, and it is an honour and a privilege to serve her. She knows my worthless body is hers to do with as she wishes, and I will bear whatever torments she inflicts upon me without complaint.

My mistress is a trained beautician, and she uses her skills to torture me in the most exquisite ways. Once a month, I am compelled to visit her at her salon, after all her clients have gone, for my regular routine.

She has always demanded that I keep my body completely free of hair, and to aid me in this process she will wax me. I cannot describe the agonies I undergo as she paints the hot wax over my chest, limbs and genitals, before swiftly and ruthlessly ripping it away. The sensation of my pubic hair being pulled out by the roots is one that brings tears to my eyes, but I must bear it in silence or risk her wrath.

Next, she will give me an enema. The nozzle is greased and inserted into my anus with ease, then I am made to take up to two pints of water at blood temperature. Soon, my bowels are churning and I am begging for relief, but she will not stop until I have taken every last drop. I am not allowed any dignity, for she will watch as I evacuate the water into a chamber pot. Once she is sure that I am completely cleansed, she will strap me to the table on which her clients receive their treatments, using wide Velcro straps which are surprisingly strong and hold me securely in place. Then she will use one of her machines on me, all of which are capable of producing electric shocks which vary in severity. Her favourite is the slimming device, which consists of a number of small pads, designed to be attached to whichever part of the body is in need of toning and firming. I never need to ask where these pads will be applied in my case, for I know it will be my penis. Once they are secured in place, she will turn the machine to its lowest setting, the electricity stimulating my poor, tormented cock in ways that are both painful and yet deliciously arousing. I know she takes pleasure in the sight of my body twitching and writhing in its bonds, and her sublime cruelty only serves to turn me on further.

I dread my visits to my mistress, and yet I love them, too, for she really is a skilled practitioner, and knows how to bring me to the peak of ecstasy again and again before finally allowing me the ultimate release of orgasm.

Nigel P.,
Manchester

DINNER FOR THREE

Ever since I met Sara, I have been training her to become my submissive slave. I am determined to have control over many aspects of her life, such as what she wears and when she uses the toilet. It really turns me on to see her asking for permission to pee, knowing that I will be watching her when she does. I am also gradually training her to offer her body to other men, and to respond to their caresses while in my presence. At first, she was often wilful, refusing to do as she was told, and had to be punished for her disobedience. Now she knows when she has done something wrong, and there is no sweeter sight than to see her crawling towards me, naked, with the whip I am about to use on her beautiful backside coiled loosely around her neck.

Recently, we went out to dinner with an old friend of mine, George. George is a wealthy businessman in his early sixties, and he is used to getting exactly what he wants. I knew that tonight he wanted Sara, and I was not going to stand in the way of him getting her. I knew this would be a good opportunity to put Sara through her paces, and to watch her reaction as George did whatever he wanted to her.

Sara was told to dress for the occasion in a long scarlet coat-dress that buttoned all the way down the front. It looked stunning against her olive skin and dark waist-length hair, and it also concealed the fact that all she wore beneath it was sheer black stockings and suspenders. Black patent leather shoes with four-inch stiletto heels completed the outfit, and she wore heavy, almost mask-like make-up that emphasised her full red lips and huge green eyes. She stood before me, waiting for my approval, and I told her that she looked almost perfect – there was just one thing missing. At that, I took a length of fine silk rope and tied her hands tightly behind her body. She had not been expecting this, but she knew better than to protest. I draped a mackintosh around her, so her bound hands could not be seen, and then we headed to meet George.

He was waiting for us in one of his favourite haunts, a West End restaurant which has a members' bar that offers utter discretion and seclusion for everyone from businessmen like himself to sports stars who do not want to be disturbed while they eat. George was drinking at the bar, and he smiled warmly as he saw us approaching. The waiter showed us to our table, and took Sara's coat. If he was confused by the sight of her tied wrists, he said nothing; I knew it was not all he would be seeing before the night was out.

When he took our order, I asked for a plate of asparagus for Sara. She was in no position to feed herself unless I chose to release her hands, and when George asked if he could feed Sara, I invited him to go ahead.

'But I wouldn't want to get butter on that beautiful dress of hers,' he said.

'Unbutton the dress, then. She won't mind,' I assured him.

George's smile widened, and he unfastened the top two buttons of her dress, revealing the upper slopes of her gorgeous breasts. I watched, barely touching my own plate of melon and Parma ham, as George offered the asparagus to Sara's lips. He made her work for every mouthful, and as she reached forward, the butter trickling out of the corner of her mouth and down her neck, I found myself wanting to lick the little golden trail away, but that privilege I deferred to George. Of course, he had to open Sara's dress further, and when the waiter came back it was to see George's mouth on Sara's neck and her dress unbuttoned practically to her waist, baring her breasts completely. She was sitting with her back to the rest of the diners, so no one else could see what was going on, and I was amused to see the waiter's stammering confusion – and the obvious bulge in his trousers which had been raised by the sight of Sara sitting half-naked and passive while George licked butter off her skin.

We skipped the main course and went straight on to dessert. Both George and I were anxious to take Sara home and use her beautiful body. George ordered Sara to spread her legs widely, and I watched as his hand, largely hidden by the crisp white tablecloth, moved between them. When the waiter came to collect our plates, he was confronted by the sight of Sara biting her lip as she struggled not to make any sound which would alert our fellow diners to what was happening, while the movements of George's hand made it perfectly clear that he was masturbating Sara beneath the table. George threw enough money on to the table to pay the bill and we left, Sara's coat once more loosely draped around her shoulders, offering the odd glimpse of her breasts as she walked.

Once outside, George handed me his car keys and asked me to drive the three of us back to his house in Kew. As I drove, I was treated to a beautiful sight in the rear-view mirror: Sara, with her dress now completely unfastened and raised so that her naked bottom was against the car's leather upholstery. George's flies were undone and, as I watched, Sara bent her head and took the head of his penis between her lips. She is an expert when it comes to sucking cock, and soon she had swallowed his entire length. As I pulled up in the drive of George's house, I turned my head to see Sara licking George's come off her lips and George tucking his wilting cock back into his trousers.

Once inside the house, Sara was ordered to strip down to her stockings and suspenders and prostrate herself on the deep-pile carpet of George's lounge. She looked so vulnerable as she hurried to obey that my cock was throbbing almost painfully in my trousers. Sara knelt on all fours, head down, knowing she was not allowed to look at us unless with permission.

'You have her well trained, Nick,' George said to me, 'but how does she respond to punishment? I should imagine the skin on her arse colours beautifully.'

'Why don't you find out?' I replied, knowing how humiliating it must be for Sara to be discussed as though she was not in the room.

'I'd love to,' George said, unbuckling his belt and removing it from the loops in his trousers. Coiling the buckle end around his hand, he flexed the thick leather thoughtfully as he looked at Sara.

'Open your legs wider, slut,' he ordered, and she did as she was told without flinching, though she must have been aware that we were now presented with a breathtaking view of the hanging pouch of her pussy and the dark pucker of her arsehole.

The next thing I heard was a whistling as the belt flew through the air, to land with a loud crack across the cheeks of her bum. Sara yelped, but held her position, and George smiled at me, acknowledging that I had taught her well. Again and again the belt came down on her taut buttocks, raising thick, red stripes that George ran his fingers over. Sara cried out at every stroke, but did not lift her head, her cries changing to gentle sobbing as George aimed the belt lower, catching the crease at the top of her thighs.

When he ordered her to thrust her pelvis towards him, she did so without demur, even though there was now more chance that the belt would strike her sex lips. I was fighting the urge to pull my aching cock from my trousers and wank as I watched, for I knew that George and I would soon be slaking our lust on Sara's body. By now, Sara's arse was a mass of reddish-purple weals, and tears were running down her face, ruining her carefully applied make-up, but I could clearly see a snail-trail of glistening juice on her inner thighs, showing just how turned on she was by what was being done to her. George finished her punishment with a couple of strokes that lashed viciously round her thighs, the very tip of the belt catching her pussy lips and causing her to shriek in a mixture of agony and ecstasy.

We spent the next hour taking it in turns to fuck Sara's juicy cunt, both of us taking her from behind so that we could savour the sensation of the heat radiating from her heavily welted backside as we thrust into her.

George has since told me that he has a couple of friends who are interested in sampling Sara's charms, and I will be more than happy to let them do so.

Nick R.,
London

The following incident actually happened to me a couple of years ago, but I have never told anyone about it until now.

I was 18 at the time, and I had taken a part-time job in a greengrocer's with the aim of putting aside some money for the autumn, when I would be starting at university. I found myself working alongside three other women: June, the manageress, and her two assistants, Marilyn and Beryl. June and Beryl were both in their fifties, and Marilyn was in her mid-thirties. It soon became obvious that Marilyn didn't like me very much. I never found out the reason for her antagonism, but I was always aware of it. She would give me the hardest and dirtiest jobs, and whenever June was out of the shop, she would go in the back room with a cup of tea and a cigarette. I looked to Beryl for some support, but it seemed that before my arrival, Marilyn had bullied Beryl, and now I was there to take the brunt of Marilyn's abuse, Beryl was only too happy to retain the new status quo.

One Thursday, June had left early to deposit the week's takings in the bank. It was almost time for the shop to close, and I was busy tidying up in the stock room when Marilyn and Beryl walked in. When Marilyn locked the door behind her, I knew something was about to happen, but I could have had no way of knowing what.

'You really are a little slut, aren't you?' she said.

'I don't know what you're talking about,' I replied, and it was true – I didn't. At that time, I did not have a boyfriend and my sexual experience was very limited.

'I've been watching you,' she said. 'That skirt of yours is so short that every time you bend over, it gives the customers a flash of your knickers. And I notice you only bend over when there are men in the shop. You like the thought of them looking at your pants, don't you?'

'That's not true,' I said, beginning to grow a little anxious.

'Well, I think you should show me and Beryl exactly what you'd like to show the men who come in here,' Marilyn continued.

'But the shop . . .' I stammered.

'We closed early. We wanted to make sure you had plenty of time to learn not to be such a little tart. Lie down on the table,' Marilyn ordered me.

I glanced at the table, which we usually sat round when we were eating our lunchtime sandwiches. When I did not move, Marilyn said, 'Do it, or we'll tell June we find you impossible to work with, and then see how long you keep your precious job.'

By now, I was getting a bit frightened, but the fear was almost delicious, too, although I couldn't let these two harridans know that. Marilyn had a strange, almost predatory look on her face, and Beryl seemed happy to back her up. Knowing I had no choice, I climbed on to the table and lay down, wondering what might be about to happen.

Marilyn's voice was harsh. 'Those knickers you're so keen to show to everyone. Take them off.'

'No . . .' I began to protest.

'Do it,' she said, in a voice that brooked no argument. I looked across to Beryl, hoping she might step in and save me from future humiliation, but she just smiled, and I realised she wanted to see me brought low in this way.

I reached up under my skirt and hooked my fingers in the waistband of my knickers. As I pulled them down, I tried to keep my legs together as much as possible, but I was sure I was still giving the two women glimpses of my pussy.

'Very good,' said Marilyn, once my little knickers were lying in a crumpled heap on the table. 'Now spread your legs. Beryl and I want to see everything.'

This was too much: if the door had not been locked, I would have shot off the table and run down the street, knickers or no knickers. But the two witches had me exactly where they wanted me. Mortified, I slowly bent my legs and let my thighs fall open. I tried to imagine what they might be seeing: the hair on my mound is fair and very sparse, and as I stretched my legs wider at their command, I knew they would have an excellent view of the shiny pink inside of my pussy.

Marilyn came close to the table, bending her head so I could feel her warm breath at the entrance to my vagina. No one had ever studied me as intently as this, and the thought that it was a woman who was taking such an interest in my body alarmed me even further. If she touched me there – with her fingers or, as seemed likely, with her mouth – I didn't know what I would do.

Then I saw what she was holding in her hand. It was a long, thin cucumber that she had brought through from the front of the shop. She presented it to my lips, ordering me to suck. I didn't want to do it, but she was insistent. Reluctantly, I opened my mouth, and she pushed the cucumber deep inside. As she had commanded, I began to suck, my lips straining around the vegetable's girth. After a few moments, Marilyn pulled it from my mouth; it glistened with my saliva and she smiled in satisfaction.

Without giving me time to protest, she put the cucumber at the entrance to my pussy, and thrust it slowly into my tight hole. I groaned at this unwanted penetration, feeling it stretching me wide. Once it was in as far as it would go, Marilyn stepped back, leaving the cucumber protruding obscenely from my cunt.

Out of the corner of my eye, I realised that Beryl was undressing, unzipping her skirt and stepping out of it, before pulling down her tan tights and big white pants in one movement, so she was naked from the waist down. The next thing I knew, she had climbed on to the table and, to my horror, was squatting over my face.

I looked up and saw her cunt, with its matted grey hair and large, fleshy lips. 'Lick me,' she ordered, lowering herself so that she was practically smothering me with her big bum and slightly moist pussy. I could do nothing but stick my tongue out and taste the folds of flesh that hovered above me. She tasted sour and unwashed, but I could not pull my head away, and had to keep licking her. Within moments, she was grinding herself hard on to my nose as an orgasm shot through her.

At last, she lifted herself off me, but there was to be no respite, as Marilyn quickly took her place. She positioned herself so that she was facing towards my feet, with her little wrinkled arsehole over my nose. She made me lick her pussy and bum, urging me to thrust my tongue into her anal hole as she grew more and more excited. When she came, her salty juices gushed into my mouth, and I swallowed them down.

When she climbed off me, she used my knickers to wipe herself dry before putting her own underwear back on. Then she pulled the cucumber from my aching pussy, laughing as she did. Finally, my ordeal was over and I was allowed to go.

The events of that afternoon were never mentioned again, but I know both Marilyn and Beryl got a real kick out of what happened. I can't help wondering if they have done the same thing to the girl who was my eventual replacement and, if so, whether she sometimes lies in bed at night and plays with herself as she relives her humiliation, as I do.

Lucy R.,
Leicester

CAUGHT IN THE ACT

When I married my wife, she was completely unaware of my cross-dressing. I have always loved the feel of silky underwear against my skin, ever since I was a teenager, and have taken great pleasure in donning women's clothes for masturbation sessions. However, my wife is the straitlaced type – or so I thought – and I never revealed my secret to her, for fear of how she might react. Perhaps if I had done so earlier, none of the following would have taken place.

I had a week off work, which I had to use or lose, but as Helen could not get time off at the same time, it meant I had the place to myself. I was really looking forward to this, as it meant I could spend the week dressing as I wished.

On the Monday morning, I waved her off to work, then headed straight up to the bedroom to raid her wardrobe. Looking through her underwear drawer, I picked out a black lace bra, matching panties, a suspender belt and stockings. The feel of the stockings as I rolled them up my legs was unbelievable, and I quickly put on the bra and panties, padding out the cups of the bra with a little cotton wool. Over this, I put on a tight-fitting red angora jumper and a black leather miniskirt. Then I sat down to put on my make-up. Raiding Helen's cosmetics, I found foundation, eyeliner, blusher, mascara and lipstick, and I applied them as skilfully as I knew how. Clip-on pearl earrings and black high-heeled court shoes completed the outfit, and when I took a look at myself in the full-length mirror on the wardrobe door, I couldn't believe what I was seeing. It was as though a beautiful woman was staring back at me.

I was still preening myself in the mirror when I heard a noise behind me and turned round to see Helen staring at me.

'What do you think you're doing, Joe?' she asked, her face like thunder.

I tried to stammer out a reply, but how could I explain to her that I got turned on by wearing her clothes?

'Well, I only came home to collect a file I'd forgotten,' she said. 'I didn't think I'd catch a prize like this.'

At her words, I began to wonder if she was really as angry as she made out. I was soon to find out.

'I didn't realise I'd married such a sissy,' she said. 'I had my suspicions that you had some kind of scene, but I never thought it was this. Well, you have a choice.'

'Choice?' I said, slightly bewildered.

She nodded. 'It depends on whether you want to keep your marriage or not. The first option is that we get divorced, which will be expensive for you. I mean, alimony payments aren't cheap, and then there's the cost to your reputation. I can just imagine how your friends, your boss and your mother will feel when I tell them you're a wimp who gets his kicks from wearing my panties.'

'What's the other choice?' I asked her, afraid to hear her answer.

'You dress as a woman full-time. Bye bye, Joe, hello, Josephine.' I was just about to say this was exactly what I had always fantasised about, but she carried on. 'You give up your job, you become my housemaid, you have sex only when I want it and only on my terms, and if I want to fuck other men, you let me.'

What choice did I have? By the end of the day, I had handed in my resignation from work with immediate effect. She then took me shopping for a whole new wardrobe. Everything I wore, even down to my underwear, was all going to be feminine from now on. She burnt all my male clothes, apart from one shirt, trousers, jacket and tie which I might need for emergencies, and made me go in the bathroom and shave off all the hair on my legs, arms and chest, and from around my cock and balls. She told me that Josephine would have to keep her body smooth at all times or be punished.

Then she showed me the clothes I would be wearing around the house. It was a maid's outfit, consisting of a very short black dress with a starched white petticoat underneath, a little white apron and a frilled cap. My underwear was to be frilly panties and a bra, stockings and suspenders, and I would wear three-inch high stiletto heels even for my housework duties.

That was the start of my new life. As Josephine, I had a strict regime. I had to take my wife breakfast in bed every morning, before bathing her and helping her to dress for work. Then I would spend the rest of the day doing chores around the house. I had to do the hoovering and dusting, keep the bathroom spotlessly clean and wash all my wife's lingerie by hand.

I soon came to realise that Helen had started to dress for work in a much sexier fashion than she had done before I became Josephine. Her skirts were shorter, her heels were higher, she wore stockings rather than tights, and all her underwear was scanty and made of silk or satin, with lacy trimmings. I began to suspect that what she had said about fucking other men if she wanted to had been no idle threat, and I wondered if she had found a lover in the office. The thought that someone else was enjoying her lovely body when I was only allowed to fuck her when she was feeling kindly disposed to me made me feel jealous and frustrated.

My suspicions were confirmed when she came home one night and told me she was having a passionate affair with Sean, a 19-year-old boy who worked in the post room. She told me that he had been very sexually inexperienced when she had first seduced him in her office one night, and that she was gradually teaching him how to become an expert lover. She told me that he had an eight-inch penis, almost three inches longer than my own, and that he knew exactly what to do with it. She also said that he knew her husband was a feminised wimp who was no longer allowed to have sex with her, and that he thought she was winding him up. She said she was going to prove to him that every word was true.

The following evening, I was taking the laundry out of the washing machine, ready to hang it up before I started getting Helen's dinner ready, when I heard her car pull up in the drive. When she came into the house, I was startled to see a young man with her. He was nearly six foot tall, with the muscular physique of a rugby player.

'Josephine, this is Sean,' Helen said. 'Sean, meet my sissy housemaid, Josephine. I'll leave the two of you to get to know each other a little better while I go to change.'

'Helen told me about you, but I didn't believe it,' Sean said. 'Now I can see she was right. She told me you're a wimp who's useless in bed, and that you like to be treated like a woman. But she said you couldn't really be a woman until you'd been fucked by a man.'

I shuddered at the implication of his words, guessing that Helen had brought him home to do more than just ridicule me.

'Show me your frilly panties,' Sean said, and obediently I raised the front of my dress to show him the white undies I wore beneath it. Sean reached out and ran his hand over the panties, his eyebrow raising when he felt the obvious bulge in the satiny material.

'Does it turn you on to be dressed like this?' he asked. 'Do you get off on being treated like the wimpy little sissy you are?'

I couldn't say anything, but he must have known from the way my cock was twitching in my knickers that his words were having an effect on me. For one so young, he was surprisingly self-possessed, and I think he was relishing the knowledge that he was completely in control of the conversation.

'Your wife says you want to be fucked like a real woman,' Sean continued, still stroking me through my panties. His voice was low and hypnotic, and I could only groan in reply.

'Take your panties down, sissy Josephine,' he said, and I obeyed his command, aware that my cock was harder than it had ever been. 'Now bend over that chair.'

There was a bottle of olive oil by the side of the cooker, and I turned my head to watch him fetch it. He put it on the kitchen table, then rapidly stripped off to reveal his fit young body. As I glanced at his semi-erect penis, I realised my wife had not exaggerated its length, and I shuddered at the thought of taking it inside me. He coated his erection liberally with olive oil, then tipped the bottle over my upraised white bottom. I felt the cool liquid dribble down between my cheeks, and knew what was coming. His finger rimmed the entrance to my bum, then slipped inside, oiling me in preparation. Like the sissy slut I was, I thrust my pelvis back at him, wantonly offering him my arse. A second finger joined the first, stretching me wider, then he pulled out, replacing his fingers with his cock. I moaned as I felt that hot, solid length thrusting into me, and reached down to fondle my own puny prick as he fucked me hard and fast.

I heard a chuckle behind me, and turned my head to see my wife standing in the doorway wearing nothing but a sheer black nightdress. 'That's it, Sean,' she said. 'Show the little sissy what it's like to be fucked by a real man.'

The amusement and contempt in her voice, coupled with the feel of that big, oily cock inside me, caused me to come, my spunk spurting over my fingers. I knew then that Helen had completely feminised me, and that I was her sissy slut, to be used and abused by whoever she wanted.

Josephine F.,
Glasgow

BARBECUE BEATING

Every year, we throw a barbecue party on the first weekend in August to celebrate my husband's birthday, and invite a mixture of his work colleagues and our neighbours. Even though it's a lot of hard work for me, I always enjoy it, and this year I was looking forward to it more than usual. You see, six months ago, Chris moved into the house directly opposite ours. He's in his late twenties and very striking, with coffee-coloured skin and black hair which he wears in short dreadlocks. I knew he was single, and I must admit I've often thought about him when Dean, my husband, has been fucking me. I was hoping for the chance to flirt with him, and possibly enjoy a slow dance or two towards the end of the evening. I had no way of knowing events would turn out as they did.

The day of the party was blisteringly hot, and by the time the guests started arriving in mid-afternoon, I had already laid the table with the cold buffet and was enjoying a cool glass of punch on the lawn. Dean, as usual, was in charge of the barbecue itself, and the air was soon thick with the smell of cooking meat and the sound of music drifting from the CD player in the living room. The French windows were thrown open, and people were encouraged to wander in and out of the house, helping themselves to food and drink.

Chris turned up around five o'clock, looking sexy in a sleeveless T-shirt and a skintight pair of cycling shorts. One of next door's kids had managed to get the ball they were playing with stuck in the cherry tree at the bottom of the garden, and it was Chris who offered to retrieve it. As he climbed up into the lower branches, his T-shirt rode up and I got a good view of the outline of his cock where the tight lycra clung to it. Even in its resting state, it seemed thick and tempting, and my pussy twitched with lust at the thought of what it might look like in its full, erect glory.

The evening wore on, and soon all the guests with young kids had drifted away, leaving about half a dozen of Dean's workmates, along with Chris and me. By now, I had had plenty of punch and was feeling horny and uninhibited, so I suggested to the guests that we go into the house and dance. Dean had driven down to the nearest off-licence to get some cans of lager and a couple of bottles of spirits, and when he got back, it was to see Chris and I dancing to a slow, bluesy track, our hands fondling each other's bum and my head resting lovingly on Chris's shoulder.

I was in my own little world, enjoying the feel of Chris's now hard cock pressing against my stomach, and I only knew Dean had returned when he switched off the music.

'You little slut,' Dean hissed, and I pulled away from Chris with a guilty start. 'I turn my back and what happens? You start throwing yourself at someone else.'

'But we were only dancing,' I protested.

'Yeah, you're dancing now, but you've spent all afternoon flirting with him. I've been watching you, so don't say you haven't.' There was a real edge of anger in Dean's voice, and the rest of the guests seemed both worried and embarrassed by the turn the party seemed to be taking. 'You've been making me look a fool in front of all of our guests, so there's only one thing I can do to stop you doing it again.'

'What's that?' I said, my voice little more than a whisper.

'Punish you,' Dean replied. 'Come on, outside. Now.'

My blood ran cold. What was he talking about? Surely he was joking? But no, he grabbed hold of my wrists and began to drag me out into the back garden. I looked around for someone to step in and call a halt to what was happening, but either the assembled guests thought that what happened between a man and his wife was none of their business, or they had some inkling of what my punishment might be and they were happy to see it go ahead.

There was a skipping rope lying on the ground that one of the neighbouring kids must have dropped.

Dean picked it up and took me, still protesting and trying to break away from his grip, down to the cherry tree Chris had climbed earlier in the afternoon. Swiftly, he used one end of the skipping rope to tie my wrists securely together, then he looped the other end over the bottom branch of the tree and knotted it firmly in place. As I'm only a fraction over five foot tall, by the time Dean had finished my toes were barely touching the ground and my arms were stretched painfully taut.

He went back into the house and ushered everyone else into the garden, Chris among them. The thought that he was going to witness whatever might be about to happen to me caused my stomach to flutter with excitement and alarm.

Dean came to stand beside me, and began to unbuckle his belt. Now I was really starting to get frightened; the thought of Dean taking that thin leather belt to my backside – which had to be his intention – was not one I relished.

'This should teach you,' he said, flexing the belt experimentally. 'But just to make sure you really learn your lesson . . .'

To my horror, he grabbed hold of the shorts I was wearing and yanked at them. With their elasticated waistband, they came down easily, but so did my knickers. With one movement, Dean had left me naked from the waist down in front of a group of people I barely knew, and with my hands tied above my head there was nothing I could do to cover myself. I could sense the eyes of all the men there staring lustfully at the wispy blonde bush which did very little to hide my pussy lips, and I felt the faint stirring of a dark, shameful excitement.

Dean gave them a couple of moments to savour the sight of me, barely dressed and totally vulnerable, then he moved round behind me to begin my punishment proper. I had a split second to register the sound of the thin, whippy leather cutting through the air, then it landed with a meaty crack on my unprotected flesh. I howled at the sudden, fiery pain that ripped across my backside, but Dean gave me no real time to come to terms with it before the belt fell again. Stripe after vicious stripe was laid across my white flesh as I howled and sobbed in agony, jerking on the end of the rope but unable to do anything to get away from the pain my husband was inflicting on me. Occasionally, as I twisted in place, my toes scrabbling to get a purchase on the dusty ground, the end of the belt would curl round and catch me on my inner thigh or the side of my hip, on more than one occasion landing frighteningly close to the pout of my pussy.

At last, Dean decided I had had enough strokes, but still my punishment was not over. As I hung there, my face blotchy with tears, my backside scarlet and blazing, he invited the assembled guests to come and inspect the marks he had inflicted. I closed my eyes, not wanting to look at any of them as they touched and prodded me. I was helpless to protest as, one by one, they came up and ran their hands over the throbbing welts that covered my bum, causing me to murmur with pain. I murmured with a very different emotion as I felt a hand move into the crease between my arse cheeks, urging me to part my legs. I had no idea whose hand it was, but I hoped it was Chris's, as it moved ever lower, searching for the juicy cleft of my pussy. My stance widened even further as the fingers stroked my soft lips and the little bud at the top of them. Soon, I was being openly masturbated, as other hands continued to trace the raised ridges on my backside. The fingers took me to the very brink, then stopped, leaving me gasping and frustrated. I begged for them to continue, aware how pathetic I sounded as I pleaded to be allowed to come but unable to stop myself. To my relief, the fingers resumed their teasing, circling motions, but just as I gave myself to the first spasms of my orgasm, I felt another finger press at the entrance to my bum hole before pushing its way inside. My shame was complete as I was forced to come in front of all these people with a finger buried deep in my anus.

When the waves of pleasure had finally died away, I opened my eyes, expecting to see Chris, or if not, then my husband standing in front of me. Instead, it was Dean's secretary, Caroline, who stood there, licking her fingers clean and obviously relishing the taste of my pussy and bum.

At next year's barbecue, I shall be on my best behaviour.

Debbie S.,
Essex

ON DISPLAY

Perhaps I should never have admitted to my husband that I got turned on by the thought of being dominated. It all started so innocently: I was reading an erotic novel in which the heroine was being trained in all aspects of her behaviour, and being gradually turned into a slave, and Trevor came home to find me with my hand down my panties, frigging myself stupid to this story when I should have been getting his tea ready. He took the book from me and quickly skimmed over the pages that had got me so excited. It was a scene where the heroine was being made to parade naked and display herself in front of her master's friends, and it must have put some ideas in Trevor's mind.

The following evening, he said we were going out for a drink with a few of his friends, and that he wanted me to look nice. He said I should wear an old black lycra miniskirt of mine, which I thought was slightly strange, as he had loved me to wear that skirt when we first started going out, but once we got married he began to object, saying that he did not want me flaunting my figure in front of his friends. He also suggested that I wear a cream chiffon top over a black bra, an outfit which he had previously described as 'too tarty' because it reveals all too clearly how big and heavy my breasts are. It was a warm summer's night, so I did not bother putting on any tights. However, when we came to leave the house, Trevor ran his hands over my bum and I was stunned to hear him say, 'You're not going out dressed like that.'

'But you told me to wear this skirt,' I objected.

'Yeah,' he replied, 'but I didn't say you could wear any knickers with it, did I? Take them off.'

I started to object, but there was a tone to his voice which told me I had better not disobey him and, reluctantly, I slipped out of the panties I was wearing and left them on the table in the hall. As we walked down the street to the pub, I could feel the evening air on my bare pussy, and I felt self-conscious and strangely vulnerable, even though I knew no one could possibly know that I didn't have any underwear on.

In the pub, we went to sit with Gavin, Chris and Simon, who all play for the same Sunday football team as Trevor. If they noticed I was dressed in a slightly more provocative fashion than I had done for a long time, they said nothing, but I could tell from a couple of the glances they exchanged that they liked what they saw.

It was when I sat down that my problems began. We were all squashed into a corner, with me sitting on the end of the row and a stool reserved for Trevor, who had gone to get a round of drinks. When he came back, he said, 'No, Clare, that just won't do.'

I started to ask what he meant, but he continued, 'I want to sit next to the lads. You go and sit on that stool.'

'But, Trevor . . .' I began. Positioned as I had been, it would have been very difficult for anyone to see quite how short my skirt was when I sat down, but if I sat on the stool, it would become obvious.

'Do as you're told,' Trevor retorted and, meekly, I went to sit on the stool. I knew as I did so that, despite my best efforts, I must have been giving the lads a flash of my pubes. I tried, discreetly, to cross my legs and tug my skirt down as best I could, but Trevor spotted what I was doing. To my mortification, he caught hold of the hem of my skirt.

'I think Clare's trying to hide her little secret from you all,' he said, 'but I think you'd like to know that I'm married to the sort of slut who likes to go out in a very short skirt and no panties.' As he spoke, he lifted my skirt, giving all three men a good glimpse of my knickerless pussy. I blushed to the roots of my hair, but at the same time I felt a dark, shameful excitement at being displayed in this way.

'You like that, don't you?' Trevor said to me. 'You like showing my friends your cunt, don't you?'

I didn't know how to react. The truth was that I did like it; it was such a rude thing to do, to let these men whom I didn't really know all that well stare at my most intimate place. But I knew that Trevor was setting me up for something, and I was afraid of what that something might be.

'Well, let them have a really good look, then,' Trevor said. 'Come on, Clare, spread your legs and show them everything.'

And I did. I parted my legs widely, knowing that even in the dim light of the pub they would be able to see the way my pussy was blooming and unfolding, drops of my sex honey beginning to shine on my lips.

'See how obedient she is, the dirty little slut,' Trevor said, with what almost sounded like pride in his voice.

'Does she do anything you tell her?' Chris asked.

'Why don't you come back to our place and find out?' Trevor suggested.

They did not need a second invitation. Drinks were finished with almost indecent haste, and soon we were on our way back home, with Chris, Gavin and Simon in tow. I thought of some of the things the girl in the book I had been reading had been forced to do, and I wondered if Trevor would do any of them to me.

Once in the house, Trevor told our guests to make themselves comfortable in the living room while he poured them all drinks. Then he told me to stand in the middle of the room and take my blouse and skirt off. By now, I knew better than to object, much as I wanted to, so I did as he asked me, standing before the men in nothing but my black bra and high-heeled court shoes. Trevor then ordered me to sit on my haunches, lean back slightly and part my legs. Even using the heels of my hands to balance myself, it was an awkward position, made more humiliating by the fact that I knew the men would have an excellent view of my wet, excited pussy.

'Can I take her bra off?' Gavin asked. 'I've always fancied playing with those big tits of hers.'

'Go ahead, be my guest,' Trevor replied. They seemed to be taking great pleasure in treating me as though I was not there. Still balancing precariously on my haunches, I was forced to endure the feel of Gavin clumsily undoing my bra and pulling the straps off my shoulders so he could grope my breasts. His fingers were rough, pinching and squeezing my tender nipples until I wanted to squeal with the pain. I knew I was powerless to stop Trevor's friends abusing me in this way, and my pussy pulsed as I acknowledged to myself how much this thought turned me on.

'Did I tell you she gives a great blowjob?' Trevor said to no one in particular, but the next thing I saw was Simon reaching for the fly of his combat trousers and bringing his cock out into the open.

'Come on then, slut, prove it,' he ordered, and I crawled over on my hands and knees and took Simon's dick obediently into my mouth.

'Why don't we make her play with herself while she does it?' Chris suggested gleefully, as though the realisation that they all had free rein to do with me as they wished had just struck home.

'Yeah, great idea,' said Gavin. 'Does she own a vibrator?'

'No,' Trevor replied, 'but I've got something that's just as good.' He went over to the mantelpiece and took my plastic-handled hairbrush from where I had left it. He told me to stop sucking Simon's cock for a moment, and thrust the handle of the brush into my mouth in its place, telling me to get it nice and wet so it would slide into me more easily.

When he was satisfied, he ordered me to thrust the hairbrush up myself. By now, I was no longer questioning anything he said to me, and I pushed it into my slippery pussy in one smooth movement. Now, as I continued to lick along the length of Simon's shaft, I was easing the fat handle of the brush in and out of my cunt. Simon, getting impatient to come, grabbed hold of my hair, pulling my head hard on to his groin so that the length of his cock filled my mouth and nudged at my tonsils. For a second I was choking on all that flesh, then I relaxed and breathed through my nose. Within moments, I felt his dick jerking, then my mouth was filling with his thick, bitter come and I was doing my best to gulp it all down. As I pulled away, a long string of spunk dribbling down my chin, I felt a saliva-wet finger – I couldn't tell whose – thrust itself without warning into my arsehole. I groaned, and began to work the brush handle into myself more rapidly. I didn't care what kind of spectacle I was presenting to my husband and his friends, all I wanted was the climax that was building inside me.

The finger that was exploring my arsehole pulled out, only to be replaced a moment later by the blunt head of an excited cock. Now I was securely plugged in both orifices, and I howled my pleasure as whoever was in my arse began to fuck me ruthlessly. I wiped my sweat-stringy hair from my eyes and looked up to see Simon, Gavin and my husband staring at me, revelling in my willing humiliation. That meant it must be Chris whose cock was in my forbidden hole, spurring me on to an orgasm that, when it came, felt as though it was tearing my body apart. I screamed like a lunatic, feeling the muscles in my pussy spasming round the brush handle seconds before Chris groaned and shot his load deep inside my arse.

That was only the start of my erotic degradation that night. By the time Trevor's friends left, each one of them had had me in every orifice. As a grand finale, they made me tell them what a slut I was, how I loved to be fucked and how I only existed to have my holes used by them, while the four of them wanked over my body until, one by one, they splattered me with their come. When they finally finished, I was left with a sore, spunk-filled pussy, and my hair was matted with spunk. Trevor had taken me to a place in my desires that I hadn't even known existed, and I know now that I want more of it. Next time they come round, Trevor has promised that they can piss on me if they want. I'm sure they will, and the thought is enough to have me fingering my pussy as I write this letter.

Clare J.,
Nottingham

TARTY TALE

I have always had a fantasy about forcing a man to wear women's clothes for sex, but I had never quite known how to manufacture a situation where this might happen. Then Sam and I got invited to a vicars and tarts party.

Of course, I was quick to suggest that we should reverse the roles, with me going as the vicar and Sam going as the tart. Initially, he was not keen on the idea, but I managed to persuade him that it would be a laugh. As he and I are roughly the same size, I thought it would not be too difficult for us to swap wardrobes, and this proved to be the case. I borrowed one of Sam's suits and wore it with a black T-shirt and a white cardboard collar round my neck. I even borrowed a pair of his briefs, and stuck a rolled-up sock into them to add to the illusion of masculinity. Without make-up, and with my short, dark hair gelled back in a masculine style, I thought I looked the part.

This, however, was nothing to the transformation I managed to impose on Sam. I lent him a black bra, which we padded out with cotton wool, black lacy knickers which cradled his cock and balls, fishnet stockings, a low-cut red blouse and a short black skirt. I spent ages on his make-up, giving him the full works with mascara, eye liner and scarlet lipstick, and used curling tongs to style his longish blond hair. By the time I had finished, I was joking that he should be careful not to find himself alone in a darkened room with any man, as he would end up being propositioned. Sam was going along with the joke somewhat reluctantly, and I could not tell him how turned on I was getting just looking at him dressed up like that.

When we arrived, it soon became obvious that everyone else had stuck to the traditional roles, and Sam found himself the butt of a lot of rude comments. Although I could barely admit it to myself, I was getting a kick out of the way he was being humiliated, and my mind was full of images of Sam being used like the tart he appeared to be by the men at the party. I wanted to see him on his knees, being made to suck the cock of one of his friends, or bent over the big pine table in the kitchen, my borrowed knickers round his ankles, as he was fucked roughly from behind. My juices were beginning to flow, dampening my underwear, and I wondered how long it would be before Sam and I could make a discreet exit and I could get him home and fuck his brains out.

As it was, we spent about an hour there before I finally took Sam to one side and whispered, 'I can't bear it any longer. I'm so horny, if we don't have sex soon, I think I'm going to burst.'

'Well, why don't we go and see if there's a bedroom free upstairs?' Sam replied.

I shook my head. 'No, I want to go home. I've got a little surprise for you.'

We grabbed our coats, made some excuse about me having a headache and headed back to the house. Once we got inside, Sam announced that he was going to go to the bathroom and take off the make-up, but I stopped him.

'No,' I said. 'I want to fuck you while you're dressed like that.' He looked at me, stunned, as I continued, 'I've always wanted to get you into women's clothes. I thought you'd make a beautiful little tart, and I was right. Now get into the bedroom and don't even think about taking anything off.'

I had never taken such a dominant tone with him, and as I ran my hands over the front of his skirt, I could feel that his cock was a big, solid bulge in his panties. Whatever he might say, I knew that he was turned on by the situation, and I realised in that moment I could probably do whatever I wanted to him.

In the bedroom, I ordered him to get up on the bed on all fours, pull his knickers down and keep looking straight ahead until I told him otherwise. He did so without question, though I'm sure he must have been wondering what was about to happen next. I went to the bedside cabinet, and took out the little toy I had bought especially for a moment like this. Sam kept staring in front of him, even though he could hear the rustling noises of my zip coming down and the sound of something being buckled in place.

When I told him he could look round, the look of horror on his face was almost comical. I was still fully dressed as the upright, saintly vicar, but now there was a big, black strap-on cock protruding from the fly of my trousers. Whatever Sam was about to say died in his throat as I walked round to his head and held the plastic phallus to his red-glossed mouth.

'Suck it,' I ordered him, 'like the dick-hungry slut you are.'

He hesitated for a moment, then his lipsticked lips closed around the tip of the strap-on and he began to lave its length with his saliva. It was such a beautiful sight to see my boyfriend, dressed like a tart, his face exquisitely made up, sucking on this big, fake cock, and my pussy was clenching with lust.

At last, I pulled away. The phallus was wet with spit and ringed with Sam's lipstick, but I still needed more lubrication for what I had planned. I took a tube of lubricating jelly and squeezed a gob of the stuff out on to my finger. Sam hissed through his teeth as I pressed that finger against the entrance to his arse and pushed it inside.

'Get used to the feeling,' I told him, 'because you'll be taking something a lot bigger than my finger by the time we've finished.'

He moaned his compliance, and I smeared more of the greasy jelly around and into his anus, before coating the length of strap-on with another generous dollop. Then I knelt behind him, and put the head of the fake cock to his tight ring. I caressed his tool with my fingers, feeling it bigger and more rigid than I had ever known it. I shuttled my fist up and down it a few times, then told him to take over.

As he wanked himself steadily, I pushed forward, the strap-on entering his arse. He stiffened, fighting against the bizarre intrusion, then relaxed. Inch by inch, I slowly eased the whole length into him, then began to thrust. It was such a glorious sensation to be fucking my feminised boyfriend while he played with his own cock, and it seemed like only moments before he was grunting and his come was oozing out over his busily shuffling fist.

We spent the rest of the night fucking in a more orthodox fashion, but I made sure that I got more than my fair share of orgasms, and it was only when I was completely satisfied that I finally allowed Sam to take off the clothes and wash off the make-up. He made such a beautiful, obedient woman that I shall have to dress him up again soon.

Victoria P.,
Torquay

THE PRIVATE PARTY

I am a dominant master who has taken pleasure over the years in finding suitably submissive females and training them to become obedient, willing slaves. For the last six months, I have been training two girls, Kim and Annette, and I had just reached the point at which I was satisfied with their progress and wanted to turn my attention to someone new when a friend of mine, Leo, contacted me. Leo was organising an event at his house on the fringes of Epping Forest, and was interested to know whether I would like the chance to put my two slaves through their paces before a selection of interested parties. Kim and Annette have always known that one day they would be passed on to someone else, without any say in the matter, and so when I told them they would be taking a trip out to Essex where they would have to perform before potential new masters, they accepted the fact without question.

I took them dressed in nothing more than simple shift dresses, with nothing underneath, and around their necks I strapped the wide silver collars which indicated my mastery of the pair. When I had talked at length to Leo about the procedure for the evening, he had told me that I was the only person who would be taking a brace of slaves, and this would be the last item on the evening's agenda. I knew then that I would be providing the highlight of the night's entertainment, and felt a glow of self-satisfaction, generated by the knowledge that I had trained Kim and Annette to the highest standards. The assembled guests, I was sure, would receive a rare treat when the two girls were shown off.

There were four other slaves on the bill, two male and two female, and I watched with interest as they were displayed. I was not in the market for a trained slave – as I have said, I much prefer to take an innocent in these matters and instruct her in the ways of submission myself – but if I had been, I would have been more than happy with the performance of a small-breasted redhead called Tia, who took a dozen strokes of the two-tailed tawse without flinching, before taking the whole length of her would-be master's seven-inch cock down her slender throat.

Kim and Annette had been kept chained by their ankles to a thick wooden post in an anteroom, and when I was asked to fetch them, I rose to my feet and made a small bow to Leo before leaving the room. Heads turned on my return, eager for a first glimpse of the two girls. Though Kim is of oriental extraction and Annette a fair-skinned brunette, I have had their hair cropped in the same identical severe style, to show their bone structure to best effect, and they were made up to achieve a mask-like effect, rendering them more alike than different. The simple dresses they wore indicated the curves of their bodies without revealing too much, arousing the curiosity of the waiting audience.

I had them stand side by side on the raised dais at one end of the imposing room, heads bowed submissively.

'Gentlemen, may I present Kim and Annette,' I said. 'I can guarantee the utmost obedience from both of them, as I shall demonstrate.' My voice was icy as I gave the first order. 'Strip, the pair of you.'

In synchrony, the girls took hold of the hems of their dresses and raised them over their heads in one fluid movement. There were appreciative murmurs at the sight of their naked bodies. Each girl wears a gold ring through each nipple, and further rings in her labia and clitoris; to show the latter to best effect, I ordered the two to stand with their legs a foot apart. As you would expect, they are expected to keep their bodies free of hair at all times, and the rings could be seen glinting in the folds of their shaven pussies.

'Assume the display position,' I told them. Again in perfect harmony, they dropped to the ground, kneeling up with their thighs splayed and their bejewelled cunts exposed, their hands linked on top of their head, lifting and tautening their breasts. This is the one area where the two girls really differ; Annette has large, round breasts which are surprisingly firm given their size, whereas Kim has the smallest breasts I have ever seen, little more than pads of flesh crowned with large, dark areolae. However, I must admit that I find Kim's form the more arousing of the two, and I love to caress those tiny swellings with my hands flat to her chest, so that her pierced nipples peep out from between my spread fingers.

I could hear the assembled guests muttering amongst themselves, and decided to move on to the next position. 'Display yourselves from behind,' I told them, and they hurried to obey. Now they were standing with their backs to the audience, bent over at the waist and with their legs wide apart. This position was designed to show off their arseholes as well as their denuded pussies, but to give an even better view, they were required to pull their bum cheeks apart with their hands. When I first told the girls that these display positions were a required part of their training, their natural shame overcame them and they were mortified at the thought of anyone being able to see the most intimate parts of their bodies. Now, however, they assumed the positions without a second's thought.

'Can we touch?' a grey-haired man who must have been well into his sixties asked eagerly. I looked across at Leo, who nodded his assent.

'Please, gentlemen, be my guests,' I said. That was the signal for the half-dozen or so men to rise from their seats and step up on to the dais. One by one, they ran their hands over the bodies of my two slaves as the girls tried their hardest not to move or make a sound – both of which they knew to be punishable offences. However, it must have been difficult for them as cunning fingers stroked their breasts and pinched their nipples, or delved between their legs to insinuate themselves into their vaginas.

Most of them were taking the opportunity to pass comments of the crudest and most uncomplimentary nature on the slave's physical attributes. One dark-skinned, balding man ran his hands over Kim's torso and muttered, 'Hasn't got much in the way of tits, has she?'

'You wouldn't believe how sensitive they are, though,' I pointed out. 'Go on, see for yourself.'

I watched as the man took hold of the ring in one of Kim's stiff little nipples and tugged it to a degree which must have been distressing for my slave. Despite all the warnings I had given her, she could not prevent herself from letting out a moan which indicated that, far from being in pain, she was becoming aroused at this man's cruel actions. A smile flitted across his face as he realised that I had been telling the truth. I have known Kim to come simply from having those tiny teats pulled and tormented, but I was sure that if he was interested in acquiring her, he would find that out for himself.

The grey-haired master who had first expressed a desire to touch the slaves was running his finger down the crease between Annette's bum cheeks. The tautly stretched skin between her pussy and anus is one of the most sensitive spots on her body, and I could see she was doing her best not to betray the reaction his touch was causing. He took his index finger and, without even bothering to moisten it with her juices or his saliva, thrust it roughly into her dusky rosebud. She flinched, and I realised he was doing his best to increase any punishment she would receive as part of the evening's entertainment.

'Isn't it time you showed us how much punishment they can take?' one of the other men asked, and the others hurried to agree with him. I could see more than one pair of trousers was tented out with a partial erection, and knew they were eager to move on to the apex of the performance.

'Very well,' I said. There was a big iron hook hanging from the ceiling, and I intended to put it to good use. I had brought a selection of restraints and implements of punishment, not knowing exactly what Leo and his circle were expecting to see, and now I began to make use of it. I ordered the slaves to stand upright and put their hands together in front of them, then I cuffed each girl's wrists together using padded leather cuffs. Then I told them to stand beneath the hook, their bodies pressed together. Using a length of chain, I secured the two of them to the hook in the ceiling, their arms above their heads. Kim, being the smaller of the two, was standing on tiptoes, and both girls' bodies were straining in position. Finally, I wound a long leather strap around them, securing them together at the waist. It was a stunningly erotic sight to see them bound like that, Annette's big breasts squashed against Kim's flat chest and their pubic bones pressing together.

'The soft cat first, then the bullwhip,' I announced, picking up the first of the two instruments. The suede cat, with its short, soft tails, is one of my favourite toys, ideal for softening up a slave in preparation for a more thorough whipping. I played it lightly over the girls' bound bodies, concentrating on their fleshy bum cheeks and the backs of their thighs. They were soon moaning as the suede thongs landed on their skin, and when I curled it around so that it landed on the sensitive pout of Kim's pussy, there was a little yelp of anguish from her and a purr of appreciation from the audience.

I knew they wanted to see the girls take a severe punishment, and that was why I had brought the bullwhip. This is not an instrument to be taken lightly; in the wrong hands it could cause severe injury. There was absolute silence in the room as I laid the whip on with all the skill I possessed, lashing it down on the girls' buttocks and watching the livid welts that sprung up where it landed. The moans changed to shrieks and sobs, and the two slaves twisted in their bonds, seeking to escape from the cruel cuts of the whip but knowing they were unable to. Cocks were being stroked at the sight of the girls' punished bodies rubbing together, and at least one of the men there had already climaxed.

Finally, I unfastened the leather strap which tied the two together and ordered the lithe Kim to wrap her legs around Annette's waist and grind her pubis hard against the other girl until the stimulation caused them both to come. The audience broke into spontaneous applause as I unchained my slaves and helped them down from the dais, delighted by what they had seen.

I am happy to say that both girls have found a good home following that performance, and I now have the delicious task of training a new slave to those same high standards of obedience.

Michael A.,
Chelmsford

My fantasy has always been to serve two equally dominant mistresses, and to be made to do whatever they require of me, no matter how difficult or demeaning.

I see myself becoming a full-time slave to the pair, being forced to relinquish my job and to hand over all my assets, including my house, my car and the contents of my bank account, to them. As I am to become their maid, they dispose of my male clothing, and make me wear nothing but a little frilly white apron and a collar round my neck which marks me as their property. My male name is relinquished and I become known to them as Snowdrop. From the moment they wake to the moment they retire to bed, I am at the mercy of their every whim and command. I sleep in the kitchen, chained by my collar to the pipes beneath the sink, so that I am ready to prepare their breakfast as soon as they wake me by ringing the bell they keep beside their beds. I have to perform all the household chores: I dust the house from top to bottom, I keep the kitchen spotlessly clean, I do the ironing and I wash my mistresses' clothes. Their expensive silk and lace lingerie has to be handwashed, and woe betide me if I am caught taking a surreptitious sniff of their feminine aromas from the gussets of their panties! Their standards of cleanliness are exactingly high, and if I slack in any respect – from leaving the smallest smear on the dressing table mirror to neglecting to clean behind the cooker – I am soundly thrashed as a reminder not to do it again.

I am also required to attend to my mistresses' sexual needs. Normally, they will torment me by offering me the merest glimpse up their long, stocking-clad legs when I am kneeling at their feet. Mistress

Tania, in particular, delights in standing above me wearing no panties, allowing me to gaze up at her beautiful blonde bush and the shell-pink folds of her sex lips. I am not allowed to get an erection without permission, but the sight of Mistress Tania's glorious cunt is usually too much for me, and she will punish me for my gross impertinence by slapping my erect penis with her gloved hand. However, I am occasionally ordered to pleasure my mistresses orally, and I find it such an honour to lick and lap at their beautiful pussies and succulent clits until they climax. Of course, I am not permitted any relief myself at these times, and before I begin I am strapped into a severe penis restraint with spikes on the inside, which prick my sensitive cock flesh as soon as it begins to rise. Sometimes my mistresses will take pity on me and allow me to wank myself until I come; my hand shuttles up and down my shaft to the accompaniment of jeers of derision from my mistresses and comments about the puny size of my prick. When my semen oozes out over my fist, they just laugh and tell me to go and clean myself up.

The highlight of my existence is when Mistress Tania and Mistress Dionne decide to throw a party, to which they will invite all their equally dominant friends. Then, I can look forward to being at the mercy of as many as a dozen cruel, stunningly attractive women, all of whom know that they have carte blanche to do with me as they will. On these special occasions, my shoulder-length red hair is put into two bunches, which are tied with pink ribbon. A third piece of ribbon is tied around my cock, and when ordered to, I must raise my apron to show this pink bow to everyone in the room. As you can imagine, this causes hoots of laughter from the assembled guests and comments about what a little cissy I am. I spend the evening attending to the guests in whatever way they desire. I move between them serving glasses of champagne and canapés, to the accompaniment of hands reaching under my little apron to fondle my cock and balls. I cannot prevent myself from getting an erection with this constant treatment, even though I know this is expressly forbidden, and when Mistress Tania spots my hard shaft pushing against the apron, she orders the punishment to begin.

I am taken to the centre of the room, and made to bend over the back of a chair, my hairy white arse exposed to the gaze of all the women there. Mistress Dionne brings out two dice and explains that throwing the first one will determine how many strokes of any particular implement I will be given, and the second determines what that implement will be. One is the hand, two is the paddle, three is the riding crop, four is the cat-o'-nine-tails, five is the tawse and six is my least favourite, the thin, whippy cane. As you can imagine, I particularly dread anyone throwing a double six! The uncertainty of what any particular punishment will consist of adds considerably to my dread and the enjoyment of my mistresses, who are always the last to take their turns. By the time they do, my backside is a mass of pain, my flesh scarlet and marked with vicious raised weals where the cane has left its mark or my skin has been caught between the tails of the tawse. However, Mistress Tania and Mistress Dionne show me no pity, and they lay on their allotted instruments with all the severity they can muster. If all they are to give me is a hand spanking, they will wet their palms first, to make the slaps more painful for me. Sometimes, I will be made to complete my humiliation by wanking for the assembled guests, often into a hollowed-out watermelon, which the guests find especially amusing. After I have been verbally abused for being a wimp, a cissy and a wanker, I am sent to the kitchen to begin the long process of cleaning up, knowing I will find it difficult to sleep that night for the dull, lingering ache in my punished bum flesh.

I would give anything to be treated like this in real life, and would love to meet a woman who would dominate me so cruelly.

Andrew J.,
Lincoln

A WEEKEND'S TRAINING

I have been a full-time slave to my master for over a year now, and in that time he has taught me what it means to be completely obedient. He never tires of finding ways to test the depth of my submission and my loyalty to him, but I was still surprised when he told me that I was in need of a refresher course and would be sent to visit a friend of his, Gareth, for the weekend. Gareth apparently had a secluded house which was ideal for entertaining slaves, and I was to expect him to assess me severely on my performance and discipline me accordingly.

On the Friday evening, a chauffeur-driven Bentley rolled up in front of our house. I had been told how I was to dress to arrive at Gareth's, and I had followed his instructions to the letter. Beneath my coat, I wore only a suspender belt and gossamer-fine stockings. My shoes had six-inch stiletto heels and my pussy was freshly shaven, displaying the silver rings in my outer labia. I was apprehensive, but determined to make sure that my master's training methods were not found wanting.

Once in the car, the chauffeur ordered me to remove my coat. I did as I was told, grateful that the Bentley's tinted windows would offer me some protection from the curious gaze of passing traffic. I was not to be spared the gaze of the chauffeur, however: following orders he had been given by Gareth, he made me sit well back on the seat, with my knees tucked up to my chest. Then I had to take hold of my ankles and part my legs, giving him an excellent view in the driver's mirror of my shaven slit and the rings that adorned it. He said nothing, and the dispassionate way in which he looked at me as I sat in this deeply uncomfortable position simply served to excite me.

'By the way,' he added, 'the master has said that if there are any stains on the seat when we arrive, you're licking them off yourself.'

I whimpered, feeling my juices starting to flow and hoping I might be made to pleasure myself while we drove, or that the chauffeur would stop the car and fuck me roughly over the bonnet so that I would spend the rest of the journey with his thick seed trickling out of me on to the expensive, cream upholstery. However, we arrived at Gareth's beautiful house without incident, and I was spared the embarrassment of having to remove the tell-tale signs of my excitement from the leather with my tongue.

The door to the house opened and the chauffeur led me inside, still naked but for my stockings and heels. A man was waiting in the hallway who I assumed to be Gareth. I caught a brief impression of a man over six foot in height with blond hair brushed back from his face and wearing a black polo-necked jumper and jeans before I dropped my head and put my hands behind my back to allow him to scrutinise me. I knew the sight I was presenting to him: I have caramel-coloured skin and long, straight dark hair that falls to the small of my back. My breasts are very firm and full, and appear even larger due to the fact that my waist is tiny and my hips flare out above the rounded curves of my bottom. I was aware of Gareth walking all the way round me, but I did not dare raise my gaze to his.

'How did she behave in the car?' I heard him asking the chauffeur.

'Just as she was asked to,' the chauffeur replied. 'It's a pity you didn't ask me to fuck her,' he added ruefully.

'All in good time,' Gareth said. 'I can promise you that you will have your fill of her cunt and arse before she leaves here.'

I shivered at the casual way in which I was being discussed, though in truth the slim, dark-haired chauffeur was almost as good-looking as his master, and the prospect of him fucking me, even in my virgin anus, was not an unpleasant one.

I felt Gareth's hand on the point of my chin and he raised my face so I was staring into his warm green eyes. 'You have been prepared something to eat,' he said. 'I'll take you into the kitchen.'

He led me down the hallway and into the kitchen. I looked around for other members of his staff, but saw no one.

'I only employ Mayfield, the chauffeur, and Mrs Christie. She's the cook and housekeeper. She's gone for the night but you'll meet her tomorrow. Your food is keeping warm in the stove. Take it out.'

I retrieved a plate of delicious-smelling stew and went to take it to the kitchen table, but Gareth stopped me. 'No, you stupid slut,' he said curtly. 'On the floor.'

I realised there was a metal ring set in the skirting board close to the cooker. As I watched, Gareth retrieved a length of chain from a cupboard, along with a wide leather collar that had a D-ring at the front. He fastened the collar tightly round my neck. 'While you're here, you will wear this at all times, to show that you are, temporarily at least, my property.' He attached the chain to the ring in the collar, then secured the other end to the ring in the skirting board. Then he took the plate from my hands and placed it on the floor. 'Eat,' he ordered.

With no cutlery offered or asked for, I got on my knees and ate my dinner like a dog. The stew tasted as good as it smelled, but that did not lessen the indignity of my position. My master had never yet treated me like this, and now I realised why he thought a couple of days under the scrutiny of Gareth would teach me to better understand the reality of servitude.

After I had licked the plate completely clean, Gareth unclipped my chain from the wall, and took me to his bedroom. By now, it was nearly eleven o'clock.

'You will be sleeping on the floor tonight,' he told me. 'If I wake you at any point and demand sexual relief from you, you will not refuse. If you behave and do everything I ask, you will be allowed to sleep on the bed tomorrow night.'

With that, he began to undress, finally slipping between the sheets naked, while I curled up in a ball on the floor and did my best to fall asleep. It was difficult; although the room was not cold, I missed the comfort of a blanket to pull over myself, and images were running through my head of Gareth waking with an erection, which he would order me to suck or take in my compliant pussy. Eventually, I drifted off, and was almost disappointed that Gareth decided against using me during the course of the night.

In the morning, I was woken by a woman coming into the room carrying a tray. Grey-haired and in her fifties, she must have been the housekeeper, Mrs Christie. She set Gareth's breakfast down in front of him as he sat up in bed, but I noticed there was no food for me.

'You'll be eating in the kitchen again,' Gareth told me. 'But first you have to use the toilet. Mrs Christie will supervise you.'

The housekeeper unchained me from the foot of the bed and led me into Gareth's en suite bathroom. I expected her to shut the door and leave me some privacy, but she just stood there, arms folded. 'The master has asked me to make sure you do as you are told,' she said. Her tone was not unfriendly, and I had peed under the gaze of my own master before now, but I had never had a woman watch me as I performed such an intimate task. I sat, shame-faced, on the toilet and voided my bladder with a little difficulty as Mrs Christie stood there. When I had finished, she tore a couple of sheets of paper off the roll, ordered me to open my legs wide and wiped me dispassionately, adding to my humiliation. Then she took me off to the kitchen to have my breakfast, which, as before, I had to eat on all fours on the floor.

After breakfast, Gareth decided it was time to introduce me to some of the implements of correction at his disposal. He took me down to the dungeon which he had had installed in his cellar, and told me I was going to learn what it was really like to be punished.

He had a large and generously padded whipping stool, over which I was told to bend. Once I was in place, he chained my wrists and ankles to the stool. My legs were widely spread apart, which I knew would give Gareth access to my pussy and anus. I shuddered at the thought of those knowing green eyes scrutinising my shaven sex and puckered nether hole.

'A few with the whip first, I think,' he murmured. Chained as I was, I could not see what type of whip he was referring to; it could have been anything from a short riding whip to a full-blooded bullwhip. However, when I felt him trailing the instrument over my backside and down the cleft between my cheeks, I realised it had many short, soft leather tails, and realised he was going to use this to soften me up before applying something more severe to my behind.

I tensed, waiting for him to lay it on. The anticipation was causing me to tremble in my restraints, yet I would be lying if I said that was purely through fear. I dreaded the punishment he was about to inflict on me, true, but I also welcomed it. The discipline I had already received at the hands of my master – limited though it was turning out to be – had taught me there was a point where pain and pleasure blurred and became one, and I was sure Gareth would know exactly how to take me to that place.

I heard the tails of the whip whistling through the air and then they landed, spreading out across the surface of my rear, each tip prickling me with a little sting of discomfort. He knew what he was doing, and his swift, methodical strokes were covering every inch of skin, moving down to stripe the soft flesh of my inner thighs. I moaned and wriggled in my bonds, but in truth I was in no real pain. Instead, I was reacting to the warm feeling in my belly and the growing wetness between my legs. I could smell my own briny excitement in the closed confines of the dungeon and was sure that Gareth could, too.

At last, he threw down the whip and went to choose another implement. This time, he walked in front of me as he returned to the whipping stool, allowing me to get a clear view of what he was holding. It was a tawse.

My master had never used the instrument on me, but I knew of the vicious instrument by reputation. A tawse was designed with two tails, so that when they landed on your skin, they would pinch a bit of it painfully between the tails. This was going to hurt far more than the whip, and I held my breath as Gareth came to stand behind me once more. He slapped the tawse against his palm, and I shuddered, knowing that he was just prolonging my agony. I wanted this to be done and over with, but he took his time.

He was just as thorough with the tawse as he had been with the whip, only this time the pain was severe. I could not stop myself from yelling as the rough leather straps landed on my bum. The pain radiated out until my whole arse was throbbing and I could feel tears pricking my eyes. Gareth paused, and ran his fingers over the ridges the tawse had raised on my skin. Even though his touch was gentle, I could not stop myself from wincing and trying to pull away.

'Have you had enough, slave?' he asked me, and I nodded, even though I knew that would only encourage him to punish me even further. But, to my surprise and gratitude, he unshackled me and let me stretch my cramped limbs. Then he led me back to the kitchen and chained me up again.

I must have fallen asleep, because the next thing I knew was a gentle kick in my ribs. I jerked awake to see Mayfield, the chauffeur, staring down at me with a grin on his face. I must have looked wretched, my face still blotchy with tears and my bum bearing the marks of the tawse, and I wondered what was about to happen. He quickly unfastened me, and led me out to the garden. Gareth was sitting in a deckchair, drinking a glass of Pimm's, and he nodded his approval at the sight of me, naked and standing meekly before him.

'Fetch Mrs Christie,' Gareth told his chauffeur. 'I want you both here for this.'

I wanted to ask what 'this' was, but dared not. I soon found out, as Mrs Christie joined us on the lawn, wiping her hands on her apron.

'I want you both to see how obedient the little slut is,' he told them. Then he turned his attention to me and I realised he was loosing his cock from his flies. 'On your knees and suck, slut.'

I could no more have dreamed of disobeying him than I could of flying to the moon. I opened my lips and took the mushroom head of his dick between them. He tasted warm and salty and I licked him with relish, oblivious to the fact that I was being watched by his domestic staff.

I was expecting him to come in my mouth, but after a few minutes he pulled out, turning to Mayfield. 'She's good,' he said, 'but don't take my word for it. See for yourself.'

The chauffeur smiled and dropped his uniform trousers. My jaw dropped at the size of his cock. Even flaccid, it was longer than his boss's, and I doubted for a moment whether I would be able to wrap my lips around it. I had no time to ponder that, as he thrust it roughly into my mouth. It hardened rapidly as I began to suck it, and soon I was almost choking on the solid column of flesh that pressed against my palate. Unlike Gareth, he didn't withdraw when he sensed he was coming, and I spluttered as a hot jet of spunk hit the back of my throat. I did my best to swallow it down, my eyes watering as I struggled to cope. I could feel Gareth's mocking gaze on me, and felt inadequate and humiliated.

That was nothing, however, to what I felt a moment later, as Mayfield withdrew his shrinking manhood from my mouth, and wiped it clean on my hair. Gareth was gesturing to Mrs Christie. 'We've seen what she can do with a cock,' he said. 'Now let's see what she's like with a pussy.'

This was not something I had expected, and I tried to object as the housekeeper lifted her skirts to reveal that she wore no knickers. I stared at the crinkled, grey hair that covered her cunt, and realised there was no way I could back out. I had never tasted a woman's sex flesh before and, as she pushed me down on to the grass and settled herself over my face, my nostrils were assailed with her ripe, tangy odour. Afraid of what Gareth might do to me if I did not comply, I reached out my tongue and began to lick along her slit.

Mrs Christie was a heavy woman, and her weight was pressing me into the grass as she writhed on my face. Her juices were starting to flow into my mouth as I lapped at her pussy, and I was aware of Gareth and his chauffeur commenting on my performance as I did my best to satisfy her. I found her clitoris and stabbed at it with my tongue, trying to pleasure her in the way I would have liked to be pleasured. Her sighs of enjoyment and the way she ground herself against my nose indicated that I must be doing something right. Suddenly, she gave a harsh cry and I realised she was coming, her thigh muscles holding me in such a tight grasp that I feared I would suffocate, unable to breathe in anything but her gushing, salty come.

At last, she released her grip on me and I rolled out from under her, gasping for breath like a landed fish and with Gareth's mocking laughter ringing in my ears. I sensed, though, that I had passed a test, however inexpertly, and knew that when I returned to my master the thought of being forced to lick another woman out would hold no fear for me.

I passed the rest of the weekend in similar fashion, alternating between being kept restrained in some part of Gareth's house and being asked to show my sexual devotion to him and his staff. Both Mayfield and Mrs Christie fucked me repeatedly, the housekeeper using a strap-on dildo of obscene proportions which I was ordered to moisten with my own saliva before she thrust it into me and to lick clean of my juices when she had finished.

On the Sunday before I left, Gareth chose to breach another of my taboos, when he compelled me to have anal sex for the first time. This was something my master had often threatened to do to me, and I could feel my stomach muscles clenching in sick anticipation as I watched Gareth grease his erect cock with a clear lubricating gel. To add to my degradation, he told Mrs Christie to hold me in place as he buggered me. The housekeeper had stripped to the waist, revealing her huge, pendulous breasts with their rubbery red nipples, and my face was crushed between them as I felt Gareth kicking my legs wide apart before placing the head of his cock at the entrance to my anus. I did my best to relax as he began to push his way through this previously unbreached barrier, but could not prevent myself from whimpering in discomfort. To stifle my cries, Mrs Christie stuffed one of her nipples into my mouth and ordered me to suck. I did as I was told, chewing on her stiff teat as Gareth thrust into my arse with increasing ferocity. It seemed to take for ever before I felt his shaft grow even bigger and thicker in the brief moment before he pumped his spunk deep into my body. At last, he pulled out of me, wiping his cock clean with a hank of my hair before hauling me back into the kitchen and chaining me up until it was time for me to leave.

I was finally returned to my master, weary and sore but knowing I had passed every ordeal Gareth had put me through. I have been warned that if I fall from the high standards of behaviour that are expected of me, I will be sent back for another weekend, and I have to admit that on one level I am almost looking forward to it.

Lorraine D.,
Folkestone

Showing Off

IN-CAR ENTERTAINMENT

When I met my wife, Holly, I soon became aware that she had exhibitionist tendencies, and I did my best to encourage them. Unlike a lot of men, who like their women to dress in as daring a fashion as possible when they first start going out and then complain about the attention this attracts once they are married, I am happy for as many men as possible to appreciate the visible delights of Holly's horny body, knowing that she will be coming home with me at the end of the evening, leaving them to nurse their hard-ons in frustration. Sometimes she would go out in a really short skirt with no knickers beneath it, or she would wear a jacket over a sheer black body stocking with no bra underneath. At some point during the evening, she would inevitably flash her tits or pussy, offering whoever happened to be nearby something to fuel their wank fantasies. We would always go home and spend the rest of the night fucking after an evening where she had flaunted herself, turned on by our daring little game.

However, after a while this was no longer enough. We wanted to take our exhibitionistic behaviour further, but neither of us was sure how. Then we were in a pub one night, and I got talking to a man who told me about what he assured me was called 'dogging'. When I asked him to explain further, he said that there was a wood on the edge of town where couples would go to have sex in their cars while other people watched. When I mentioned this to Holly, she admitted the thought of fucking in such a public spot was something she had often fantasised about. It gave her another chance to flaunt her body and take her exhibitionism to the next level, but in what she felt was a relatively safe environment. A couple of nights later, we drove up to that spot to see if what I had been told was true.

When we got there, we couldn't believe what we saw. A rusty white van was parked up, of the sort painters and decorators often use, with about three or four men gathered round the back. After a couple of moment's speculation about what might be going on in the van, Holly and I worked up the courage to get quietly out of the car and join the crowd. The back doors of the van were thrown open and there, among a litter of paint pots and rags which gave off a strong scent of turpentine, we could see a bare-breasted blonde straddling a man's body, facing his feet. She was bouncing up and down and playing with her nipples. Every time she pulled herself up off him, we could see that she must have been sliding up and down on a good nine inches of solid cock flesh. Although she must have been completely aware of the audience's presence – after all, this was not the vision we had had of a snatched glimpse of a fucking couple through a steamed-up car window – she seemed completely oblivious to them.

This was all the encouragement Holly and I needed. We got in the car and drove home so fast I'm amazed I didn't get clocked by a speed camera. Then we spent the rest of the night fucking. As I pounded into Holly's wet quim, my head was full of the vision of that big, blue-veined cock sliding in and out of that blonde's juiced-up pussy.

Holly and I talked it over the following morning, and decided that although we were not prepared to go quite as far as the couple we had seen – after all, anyone could have reached into the back of that van and joined in the action – we really wanted to give it a go.

A week later, we drove up to the dogging spot. The clearing where we had seen the white van was empty, so we parked there, climbed on to the back seat and got down to the sort of petting that is usually indulged in by young couples who don't have a private space of their own where they can fuck.

I could feel Holly's heart pounding in her chest as I pulled her top up and unclipped the fastening of her bra, and knew she was as nervous as I was. I suckled on her nipple as she unbuttoned the fly of my jeans. I never wear underwear, so the next thing I felt was her warm hand on my rapidly hardening cock. She wanked me expertly with one hand, cupping my balls and squeezing them with the other, while my mouth feasted on her tits.

Suddenly, we became aware of shadows against the car window, and knew that our audience had arrived. Hoping we had been joined by a keen voyeur or two, rather than a couple of members of the local constabulary, I pushed Holly down so that she was lying on the seat, and pulled her knickers off. Even though there was plenty of condensation on the windows, I was sure whoever was watching was getting a good view of her creamy pussy as she raised her bum to let me undress her more easily. I fingered her for a moment or two, hearing the urgent groans which always let me know she's ready to feel my cock inside her, and then I knelt over her, put the head of my glans to her moist entrance, and slid home. The force of our fucking made the car rock on its axles, and I knew that even if people could not see what we were doing, the noise would be a giveaway. Holly was begging me to fuck her harder, and I was happy to oblige, as my balls grew tight and I knew I was about to shoot my lot inside her. Her semi-clad body stiffened beneath me and then stilled, and I knew she had peaked, my own climax following only moments behind.

When we had recovered and dressed, I wiped the steam from the window and looked out to see that our audience had gone. When we got home and got out of the car, I saw that there were long streaks of what could only be dried come on both the rear doors, proving that at least two people had been wanking while they watched us fuck.

Since that evening, we have returned there a few times, and the number of people watching us has grown. We are even talking about fucking with the door open, or even getting out of the car. I love the idea of pressing Holly up against the bonnet, naked, while I pump my cock into her from behind and our audience cheers us on, urging me to use her in whatever way takes my fancy.

John M.,
Doncaster

YOU'VE BEEN FRAMED

My boyfriend Warren and I have always been turned on by the idea of fucking in public. For some reason, just the thought that someone else might be able to see what we're doing gets him hard as a rock and has me juicing my knickers like no one's business. We were reading through a contact magazine one time, and we came across an advert from a bloke who was looking for couples who he could video in action. Of course, this really appealed to us: not only would we be able to perform for him, but we would get a copy of the tape that we could show to all our mates. We replied to the ad, sending photos of ourselves that showed off my perky little tits and shaved pussy and Warren's hard nine-inch cock, and a week later we got a phone call from a guy called Roger who said he liked what he saw and wanted to meet us.

We arranged to meet in a motorway service station a few miles away from where we live. The idea was that Roger would bring his camera and, if we all got on, we would drive back to our place and he could video us that afternoon. Roger turned out to be a weaselly looking bloke in his early forties, with a greasy black quiff, but after talking to him over a couple of cups of foul-tasting coffee we realised he was on the level, and we were more than happy to let him film us fucking. Forty minutes later, we were pulling up in the drive of our semi, with Roger in tow. I had been playing with Warren's hard-on through his jeans as he drove, and fingering my own pussy as I thought about what we were going to do.

Roger took a quick look round the house and decided he wanted to film us fucking over the kitchen table. That was fine by me, as I love it when Warren slides that big, firm dick of his into me from behind. Roger was definitely going to get the hot, raw action he had told us he was looking for.

When he got his camera out, I could hardly believe it. The thing was only as big as his palm, but he assured us it was the latest digital technology, and the results would be great. We needed no further persuasion to get down to it and, by now, all I could think about was how it would feel as I creamed myself on Warren's cock.

Roger said he was not going to give us any direction, as he never dubbed a soundtrack on to these tapes afterwards; we were just to go as the mood took us. Well, I knew exactly where the mood was taking me, and as Roger trained that little camera on me, I dropped to my knees in front of Warren and unleashed his manhood from his jeans. It rapidly unfurled to its full length as I wanked it with swift, steady strokes, the foreskin peeling back to reveal the big mushroom head. Juice was already oozing from the little eye in its tip, and I took as much of it as I could between my lips and began to give him a long, lingering blowjob. I had purposely worn loads of bright red lipstick, and as I sucked Warren it smeared along the length of his shaft. He was hot and pulsing in my mouth, and as I caressed his taut bollocks I knew it wasn't going to be long before he was coming. I let his cock drop from my mouth, a long trail of saliva stretching out and then breaking as I did so, and urged him to fuck me.

I was wearing a tight blue lycra top, and Warren pushed it up so that my tits emerged from underneath. They're only tiny, and his big hands can easily cover them so that only the hard little nipples emerge. I groaned as he squeezed the tips tight between his fingers, and thrust my pelvis back at him. He lifted up my skirt and pulled my knickers down so they were around my knees, then I quickly wriggled out of them, hoping Roger was focusing his camera on my juicy, excited pussy. Warren bent me over the table, guided the head of his cock to my waiting hole, and shoved it inside me. I gasped at the force of his penetration, knowing he was going to be rough with me and loving him for it. I hung on to the sides of the table for dear life as he fucked me, feeling my pussy mound banging against the hard wood with every stroke. I was aware of Roger moving around us, stepping back to take in the whole picture, before coming in close to focus on Warren's shaft sliding in and out of my creamy cunt.

Warren's thrusts were speeding up, and I knew he was about to come. To my disappointment, he pulled out of me, and I almost went to grab his cock and push it back inside me, when I realised what he was going to do. He gave a grunt, and I felt his warm spunk splattering my arse cheeks for the benefit of Roger's lens. Not to be deprived of my own orgasm, I reached between my legs and diddled my own clit, crying out as my love juices gushed out on to my furiously rubbing fingers.

Three days later, Warren and I got a tape in the post from Roger. It featured our kitchen-table fuck, immortalised in all its hot, sweaty glory. It's now become our favourite viewing when we want to get in the mood for sex, and we've even shown it to friends who reckon we'd have a good future as porn stars. Roger is going to come round and video us again; we'll let you know how it goes.

Paula T.,
Bedfordshire

WET AND WILLING

I would like to tell you about a party I went to last summer, which ended with me making a complete exhibition of myself. It was my cousin Gill's twenty-first birthday and, as it was a beautiful July day, she had decided to have a pool party. I was really looking forward to it, until she told me she had invited a girl she works with called Isabel. Now, Isabel and I were at school together, and we were never able to stand each other after I pinched a boy she fancied from under her nose when we were both in the sixth form. I knew I would have to try to be sociable but, as soon as I saw Isabel, I realised just how difficult that was going to be.

She was bragging to everyone about how she had just got back from a week in an exclusive Spanish holiday resort, and wearing a tiny white dress that really showed off her honey-coloured tan. Her long, blonde hair was cut to flatter her elfin face, and her make-up was immaculate. I had dressed much more casually, in cut-off jeans and a bright pink bra top, and I felt dowdy in comparison.

It soon became obvious from her conversation that Isabel was doing much better for herself than I am. I have a decent job in a branch of a well-known building society, but Isabel had just been promoted to the role of PA to a merchant banker in the City. She also, she claimed, had a rich boyfriend who was fantastic in bed, and could not do enough to please her. I had recently split up from a guy I had been seeing for a couple of years, and Isabel's boasting on the subject of her boyfriend was the last thing I wanted to hear.

After half an hour or so of her incessant chatter, I just could not take any more. I was sitting on the edge of the pool, dangling my feet in the cool water, when she walked past on the way to the buffet table in the dining room. I could not resist it. I caught hold of her ankle, and sent her flying into the pool. Everyone's head turned as there was a startled cry from Isabel, followed by a huge splash. When she rose to her feet, her beautiful outfit had been ruined. Her long hair was plastered to her skull, her make-up was running down her face and her dress had gone transparent, the dark circles of her nipples proving that she was braless underneath it.

I tried to make my apology as sincere as I could, but Isabel must have known what had happened was no accident. A few of the other guests were pointing at her and sniggering as she stood waist-high in the water, and her injured pride demanded only one response from her. She grabbed my leg and hauled me into the pool to join her. I squealed as my body was completely submerged, and struggled to the surface, pushing my wet hair out of my eyes.

'OK, so now we're even,' I said, and went to climb out of the pool, but Isabel caught my arm. She was surprisingly strong, and I tried to break free of her grasp without success.

'We're not even, not by a long way,' she replied. 'I've never paid you back for pinching Neil off me, not properly, but now I'm going to.'

'What do you mean?' I asked, worried by her venomous tone.

'You humiliated me, and now I'm going to humiliate you,' she said. The next thing I felt was her fingers fumbling with the fastening of my bra top. She knew exactly what she was doing, and it fell free from my body to float on the surface of the water. Suddenly, my little breasts were visible to everyone who had gathered round the pool, the nipples standing out proudly. I should have gathered up my top and what was left of my dignity then and there, but I was so incensed with rage at what Isabel had done to me that I just went for her in a fury.

I gripped the neck of her thin cotton dress and pulled, ripping the front in two so that it flapped apart. Now two pairs of tits were on display, Isabel's significantly larger than my own, I could not help but notice.

Isabel's response was to grab me by the hair and haul me out of the pool, her grip hard enough to make me think my hair would be pulled out by its roots. We squared up to each other on the grass, our audience almost forgotten, and then we were wrestling each other in a tangle of arms and legs. We scratched and clawed at each other, Isabel's fingers finding the fastening of my cut-offs. Once it was undone, despite my frantic efforts to prevent her, she dragged them down, together with my knickers, so that they caught around my ankles. I tried to pull them back up, but as we rolled over and over on the grass they were ripped off by our movements. Now I was stark naked, while Isabel was still wearing her panties and the remnants of her dress. I managed to manoeuvre her into a position where I could make a grab for her panties and shred those, too – silk may look nice, but you would be surprised how easily it rips when you try.

Neither of us cared what kind of a spectacle we were presenting, even though I was vaguely aware of cheers and cries of encouragement from a couple of the guys who were watching us; all that mattered was making the other one submit. Grievances which had festered for years had come to the surface, and now each of us was seeking retributions for slights both real and imagined.

Eventually, it was Isabel's extra strength which told. She had me pinned down on the ground and as she squatted over me, her bum directly over my face, I suddenly realised what it was she intended to do.

'Lick me,' she ordered.

'I – I can't,' I replied. 'Not in front of all these people . . .'

Her only answer was to lower herself until her pussy was pressed against my mouth. I had no other choice but to do as she wanted, tasting another woman's cunt for the first time and smelling the pungent scent of her arsehole. She ground herself on to my face as I licked away, until I thought I might almost suffocate from the weight and the strength of her. Finally, she lifted herself up and I had a moment's respite, but all she was doing was shifting round so that she was facing my feet. When she settled herself again, I felt her pulling my legs apart, and realised she was giving everyone around me the chance to look at my open pussy. I felt completely humiliated as she urged me to lick harder and faster. At last, she had a noisy climax, her juices dripping down into my mouth as I lay pinioned beneath her.

Our audience, sensing that the show was over as Isabel had no intention of reciprocating what I had just done to her, began to drift away, and I was left to gather up my scattered clothes and make my way home.

If by any chance Isabel is reading this, I would like to assure her that next time I see her the boot will be on the other foot, and she will be the one who has to submit to me. I shall really enjoy making sure that she does.

Megan D.,
Guildford

All Wrapped Up

HIS LITTLE PONY

If you had told me six months ago that I would enjoy being treated like a pony and made to pull a cart, I would never have believed you, but that's what happened after I met Pete. He has been going to fetish clubs for much longer than I have, and in that time he's got heavily into the pony scene. So much so, that when he and I started dating, he said he would introduce me to the joys of being a pony girl.

Pete is friendly with a couple called Roger and Melissa, who own a big house on the outskirts of Bristol, and he told me that they held regular events at which masters and mistresses would race their ponies. He had mentioned he had a new, very submissive girlfriend who he thought would make a good pony, and Roger and Melissa had suggested he bring me along to their next racing day.

I really wasn't sure what to expect when we arrived, but Pete's friends soon put me at my ease. Roger was a successful businessman in his fifties, and he and his wife had spent a great deal of time and money on renovating the house, which had been in a fairly bad state of repair when they had bought it. They told me that one of the reasons why they had particularly wanted the house was because of the large grounds which came with it – grounds which were ideal for staging pony-cart races.

After a few drinks and some delicious canapés, Roger announced that it was time for the owners to prepare their ponies. Pete and I went up to one of the house's many bedrooms, where we were to change. When Pete showed me what I would be wearing in my new role, I could hardly believe it: my outfit consisted of nothing more than solid-looking, platform-soled shoes, a head-dress sporting a plume of pink feathers, and a tail which was brown, to match my hair. I was obviously expected to parade naked for the benefit of the more dominant among Roger and Melissa's guests.

Roger had told me if I had any reservations about what I was to do, I could back out, but I knew that would be letting him down – and surely he would not force me to do anything I didn't want to?

The tail was fixed to what was unmistakably a butt-plug, and while I stripped off my clothes, Pete greased the butt-plug with lubricating gel. Once I was naked, he helped me put on the shoes and the head-dress, then he ordered me to bend over. His fingers moved between my legs, stroking me until I started to get turned on, then, without ceremony, he pushed the butt-plug firmly into my tight bum hole. It felt strange to have something up there, and I fought the urge to expel the greasy plug, but as I looked at my reflection in the bedroom mirror, I had to admit there was something oddly exciting about sporting my new tail.

Pete swiftly changed into tight-fitting riding breeches and a tail coat, and produced from his bag a dressage whip I had not, until that moment, known he possessed. I shivered at the thought of why that whip might be used, and how it would feel. He pronounced himself satisfied with his appearance, and we went back downstairs to join the others.

I discovered that I was one of seven ponies, all but one of whom was female. The contrast between our nakedness and our owners' elaborate riding gear made me feel even more aware of who was in control. We were led outside, where we were attached to beautifully made wooden carts. I was strapped in place, and a bridle was fitted in my mouth. As Pete climbed into the cart, I was surprised to discover how light it was, even with him in place. The designer had obviously taken into account the fact that most ponies were female, and therefore not as strong as their male masters, and I realised that my worries about being able to pull Pete round in the cart were unfounded.

Roger announced that a series of elimination races would take place, with two carts racing against each other around three circuits of the track, and that the winner of the final would be allowed to discipline any of the other ponies in whatever way he or she saw fit. I remembered Pete's dressage whip, and shuddered at the sound of the word 'discipline'.

Pete and I were drawn in the third race, against a well-built, red-haired woman in her late thirties, who was the owner of the male pony. Pete had told me that my pony name was to be Fenella (as you would expect, I didn't have any choice in the matter), and as Melissa called Fenella and Rocky to their starting positions, I felt a thrill of anticipation pass through me.

Even though Rocky was a much more experienced pony than I was, Pete and I ran him very close, but in the end we were beaten by a couple of yards. After that, we stood and watched the other races take place, as gradually the field was whittled down to Rocky and his owner, Caroline, and a blonde-haired pony – or, as Melissa called her, a palomino – called Petal and her owner, Jim. As they raced round the little track, the other owners cheered for their favourite horse. By then, I had got into the spirit of the afternoon completely, and I found myself stamping my foot and shaking my head-dress, as though I really was a fidgety pony. Pete had come to stand beside me, and he ran his hands over my flanks affectionately.

In the end, Caroline and Rocky beat Jim and Petal quite easily, which gave Caroline the choice of whichever pony she fancied to discipline. She looked around at the assembled ponies, and at last her gaze settled on me. 'I've taken a shine to the pretty little newcomer, Fenella,' she said, smiling. 'Would you mind if I put her through her paces, Pete?'

'Not at all,' Pete replied, and together he and Caroline unhitched me from the cart. She led me to the centre of the racing circuit, and I realised to my horror that she was going to discipline me in front of everyone else. I had never taken a public punishment before, and I shivered nervously as she walked round me, brandishing her riding crop.

'A very pretty little pony,' she said, touching me as Pete had done, 'but so sadly inexpert when it comes to racing. Still, I'm sure we can improve on your times. I find judicial use of the whip helps.'

With this, she slashed the riding crop down hard on my buttock. Hot, sharp pain shot through me, and if I had not had the bit in my mouth, I would have cried out.

'Yes,' she said, 'a lazy pony can always be encouraged with the whip.' Again and again the crop landed on my bum cheeks, each one laid with devastating accuracy, until my entire backside was a throbbing mass of pain and hot, shameful tears were flowing down my face. I glanced round at the watching crowd, and realised that more than one of the men there had a sizeable bulge in his jodhpurs. Even Rocky was sporting an erection, for which I was sure he would be punished once Caroline had finished with me.

At last, Caroline threw down her crop. My punishment was over.

'Poor little Fenella,' Melissa said, coming to run her fingers over the raised, purple weals on my bottom. 'That's going to be sore in the morning. Let's go and put some soothing cream on it.'

She led me into the house, and up to her room, where she told me to lie face down on the bed. The next thing I felt were her fingers delicately rubbing cream into my abused flesh; the feeling of the cold cream on my hot bottom was wonderful, and when her fingers strayed into the cleft between my cheeks and then down to my quim, I did nothing to stop her. Within moments, I was enjoying a powerful orgasm, made even more intense by the feeling of my anal muscles clenching round the butt-plug to which my tail was still firmly attached.

That was my first race day, but it wasn't my last. Pete and I have been to several of Roger and Melissa's events, and our race times are improving all the time.

Fenella J.,
Cheltenham

A VERY NAPPY LITTLE GIRL

Ever since I was young, I have always had a problem with bedwetting. I was kept in nappies by my mother until I was eight years old, and even as I grew older, I always had to have a rubber sheet on the bed in case I had an accident. When I finally met the man I was to marry, I was embarrassed to let him know about my little problem, in case it put him off me, but to my surprise, his reaction was very different.

Robert told me he found the thought of a grown woman who wore nappies and wet herself an incredible turn-on, and he said that he would love to treat me as his big baby girl. We would try it on our honeymoon, and see how things progressed from there.

Robert booked a cottage in the Lake District, where he was sure we would have the privacy to do as we wanted. I don't know what most new brides pack in their trousseau, but mine included half a dozen adult-sized terry nappies, waterproof plastic pants and big pink nappy pins. It took us an hour to drive from the reception to the cottage, and by the time we got there it was almost midnight. 'Baby's up past her bedtime,' Robert told me. 'She needs to be put into her nappy to make sure she doesn't have an accident.'

He ran a bath, and bathed me as I splashed away. He had even brought along a couple of plastic ducks that I could float in the bath; he really had thought of everything. Then he dried me using a big, fluffy white towel, and told me he had a surprise for me. He said that big babies didn't have pubic hair, and that he was going to get rid of mine. He smeared depilatory cream all over my mound and my outer lips, and when he washed it off five minutes later, my pussy was beautifully smooth. Then he took me into the bedroom.

Lying on the bed was a terry nappy, which he urged me to lie on. He sprinkled talcum powder all over my newly naked sex, then pinned the nappy in place. Finally, he pulled a pair of plastic pants over the nappy. My transformation was complete.

I slept well that night, but when I woke up in the morning, it was to feel the bulkiness of a wet nappy around my bottom. There was something delightfully sexual about the feeling, and I wriggled, enjoying the sensation of the folds of terry cloth against my bald pussy. I was aware of Robert watching me with an amused expression. To my delight, he pulled down my plastic pants, put his hand into my wet nappy and rapidly frigged me to a climax.

The rest of the week was spent in similar fashion. Every night I would go to bed in a clean nappy, and every morning I would wake up wet. There would always be freshly washed nappies hanging up to dry outside the cottage. Robert got very turned on when he felt my soggy nappy, and he would usually fuck me as I lay there on the soaked terry towelling.

Robert enjoyed babying me so much that we continued the scenario on our return from honeymoon. One Friday, he told me that he had to go away on business overnight, but that he had arranged for a babysitter to look after me. True to his word, a grey-haired motherly woman in her forties turned up at the house, announcing that she was here to look after the baby. She said I was to call her Aunty Madge, but she warned me that she was very strict, and that if I misbehaved, I would be punished. Robert and I had reached the stage where he would give me a bottle feed of milk before I went to bed, and I was expecting Aunty Madge to do the same. However, she told me she believed breastfeeding was much better for babies and she proceeded to unbutton her blouse. Beneath it, she was wearing what I recognised to be a nursing bra; she took me in her arms, freed one of her massive, pendulous breasts from the cup and presented the stiff, rubbery nipple to my lips. For a moment, I was reluctant – after all, I had never done anything like this with a woman before – but then I remembered what Aunty Madge had said about punishment, and so I took her nipple into my mouth and sucked on it. It felt strange at first, but I was soon enjoying it, as was Aunty Madge, who had her eyes half-closed in pleasure. I wished Robert was here to see me being breastfed, as I knew the sight would have made him really horny.

In the morning, as usual, I woke up with a wet nappy. Aunty Madge pulled the covers off me and tutted her displeasure. 'At your age, you should be able to stay dry overnight,' she told me. 'Naughty babies who wet themselves have to be punished.'

I couldn't believe it as she hauled me out of bed and over her solid lap. She pulled my pants down and unfastened my nappy, running her hand over my damp bottom. 'No sign of nappy rash, which is good,' she said. 'But you have to be taught to stay dry.'

She raised her hand and brought it down matter-of-factly on my bum. The slap stung more than it should have done because my skin was wet and sensitive, and I wriggled and squealed. She ignored my protests and set about peppering my cheeks with a volley of slaps. I could just see my reflection in the bedroom mirror, and I watched as my skin turned from a creamy white to a flaming scarlet. I also watched Aunty Madge's nipples start to push against the blue overalls she was wearing, and I realised that she was taking her own kind of pleasure in disciplining me in this way. As I squirmed against the sodden, bunched-up towelling on her lap, it began to stimulate me in a delightful way, and soon the pain of the spanking was being replaced by the sweet pleasure of my impending climax. As I came, I thrust my fist in my mouth to stifle my cries, though it must have been obvious to my babysitter what was happening.

When Robert returned from his trip, he found me sitting up in bed while Aunty Madge read me a bedtime story. I do hope he has to go away on business again soon, so I can be looked after by my stern but loving babysitter.

Meryl P.,
Manchester

BREAST INTENTIONS

I'm what you'd call a breast man, but with me, the fetish goes further than just admiring a nice pair of tits in the street, or spending a long time licking and sucking my wife's glorious nipples. For as long as I can remember, I have had the urge to taste a woman's breast milk. Nothing would give me greater pleasure than to suckle my wife and taste her milk, but Grace and I have decided not to have children, and so it seemed that my fantasy was destined to stay just that.

Three months ago, Grace's sister, Ellen, gave birth to a baby son, and everything changed. Often, when I was fucking Grace, I would imagine that I was with Ellen, fondling her breasts, which I knew were heavy and swollen with milk. I had thought that Grace might be upset at seeing her sister achieve something she never would, but she took it very well, spending a lot of time babysitting her little nephew and buying him presents. Grace told Ellen that if there was ever anything she needed, we would be more than happy to oblige.

Ellen's husband, Rick, works out on the oil rigs, and while he'd managed to get a certain amount of leave to see his new son, that soon ran out, and Ellen was left on her own. That's when she started to invite Grace round more frequently, because it was company for her and because Grace loved spending time with the baby. It was an arrangement that seemed to suit everyone.

One afternoon, however, Ellen rang up in some distress. Her washing machine had broken down, and she didn't know what to do. There was water all over the floor, she said, and she couldn't really struggle to the launderette with a load of dirty washing and the baby in tow. As luck would have it, I'm a plumber by trade, so I told Ellen to sit tight and I would be straight round to take a look at it.

When Ellen greeted me at the door of her flat, the most beautiful sight greeted my eyes. She was apologising for the fact that she looked a mess, but I barely registered her unbrushed fair hair and the dark circles of tiredness that ringed her eyes. I couldn't tear my eyes away from her chest. She was wearing a navy blue T-shirt, and it was obvious that her breast milk was leaking through her bra, and soaking the cotton material even darker. Even though this was my wife's sister, I could feel my cock stirring in my overalls as all my fantasies came flooding back.

The washing machine was easy to fix – it was a simple problem with the door seal that only took me twenty minutes to sort out. By the time I'd finished and we'd mopped the soapy water from the kitchen floor, I was dying for a drink. Ellen offered me a cup of tea and I accepted, even though I had another kind of drink in mind, as I'm sure you can imagine.

Ellen and I sat in the lounge, drinking our tea, and that's when she dropped the bombshell. She told me that since she'd had the baby, as far as Rick was concerned, she had completely lost her sex appeal.

She claimed he could hardly bear to touch her, and she was sure he found her ugly, with her stretch-marked stomach and her swollen, leaking tits. I told her she was talking rubbish; I had never seen her look so beautiful, and as for her breasts ... Despite myself, I began to spill my secret: the fact that I had always wanted to drink breast milk. I would never do anything to hurt Grace, I swore, and yet looking at Ellen, with her big tits so obviously full of milk, I was struck with the overwhelming urge to sink to the floor and bury my face in that wonderful, ripe cleavage.

'Do it,' Ellen urged. 'Please, Martin, do it. The baby's been fed and I've got more than enough to spare.' As she spoke, she was pulling her T-shirt over her head. Her breasts were cradled in a white cotton nursing bra, the material wet through where it pressed against her dark, stiff nipples. As she unhooked the catch of her bra and let her tits fall free, I knew my ultimate desire was about to be realised. I raced over to the settee where she was sitting, and rested my head on her breast. She stroked my hair as my lips clamped hold of her rubbery nipple and I began to suck. Instantly, my mouth was filled with rich, sweet-tasting milk, and I gulped it down like a thirsty man who's found an oasis in the desert. My hand caressed the soft, cushiony flesh of her other breast, and as I looked up briefly I could see that her eyes were half-closed and she seemed lost in a world of her own.

I know I shouldn't have done what I did next, but I couldn't help myself. The skirt she was wearing had rucked up, and I slipped my hand under its hem, stroking the soft flesh of her thighs. She made no move to stop me as my fingers moved higher, until they touched the fabric of her panties. They were as wet as her bra had been, and I knew then that she was taking a deeply sexual pleasure in what I was doing to her.

By now, my cock was desperate for relief, and Ellen made no protest as my lips finally released their grip on her nipple and I laid her back on the settee. I quickly stripped off my overalls, before pulling down her panties and spreading her legs wide. Her crease was shining with her juices, the lips peeling apart easily to give me access to her cunt. With one firm thrust I was inside her. She groaned in pleasure as my shaft lodged between her ribbed velvet walls. I paused for a moment, savouring the sensation, before I began to fuck her steadily. Within moments she was coming, her pussy spasming around my cock, and I wondered how her husband could be so stupid as not to appreciate what a beautiful, sexy woman he had. That was my last coherent thought before my own orgasm hit and I pumped my load inside her.

Ellen and I promised each other that afternoon would be a one-off, and so far we've stuck to that promise. However, I can't deny that I'd love to suckle from those beautiful tits again, now that I know they taste as good as they look.

Martin K.,
Edinburgh

NURSE IT BETTER

My girlfriend Alison and I have found our sex life improving no end since we discovered the medical fetish. She has always taken the dominant role, but now she finds that when she plays the strict nurse and I am her helpless patient, she can push me to my very limits.

We have invested in a selection of equipment which we found via the fetish magazines and from some genuine medical suppliers, but the basic scenario is always the same. I have been sent to the nurse for an intimate internal examination, and as I am somewhat apprehensive of what this will entail, the nurse has to take precautions to ensure that I do not attempt to leave or fight her off when she tries to examine me.

I am dressed in one of those white hospital patient's gowns which fastens at the neck and is loose all down the back of my body, to give her easy access to whichever part of me she wishes to inspect. Alison makes me lie face down on the couch – a rather unorthodox position for an internal examination, you might think – and then straps me firmly in place. The straps are made of wide leather and buckle in place, and offer me very little in the way of movement. However, I am able to move my head enough to watch Alison as she walks around the room, taking pieces of equipment from a low table.

She wears a breathtaking nurse's outfit, made from white rubber that clings to her gorgeous breasts and is so short it only just skims the curve of her arse. Sometimes, she will not wear any knickers beneath it, giving me tantalising flashes of her cunt, which I am not allowed to touch without her permission. My own sex is kept shaven, and the first thing Nurse Alison does is inspect it to make sure I have not allowed any stubble to mar its smoothness. If I have, I know there will be trouble. This time, however, she is satisfied, and goes on to the next part of the examination.

She slips on a thin latex glove, and squeezes a generous dollop of lubricating jelly on to her rubber-clad fingers. As she bends over the table, I make the most of the brief glimpse the short uniform offers me of the contours of her beautiful pussy. She tells me she has to check that my cunt and anus are in good health, but warns me that if I make any noise as she inspects them, then I can expect to be punished. Her digits first ease into my vagina, and she probes its depths expertly. As the pads of her gloved fingers brush against my G-spot, it is all I can do to stop myself from moaning with pleasure. Sometimes she will rub me there until my body convulses in orgasm and my juices spurt out with great force, but not today. Instead, she slips a second finger and then a third into me, as if to see how widely I can stretch. On occasions, she will use a speculum on me, knowing how much I hate the feel of the cold metal entering my vagina and pushing its walls apart but aware that I am powerless to prevent her.

Finally satisfied, she turns her attentions to my anus. Her gloved fingers, now slippery with a mixture of the lubricating jelly and my own intimate moisture, breach the ring of muscle, and she examines my back passage with the same thoroughness with which she checked my vagina. I am growing increasingly excited, my arousal intensified by the impersonal way in which she is treating me, and I know that I am in danger of coming without her permission. She acts as though she is completely oblivious to the state I am in, and merely disposes of the soiled latex glove in the waste bin.

The last test, she tells me, is to examine my clitoris. We sometimes use the pretence that I have made an appointment to visit her because I am worried about my inability to reach orgasm, and she wants to see what is causing the problem. The point of this exercise is that I am to hold off from coming until she says everything is in complete working order and gives me her permission to do so, but by this time I am so turned on that it usually only takes the most cursory swipe of her fingers over my clit and I am bucking in orgasm, my movements restricted by the tight leather straps that bind me to the bed.

When this happens, Nurse Alison's demeanour changes abruptly as she tells me that such wanton behaviour in the clinical surroundings of the examination room are deserving of punishment. Usually, the form this punishment takes is that of an enema, which I hate. She unbuckles me from the couch and guides me to the bathroom on slightly shaky legs. Knowing that I am almost always unable to prevent myself from coming on the examination couch, she has prepared a saline enema in advance. I am made to strip off the hospital gown and crouch on all fours in the bath. The next thing I feel is the greased nozzle of the enema tube being inserted into my rectum and then the carefully controlled flow of water flowing into my bowels. Nurse Alison loves to keep the water pumping until I am uncomfortably full and my whole body is trembling with the need for relief. She likes me to beg for her to stop, as she knows how humiliating I find the whole procedure. At last, she pulls out the tube and I almost scream with the joy of being able to void the water into the bath. The relief is so intense that I find myself on the verge of orgasm again; if Nurse Alison is feeling kind, she will gently stroke my clit until I come.

At last, I am allowed to shower, while Alison puts away all her equipment, ready for the next time she feels the need to give me such an intimate examination.

Nicola G.,
Brighton

VERY LADYLIKE

I love going to fetish clubs, because you never know what might happen to you or just who you might meet. Take a recent example. I was at one of my favourite clubs on the London scene, when I spotted a beautiful woman ordering a drink at the bar. Now, I am not particularly into playing a dominant or submissive role, I just like to meet other people who enjoy dressing for pleasure, and it was obvious from the moment I saw her that she did. She was wearing a red, long-sleeved rubber dress that clung erotically to her small breasts and slim hips, fishnet stockings the tops of which were just visible beneath the hem of the dress, and red patent stiletto-heeled shoes which boosted her already impressive height to well over six feet. Her long, black hair fell in a shining wave to waist length, and her make-up was immaculate. It was lust at first sight, so I went over and introduced myself.

She told me in husky tones that her name was Simone, and when I offered to pay for her vodka and tonic she accepted graciously. As we chatted, we seemed to have so much in common that I sensed some hot sex was on the cards. After all, people reckon I am pretty good-looking, with my closely cropped peroxide blond hair and muscular body, and I got the impression Simone liked what she saw. That impression was confirmed when, after a couple of drinks, she suggested we go somewhere to get to know each other a little better. I wanted to know what she had in mind, and she asked how I felt about a quick fuck in the toilets? I was a little taken aback, I have to admit, as she seemed much more forward than some of the other women I have met on the scene, but I would have been lying if I said my cock did not twitch in my pants at her suggestion.

We headed for the ladies', nobody turning a hair as we squeezed in one of the cubicles together. It's pretty much a given that someone will end up screwing in the loos before the end of the evening at one of these places, and as long as you don't hog a cubicle when there is a queue you can usually get away with it. It also goes without saying that the ladies' is always more salubrious than the gents'.

When the door was safely locked behind us, I urged Simone to push her dress up towards her waist and pull down her panties, and that was when I got a massive shock. For there, tucked out of the way, was what was unmistakably a penis. Simone was not what she seemed – in fact, she was Simon.

My mouth gaped open for a split second, and then I thought, What the hell? As Simone brought her cock out of its hiding place and began to stroke it, I dropped to my knees and took it between my lips. It tasted warm and salty, and not at all unpleasant, and as it expanded in my mouth to its full six inches I fell to my task with relish. Simone was moaning and urging me on, her hands with their false red fingernails raking my scalp as I sucked away. The sleazy backdrop to what we were doing must have been acting as a powerful turn-on for Simone, because sooner than I might have expected, she was coming, her spunk hitting the back of my throat in a series of powerful jets.

Then she turned round, and offered me her arse. By now, my cock was aching for relief, so I freed it from my leather jeans and told Simone to grab hold of the toilet cistern. She wriggled her backside at me lewdly, squealing out loud as I thrust my dick up her arsehole with some spit for lubrication. The novelty of fucking a transvestite in the toilets of a fetish club, knowing anyone outside would be aware of exactly what we were doing from the noises we were making, excited me beyond belief, and I came as quickly as Simone had done. When we came out of the cubicle, giggling, a couple of girls looked at us and winked at Simone, as taken in by her authentically feminine appearance as I had been. If only you knew, I thought, as we went to get a well-earned drink. If only you knew . . .

Danny S.,
East London

WRAPPED IN PLASTIC

I know that what I am about to tell you will sound unbelievable, but I can assure you that it really happened to me. It was my love of nude sunbathing which caused me to get into such a mess. The problem is that I live in a block of flats which has a shared garden and no privacy, so I had got into the habit of taking a trip out to a local beauty spot about five miles away, finding a secluded spot and stripping off there to enjoy the sun.

It was Bank Holiday Monday when I last went up there, and I had packed a little bag with everything I would need: sun-tan lotion, a good book, a bottle of mineral water, a plastic mac in case it rained and my bus fare home. I got to my favourite spot about mid-morning, and was pleased to see there was absolutely no one else about. I undressed completely and rubbed the sun-tan lotion all over my body, paying particular attention to my breasts and big, pink nipples, which are very sensitive. Then I lay back to read my book.

The sun was hotter than I had expected and, despite my best intentions, I soon nodded off. When I woke up, I had a dreadful shock. My clothes, which I had placed in a neat pile by my side, had disappeared! I looked round everywhere, trying not to panic, but could not find them. Obviously someone had come along while I was asleep, and thought it would be a joke to take my clothes. I supposed I was lucky, as they could have done anything to me while I was sleeping, but that thought did little to comfort me. At least they had left my shoes and my bag, so I had the plastic mac to cover me and the money to get home. I unfolded the mac, put it on and zipped it up to my chin; it was not the ideal thing to be wearing in such hot weather, but it was all I had.

I headed to catch the bus as quickly as I could, knowing how bizarre I must look and hoping I would not bump into anyone else. As I rounded the corner, I saw to my horror the bus pulling away. On Bank Holidays, there was only one bus an hour, which meant I had the choice of hanging around for the next one, or setting off to walk the four miles home. Neither was a prospect I relished, but the walk seemed marginally better, so I began to trudge down the road that led back into town.

By the time I had gone half a mile I was beginning to sweat heavily. The thin plastic of the mac was rubbing uncomfortably against my bare skin, and as it stuck to me it was accentuating every contour of my bare form. I thought about unfastening it, but I did not want it flapping open, offering anyone who might be passing a peep at my nakedness, so I just unzipped it a little way, hoping it would let the air circulate around my sticky skin. I was aware of the odd car passing, and I just kept my head down, not wanting to attract any undue attention. After all, I was in no position to try to thumb a lift. As one drove by, I heard a horn hooting and some rude comment from the driver, but I ignored it and tried to pick up my pace so I would get home sooner.

It was not long before I developed a second problem. I had been swigging the mineral water as I walked, in an attempt to cool me down, and now I desperately needed to pee. There was a dry stone wall to the side of me, and I decided to nip behind it, as it would offer me some protection from any passing traffic. I had just squatted down and was letting my pee out in a long, gushing stream when I heard a voice behind me.

'What's all this, then?'

I glanced round, startled, to see a man standing behind me. He was an ugly-looking man in his late fifties, weather-beaten and scruffily dressed.

'What are you doing in my field?' he demanded. I tried to scramble to my feet, but I could imagine how I looked to him, the thin plastic mac clinging to my sweaty breasts and my bum on display as I pissed in front of him.

'I'm sorry,' I replied. 'I only wanted . . .'

'I know what you want dressed like that, you little slut,' he said, and caught hold of my arm. I tried to wriggle away, hoping I could make a run for it, but his grip was very strong. I tried to stammer an explanation, but he was in no mood to listen to me. What he was in the mood for I soon realised as his hand cupped one of my tits through the plastic mac.

'You were trespassing on my land,' he said, his fingers twisting my nipple almost painfully, 'and trespassers get firmly dealt with.'

I knew what my fate was likely to be, and I was ready to accept it. It seemed like everything which had happened to me today had been one humiliation after another: I had been spied on as I slept naked, I had been forced to walk a couple of miles wearing nothing but a flimsy, clinging plastic mac and now I had been caught by a farmer as I peed in his field. I realised he was going to beat me or fuck me or both, and the really shameful part of it was that, old and ugly as he was, I wanted him to.

'Take that stupid mac off,' he told me, and I quickly did as I was told, dropping it to the ground to stand naked before him. His eyes roved over my body, taking in the sight of my big breasts and bushy pussy. 'Now suck my cock.'

I dropped to my knees before him and loosed his cock from his flies. It looked as though he had not bathed too recently, and I wrinkled my nose at the sour smell of him, but I put his glans to my lips and began to suck tentatively. As I worked on his penis, it began to grow and lengthen, and soon I had what must have been eight inches of warm, throbbing flesh in my hands. Despite my reluctance, the thought of taking so much cock inside me, as I knew I ultimately would, was making me feel strangely turned on, and I could feel myself beginning to get wet.

After a few minutes of me licking his cock, the farmer pushed me on to my back, and told me to spread my legs wide. Then he was on top of me, his heavy, unwashed body pressing me into the ground. He made me spread my pussy lips with my fingers, and then he guided his dick into me, my juices easing his passage. He thrust into me as though I was just there to be used for his pleasure, his hands groping my tits as I writhed beneath him. It must have been a good twenty minutes before he grunted and came, his hot spunk shooting deep inside me.

'Now don't let me catch you on my land again,' he said, as he fastened up his flies and threw my mac at me, 'or I might have to take my belt to you.'

There was no way I could catch the bus now, stinking of sweat and sex, so I walked the rest of the way home, my gait slightly cautious as my pussy was so tender from where his thick cock had pounded it. The second I got in, I threw myself down on the bed and wanked myself to a frenzy, imagining that dirty old farmer leathering my arse with his belt. You would think that what happened to me should have taught me a lesson about putting myself in such a vulnerable situation but, deep down, I know that come the next sunny day I'll be out there again, naked and with only my thin plastic mac to protect my modesty.

Janet J.,
Shrewsbury

ADVENTURES IN CYBERSPACE

My sex life has improved beyond all recognition since my husband bought his computer. He hooked it up to the Internet and encouraged me to go surfing, perhaps because he thought it would enable me to keep in touch with my relatives in Australia. What he does not know is that I am getting plenty of use out of it, but not for the reasons he might expect. Basically, when he is working nights and our two kids are tucked up in bed, I make myself a cup of Irish coffee, go to the PC and log on to an adult chat room.

I have had some incredibly exciting cybersex adventures over the last month or so. The first one was with someone who called himself Easy Rider. I was in the mood to talk about sex with someone, so I went into a chat room and that was where I met him. After making a little flirtatious conversation, we decided to have a one-to-one talk, and things soon got very hot. Easy Rider asked me to describe myself, and I told him I am petite and blonde with very big breasts, none of which is a lie. Then he typed in the words, 'I'd really like to see those big tits of yours naked. Why don't you take your top off?'

Just the thought of that was a turn-on, so I typed in, 'It's off. What do you think?'

His reply came back instantly. 'You have really gorgeous tits. I'd love to suck your nipples.'

By now, I was starting to get wet between my legs. Even though I knew absolutely nothing about this man, the idea of someone I had never had any contact with before tonight licking my nipples was so exciting that I replied, 'And when you've sucked them, why don't you lick my pussy? It's all wet and juicy for you.'

The conversation continued in that vein as we each got more and more horny. He described how he was pulling down my knickers to feast on my cunt, while I responded by telling him that I was stroking his eight-inch erection before taking it in my mouth and sucking on it. My typing was getting ever more erratic, and by the time we described how we were both coming, I really was on the verge of orgasm. When I finally logged off, I simply plunged my hand down the front of my knickers and frigged myself to climax as I sat in my chair in front of the computer.

I had never done anything like it before. It was so thrilling, and yet there was something dirty about it, as though I had been taking part in an obscene phone call. I never use such crude or direct language when my husband is fucking me, and the fact that I had used it to a complete stranger made it all the more exciting.

I did not have any regrets about what I had done; in fact, after that evening, I was hooked. I have always liked the idea of playing domination and submission scenarios and trying a little light CP, but whenever I have broached the subject with my husband he makes it clear he is not interested, so I go to the chat rooms to get what I cannot get at home. I use the name Bambi, and say that I have been bad and need to be punished. As you can imagine, this always gets an instant response, and soon I have picked out someone who is prepared to discipline my bottom the way it craves.

Let me tell you about a recent encounter. I went for a one-on-one conversation with someone called Master Severin, and within moments he was telling me to bend and present my bare bum for the cane. He told me it was a thin, bendy cane which was really going to hurt when it landed on my cheeks, and I replied that I must have done something very bad to deserve it. He told me simply to count the six strokes he was going to give me, and tell him how it felt as each one landed.

I counted the first, and told him I could not believe the pain; it was almost as though my defenceless little bum was being cut in two. He told me to steady myself and prepare for the next one. I did, thanked him obediently for it, and said it had been just as painful as the first. He replied that it had landed just a little lower than the first, just below the crown of my bottom, and that I looked so beautiful with those two scarlet lines running parallel across the white flesh of my arse. He delivered the next three, each time commenting on how the stripes looked. His descriptions were so vivid that I could almost feel the fiery pain, and I was certain that if I ran my fingers over the skin of my bottom I would find vicious, raised welts. When it came to the sixth stroke, I knew exactly where Master Severin would want to place it: just on the fleshy crease at the top of my thighs, where the skin is most sensitive. This time, I told him the pain was unbearable, and I begged him to soothe it. He replied that he was running his fingers between my legs, and that I was as juicy as a ripe peach. There was only one way, he told me, to soothe my ache, and that was to slide his massively erect cock into my wet cunt. By now, I was typing with one hand and the fingers of the other were playing with my clit, and at the moment he said he was lodged between my velvet walls, filling me more full of cock flesh than I had ever been, I came explosively.

My husband, as you can imagine, has no idea that I am leading this secret life. He sometimes gets into bed beside me when he comes in from his shift and when he touches my pussy, he comments on how wet I am. He wants to know what I have been doing in his absence to get me so excited and I just tell him I have been thinking of him. Well, I can hardly tell him the truth, can I?

Barbara G.,
Chester

Bring a Friend

COSTA DEL SEX

My wife Jane and I had often fantasised about what it would be like to have sex with another couple, but we never knew quite how to turn that fantasy into reality until we went on holiday to the Costa del Sol. On our second day, we found ourselves sitting by the pool in our apartment complex alongside a couple in their late twenties. She was sunbathing topless, and I found myself getting an unexpected erection at the sight of her large breasts with their very pale nipples. I ended up jumping into the pool to cool down, and as I swam a few splashy lengths, I noticed that Jane had got talking to the couple. When I rejoined her, she introduced them as Barry and Linda, from Bradford. As we talked, we found out we had a lot in common, and when Barry suggested that we go for a meal together that evening, Jane and I agreed happily.

That night, we had a nice dinner in a local restaurant, and over a big jug of sangria, we found the conversation turning almost inevitably to the subject of sex. Thinking of Linda's firm tits as they had been displayed earlier that morning, I asked them if they had ever thought about swapping partners.

Barry and Linda admitted that not only had they thought about it, they had done it on several occasions, but it could be hard finding other couples who were amenable to the idea. Driven by my fantasies and the effects of the alcohol, I confessed that Jane and I were keen to try it.

'Come back to the apartment, then,' said Barry, 'and we'll show you what to do.'

Jane and I were nervous but excited as Barry ushered us into their apartment. There was a double bed and a single bed in the room, and I helped Barry push them together to give us all the room we would need. The French windows that led out to the balcony were open, and we could hear the faint noise of the disco in the complex's main block, coupled with the chirping of insects in the bushes below us.

Barry urged Jane to sit down on the bed, and they began kissing and caressing. It felt strange seeing my wife being fondled by this virtual stranger, but as he reached for the zip on her dress and pulled it down, before pushing the straps off her shoulders and baring her small, braless breasts, I was beginning to get very turned on. I felt Linda's hands around my waist, and as she reached to pull my shirt free of my trousers and unfasten it, I relaxed into her embrace.

Soon, Jane was lying on the bed wearing nothing but her thong panties, and Barry's dark head was bent over her, as his mouth feasted on her little tits. She was moaning softly, and her hand moved down to cup her pussy through her panties and begin stroking it.

Linda broke away from me. 'Let me do that,' she murmured, and I watched, mesmerised, as Linda pulled down my wife's panties. I could see that Jane's pussy lips were already swelling, a damp patch clearly visible on the gusset of the panties as Linda tossed them into the corner. I knew that Jane had never been touched intimately by another woman before, and I half expected her to protest as Linda's fingers began to probe her juicy cleft, but she seemed almost hypnotised by what was being done to her. I stripped off quickly, eager to join the tangle of bodies on the bed, and then got behind Linda. She was wearing a halter-necked top, and I untied it, giving myself access to those big, succulent breasts. As she continued to play with my wife's pussy, I rolled her nipples between my fingers and thumbs, feeling them peak beneath my touch.

When Linda slid two fingers deep into my wife's cunt, I knew Jane was ready to be fucked. Barry had sensed it, too, and he undressed. As he slipped down his briefs to reveal his cock, I noticed that while it was no longer than mine, it was very thick, and the thought of it stretching Jane's pussy wide made my own penis twitch with envy and excitement.

Barry urged Jane up on to all fours, and I realised he was going to fuck her doggy-style. That is probably her favourite position, and I knew she would really appreciate the feel of that fat shaft as Barry thrust into her. She groaned as she tried to accustom herself to its unexpected girth, and I gave my own cock a few swift rubs as I watched Barry gradually ease himself home. I did not have too long to enjoy the spectacle, though, before Linda had dropped to her knees and taken my erection between her wet, skilful lips. I was torn between watching Barry give my wife a good shafting and luxuriating in the feeling of the languid blowjob I was getting from Linda. She knew exactly what she was doing, and as her tongue moved in wicked little circles over the head of my prick I knew it wouldn't be too long before I came. She must have realised how close I was getting to coming, because she suddenly spat out my cock and told me to lie down on the bed. The next moment, she was straddling my body, her hot, wet quim enveloping my hard-on as tightly as her mouth had done. As she bounced up and down on my rigid six inches, I was able to reach up and maul her big breasts, squeezing them with my fingers till she moaned in a mixture of pain and ecstasy. The feel of her cunt muscles milking my cock was too much, however, and while Barry continued to fuck my wife with increasingly rapid strokes, I gave up the struggle and came inside Linda's sweet cunt.

Jane's throaty little cries indicated that she was in the throes of her own orgasm, and as I lay there, recovering, Linda used her own fingers to bring herself off. Barry groaned and announced that he was coming. He gave one last, hard jerk, and then pulled out of Jane's body to let the last spurts of his climax spatter over her arse cheeks. To my surprise and delight, Linda pushed her husband out of the way, and set about licking her husband's come off Jane's backside, before moving lower to let her tongue dip into my wife's honeypot. She must have been tasting a mixture of Barry's spunk and Jane's love juices, and she was licking it up with relish.

Jane relaxed on the bed, and let Linda give her a thorough tonguing. From the smile on her face, she was clearly enjoying every moment of what was being done to her. When Linda turned round and climbed over Jane's body, so that her sex was inches away from my wife's face, Jane merely stuck out her tongue and began to sample the taste of another woman's pussy for the first time.

'It's a beautiful sight, isn't it?' Barry said softly in my ear. 'Two people of the same sex enjoying each other's body, I mean.'

I had barely had time to register his words before I felt his hand reach down and grasp my cock, which had begun to stiffen again at the sight of the two women in the sixty-nine position.

'That's the great thing about being on holiday,' Barry muttered as he began to wank me with smooth, efficient strokes. 'You can do anything you want – be anything you want – and no one will ever find out.'

His touch on my cock was skilful, his other hand coming down to cup and gently stroke my balls. When he urged me to get on the bed, in the same kneeling position my wife had so recently adopted to receive him, I did not object. I saw him spit on his hand, using his own saliva to lubricate his shaft, then I felt his wet tongue rimming my arsehole. I found myself enjoying the sensation, and turned my head to watch my wife lying beside me, her mouth working hungrily on Linda's hairy quim.

I felt something warm and hard replace Barry's tongue at the entrance to my anus, and knew it was the head of his cock. I relaxed, doing all I could to ease his entry, almost crying out as his glans breached my virgin arse. Within moments, the pain subsided and was replaced with the first stirrings of pleasure as he buried himself in me to the hilt. As Linda and Jane moaned and sighed and moved towards their orgasms, Barry began to fuck me with strong, steady strokes. I reached down and wanked my own cock in time to Barry's thrusts. All too soon, we were both coming, my spunk arcing out powerfully enough to hit the iron bedstead. Linda was more than happy to lick both of us clean, and then the four of us fell asleep, curled up together on the bed.

Jane and I got together with Barry and Linda almost every night of that holiday. We have not yet found anyone to swap with at home, but I'm sure it can only be a matter of time.

Pete M.,
Crewe

JOINING THE CIRCLE

Greg and Anna were the first couple I got friendly with on the fetish scene. They took me under their wing when I turned up at my first ever club night, shaking in my thighboots and not really sure what to expect. They introduced me to a lot of people and made me feel welcome and a part of the scene. They were also the only couple I knew who switched – whereas it was easy to see who was the dominant one and who the submissive in most relationships, sometimes Greg would be the master and Anna his slave, and sometimes the roles would be reversed.

Before long, I had been fucked by both of them, individually and together. When Anna was dominant, she would wear a thick, black strap-on dildo that protruded aggressively from her crotch, and she would order Greg or me to suck it to get it nice and wet. Then she would thrust it hard and fast into my cunt or Greg's arse, till we were screaming with pleasure. When Greg was in charge, he would order Anna and me to lick each other's pussy while he watched, and then he would fuck either or both of us. Sometimes, I would be feasting on Anna's juicy sex while she was sucking Greg's cock, and other times I would have Anna's mouth nuzzling at my clit while Greg pounded hard into me from behind. Until I met them, I had never realised I had the capacity to fuck or be fucked by another woman, but I had always known I wanted to be spanked and taken anally, and both of them were more than happy to indulge me in those desires.

I thought that a threesome would be the limits of my experience, but then Greg announced that a friend of his, Jon, was holding one of his special party evenings at his home in East London. I had heard about these parties, and knew that anything and everything could happen there, but attendance was strictly by invitation only, and that Jon and his wife, Maura, were very fussy about who joined their select circle. I was delighted and, I must admit, more than a little scared when Greg told me that Jon and Maura wanted me to be there. He explained that single, submissive women were at a premium, and that someone who was as willing to be used as I appeared to be would be very popular with the experienced masters and mistresses among Jon and Maura's group of friends.

The evening of the party, I spent a long time choosing what to wear. Greg had told me that, as a newcomer, I could expect to receive a lot of attention. Maura, in particular, liked to put new subs through their paces for the benefit of an audience, and though she could be very cruel, she was also capable of giving a lot of pleasure in reward. Finally, I settled on a long-sleeved all-in-one bodystocking in very sheer net, which had an open crotch. Over it, I wore a skimpy pair of PVC shorts and black patent court shoes with four-inch heels and little padlocks at the ankles. My nipples I covered with strips of gaffer tape, hoping that this would attract curious and admiring gazes. I left my waist-length blonde hair loose, and made my face up carefully, emphasising my full lips and big, green eyes. When Greg and Anna turned up to collect me, I could see from the expression on their faces that they had made the right choice.

'You look innocent, but with just a touch of the slut,' Anna told me. 'Jon will be hard as a rock the moment he sees you.'

Jon and Maura owned a big, three-storey Victorian house, the only one in its road not to have been converted into flats, or so it seemed. When I had asked Anna what the couple did for a living, she had said that Jon was a lawyer who specialised in libel cases, and Maura was a television producer. That explained their lavish lifestyle.

The house itself was beautiful. Jon and Maura were holding court in the living room. He was in his forties, with steel-grey hair and piercing blue eyes, while the red-haired Maura was as tall and slender as a supermodel. There was a cold buffet spread out on the table, and the two dozen or so guests were encouraged to help themselves to food and drink. I couldn't help but notice a couple of bowls of condoms, of all colours and textures, it seemed, sitting on the coffee table. The couple had thought of everything.

It was hard to pinpoint exactly when the socialising stopped and events moved on to a more sexual level. At first, it was nothing more than a caress of a breast or a buttock as people talked to each other, but I soon noticed that one girl had removed her top and was allowing her male partner to suckle her pierced nipples, while another was down on her knees, vigorously sucking the penis of her well-endowed partner. His hands were on the top of her head, forcing her firmly into his groin, and I marvelled with the ease at which she was taking what must have been a good seven inches of rigid cock flesh down her throat.

'Why don't we see what's under those little shorts of yours, eh?' a soft, Scottish-accented voice whispered in my ear, and I realised with a start that it was Maura speaking. Without waiting for an answer from me, she rapidly unzipped my shorts and pulled them down my legs. She smiled in approval at the sight of my freshly shaven pussy. 'Mouthwatering, my dear, simply mouthwatering,' she said with a smile, and ran a hand casually between my legs, as if checking to see how wet I was.

I looked round frantically, trying to spot Greg and Anna, but they were nowhere to be seen. Jon had mentioned when we arrived that most of the action would be taking place in the playroom, and I wondered if the two of them had gone there. I was aware that heads had turned, watching as Maura played with me as though I was her latest toy. I had not expected to be the centre of attention so soon, and I was excited and frightened by the thought of what might be about to happen.

'You mustn't come without my permission,' Maura warned me, as her hand moved faster. Her index finger slipped inside me, drawing out my juices, which were beginning to flow freely. She knew exactly what she was doing, and I was fighting hard against the orgasmic sensations which were beginning to build somewhere deep within me. I was afraid that if I came before she let me, she would punish me, and even as I strove to avoid giving her that satisfaction, the pleasure became too much. I groaned as her finger stroked unerringly over my G-spot, feeling my cunt honey gush out and down her wrist.

Maura's soft tones became a threatening growl. 'You were warned, slut,' she said, and grabbed hold of my wrist. I was dragged out of the living room, leaving my shorts forgotten on the deep-pile carpet, my high heels clattering on the polished wooden floorboards in the hall. I was dimly aware that several of the people who had been watching Maura wank me were following us, and I knew that they would all take great pleasure in seeing the mistress of the house give me whatever punishment was my due.

As I had suspected, Greg and Anna were in the playroom when we got there. Greg was chained facing the black-painted wall, and Anna was applying a short, many-tailed whip to his backside. From the weals that already marked his skin, it was obvious they had been there for some while. Anna stopped what she was doing as Maura and I arrived.

'When you bring guests, I expect them to do as they are told,' Maura explained to a smiling Anna. 'I told this weak-willed slut she wasn't allowed to come, and yet she creamed herself all over my hand like the disobedient little whore she is. I think the only answer is a taste of my whip.'

Ignoring the protests I was making, Maura bent me over a padded whipping horse which was standing in the middle of the playroom. With Anna's help, she pushed my legs apart and secured them in place with a spreader bar, then she fastened my wrists to straps on the far side of the whipping horse. Satisfied that I could not move, she took down an evil-looking whip with three short, plaited tails from a rack on the wall. Giving me no time to prepare myself, she brought it down hard on my cheeks, the thin net material that covered them offering scant protection. I howled, but could do nothing to prevent her slashing the vicious instrument across my buttocks again and again.

At last, she tired of punishing me, and came round to stand in front of me. She smoothed away a strand of my hair from where it was clinging to my tear-stained face, and told me I had taken my punishment well. She then announced that I was now available to whoever wished to use me.

For the next hour or so, I was at the mercy of Maura, Jon and their guests. I was fucked by a succession of condom-clad cocks, including, I was sure from the feel, at least one strap-on. My cunt and arse were taken repeatedly, while I moaned and writhed, trying to press my mound hard against the padded top of the whipping horse to give my clitoris the stimulation it craved. Then, I was freed and ordered to pleasure Maura and Anna orally in turn, my tongue working overtime as I sought to bring each of them to orgasm. Finally, I was fucked by Jon as I lay on the floor with Maura squatting over my mouth, urging me to lick her. When she came, she peed over my face in her excitement – a first for me. At last, I was allowed the privilege of showering in the couple's en suite bathroom, to wash the semen, sweat and love juice from my exhausted body.

Next time I go, I won't be the new kid on the block and, hopefully, I will get the chance to watch someone else endure the pain and wonderful pleasure I experienced that night.

Melanie G.,
London

THEY SHOOT, THEY SCORE

Recently, I had to go to South Yorkshire on business, and I had what I am happy to admit was the rudest sexual experience of my life. I was staying in a hotel on the outskirts of Rotherham, and when I booked in, I couldn't help noticing a group of fifteen or so young men who were chatting noisily as they had their bags brought in for them. The receptionist told me they were the members of a football team who were stopping overnight before playing a match the following day. Now, I know nothing about football and care even less, but a couple of these men were very good-looking, and I found myself hoping I might bump into them at some point during my stay.

After dinner, I went for a drink in the bar, and noticed that several of the footballers were sitting talking, nursing glasses of orange juice. It wasn't too hard to get talking to them – after all, I'm tall and blonde, with a voluptuous figure which was squeezed that night into a tight dress – and soon three of them in particular were paying me the sort of attention any girl would find extremely flattering.

It turned out that two of them were sharing a room, and they said that although they were under strict instructions from the team manager to get an early night, none of them was in the least bit tired. By this time, I had taken a distinct liking to one of them in particular, who was tall and blond and only just nineteen. The other two were equally young; one was a stocky redhead and the other was black and on the lanky side. I told them I was not sleepy, either, and if they came up to my room, I was sure I could find a way to pass the time until they felt like nodding off.

I went upstairs first, hoping that none of them would bump into their manager on the way up to join me. However, within five minutes I heard a knock on the door, and the blond slipped into my room, swiftly followed by his two friends.

'So how did you plan to entertain us?' he asked.

'Like this,' I replied. I switched the bedside radio to a station that was playing dance music, and began to sway to the beat. As the three of them sat on the bed and watched with rapt expressions, I began to slowly peel out of the sleeveless navy-blue dress I was wearing, slipping it down off my shoulders to let it pool at my feet. Their eyes widened as they saw the white lacy bra and panties I was wearing beneath it, and which they realised I would not be wearing for much longer. I made the removal of my underwear as drawn out and tantalising as I possibly could, unfastening my bra and pulling the straps down my arms, but holding the bra cups over my nipples like a shy virgin who did not want anyone to see her nakedness. By the time the bra dropped to the floor, three hard-ons were making themselves obvious in three pairs of trousers. I wanted to go on teasing them, making them wait as long as possible till I removed my panties, but my pussy was beginning to throb with lust and all I could think about was getting one of those hard young cocks inside me. Footballers are renowned for having a lot of energy and stamina, and I sensed that when we got down to fucking, as I was sure we inevitably would, they would be able to keep going long enough to give me as many orgasms as I wanted.

I pulled down the front of my panties, giving them the merest flash of my pussy. What little hair I have on my mound is so fine it almost looks as though I shave myself, and I could tell the sight had whetted their appetite. At last, I pulled the flimsy garment off and tossed it to the blond, who sniffed at the gusset appreciatively, as though it was his favourite perfume.

Meanwhile, his two companions had undressed down to their underwear and were all over my body like a rash. The black guy was kissing and licking my stiff little nipples while the redhead's fingers probed between my legs, seeking out my juicy cunt. I sighed with undisguised pleasure as his fingers delved inside me while his thumb circled my clit. I'm one of those lucky girls who can come very easily, and it only took a few swift rubs before my legs were shaking and I was moaning in ecstasy.

Much as I was enjoying the feel of that hot, wet mouth on my tits and the fingers that were wanking me so skilfully, I wanted the blond to join in. As I looked over to where he was sitting, however, I had the feeling that this was not the first time he and his friends had seduced a woman in this way, and that they were working to some pre-arranged plan.

My suspicions were confirmed when he began to strip out of his clothes, slowly and with complete self-assurance, as though he was in charge of the situation. When he was naked, I realised why he was quite so confident. He had the biggest, thickest cock I think I have ever seen, rising from a bush of wiry, sandy hair to curve slightly away from his flat belly. My cunt muscles quivered in anticipation of feeling that beautiful tool inside me but, before that happened, it looked like the other two were going to fuck me first.

I was guided on to all fours, and the black guy pulled down his boxer shorts to reveal his own cock. It was not as big as the blond's, but its rigid ebony shaft gleamed beautifully, and I put out a hand, greedy to touch it. Pulling away from my grasping fingers, he came behind me and guided his glans between my swollen pussy lips. I sighed as I felt him ease into me, shuffling forward on his knees until he was in me up to the hilt and I could feel his balls resting against my bum cheeks.

As I was growing used to the feel of him and waiting for him to start thrusting, the redhead presented the head of his dick to my mouth, urging me to wrap my lips around it. Now, the next best thing to the feel of a cock is the taste of one, and I happily swallowed as much of his meat as I could. I was firmly skewered as the two began to move, awkwardly at first, but then the rhythm caught fire between them and I was being pushed backwards and forwards on the carpet, every thrust of the cock in my cunt pushing me hard on to the one in my mouth.

I must have orgasmed two or three times before the redhead gasped and called out that he was coming. I think he was expecting me to pull my mouth away, but instead I kept on sucking until I had taken every drop of his creamy emission down my gullet.

My black lover was showing no signs of reaching his climax, and my cries became more animalistic as I came again and again in a series of little orgasms that, far from satisfying me, simply left me hungry for more. My head was down, and I pushed my hair out of my eyes, feeling sweat trickling out of every pore in my body. At last, I felt his body give a final jerk as he flooded his spunk into me.

As he withdrew, my cunt muscles clenched in anticipation of clasping the blond's big, gorgeous cock, but I was in for another surprise. He lay back on the floor, his erection pointing up into the air, and his friends helped me into position so that I was squatting over him. However, instead of his cockhead slipping between my expectant sex lips, I gasped as I felt it nudge against the entrance to my anus. My juices had been leaking out of me at such a rate that they had pooled in my arsehole, but I was apprehensive at the thought of something that size breaching my virgin hole. Knowing that all I could do was trust him, I sank down as gently as I could, doing my best to relax the little ring of muscle and help him enter me more easily. There was an initial moment of discomfort and resistance, then I felt something give and he was inside me. With the help of his two friends, who held me securely by the arms, I began to shift up and down, taking as much of that warm, solid length into my arse as I could. I had never known anything like it; it felt like such a dirty thing to do, particularly with an appreciative audience, but I had found myself coming again as he thrust up inside me, and I was on a strange, orgasmic high. Fingers were playing with my clit and nipples and my body felt supremely sensitive. Given the tightness of my anal passage, the blond came quicker than I think either of us would have wanted, and as I felt his hot semen jetting up into me, I reached the biggest and most spectacular orgasm of the whole evening.

I think the three of them wanted a repeat performance, but by this time I was utterly exhausted, and so the blond helped me run a bath before the three of them quietly made their way back to their own rooms.

As I said, I'm no football fan, but I found myself looking out for the team's result the following day. They won, and my cute blond stud got two goals, so it was nice to see he kept up his scoring prowess.

Helen S.,
Bristol

Me, Myself and I

CAUGHT IN THE ACT

My work takes me down to the south coast for a couple of days every month, and when I go, I know that my old friend John will always put me up overnight. We were at university together, and there had always been an attraction between us, though we never acted on it as we thought that was a pretty good way to ruin a friendship.

One of my visits to his place was during last summer's heatwave. My business finished early, for once, so I decided to take advantage of the good weather and do some nude sunbathing before John got back from work. John has a first-floor flat with a balcony that is not overlooked, so I figured I could get an all-over tan without anyone seeing me. I took out the sun lounger he kept in a cupboard and a book, covered my naked body generously with sun-tan lotion and lay back to soak up the rays. It was beautifully warm out there, and I couldn't stop myself falling asleep. I was only woken up when a cloud covered the sun and it started getting cold. I sat up, disorientated, and realised I was not alone. John had got back from work and was looking at me through the French window that led out to the balcony, a wolfish smile on his face. What made it worse was that he had someone else with him!

All I had to cover my embarrassment was my paperback, and I shielded my pussy with it as I went to open the French window, sure I could laugh the incident off. When I tugged at the door, I found to my surprise that it was locked.

'John, what's going on?' I asked, panicking slightly. I had to press myself close up to the window to make myself heard, and I tried not to think of the show I was giving him, with my big breasts squashed against the glass.

His reply was muffled. 'This is Matt,' he said, indicating his companion. 'He's been enjoying what he's seen so far, but I don't think he's really seen enough. Sorry, Liz, but you're not coming in without putting on a show for us.'

I wondered what he meant by that, but his next words made everything clear. 'We want to see you play with yourself.'

I felt myself blushing with shame, but there was nothing I could do. I had managed to put myself in a position I could not easily get out of. There was no way I could climb off the balcony, and I was stuck until John and Matt decided to let me in – and I quickly realised that wasn't going to happen unless I did as they requested.

I dropped the book and stepped back a couple of paces from the French window. Now they would be able to see the bush of soft brown curls crowning my mound. More than that, I like to keep my pubes neatly trimmed, which means that my very long inner pussy lips are always slightly visible.

I cupped my breasts in my hands, and pushed them together. As I stroked my large, brown nipples with my thumbs, I realised that for all the vulnerability of my situation – or perhaps because of it – I was starting to get aroused.

Bringing my breast up to my mouth, I circled my tongue round the nipple. If I had to give them a show, it would be one to remember.

At last, I turned my attention to my pussy, which was already starting to get wet with excitement. Slipping a finger between my lips, I brought it away shining with my juices, which I licked off. I could see the two of them staring at me through the glass, and I glanced down, trying to see whether I was causing their cocks to grow in their suit trousers. I found myself wanting to get them hard, wanting them to be so turned on by my performance that they would start wanking, too. A vision flashed across my mind of the two of them, each with the other's cock in his hand, then John kneeling to take Matt's fat shaft in his mouth, his blond head bobbing up and down as he sucked. My pussy twitched with lust at the sheer rudeness of my fantasies, and I rubbed my clit hard and fast, slipping first one, then two fingers of my other hand into my aching channel. Eventually, I was frigging myself with three fingers, pumping them in and out of me, but it wasn't enough; I craved something more inside me. I glanced round, and my gaze landed on a coil of hosepipe lying on the balcony floor. It was an outrageous thing to do, but I was so frantic to come that it seemed like the ideal solution. As John and Matt watched, I took the end of the hosepipe and began to insert it slowly into my quim. It felt strange, warm from the sun and slightly slippery, the ridges in the plastic stimulating me in a way I had never known before. I lay back on the sun lounger, vaguely aware that John had unlocked the French windows so he and Matt could come and watch me more closely, but I was oblivious to everything but my own pleasure. I thrust the hosepipe as deeply up me as it would go, clamping my pussy muscles around it, and came, screaming in ecstasy as I did.

John told me afterwards he had never believed I would go as far as I did, but then, however long you have known someone, they can still be capable of surprising you.

Liz B.,
Sheffield

SEE EMILY PLAY

I would like to tell you about what happened the last time my wife's best friend, Emily, came to stay for the weekend. Claire and Emily have known each other since they were six, and though their lives have taken very different paths – Emily went to university and has a job working for a TV production company in London, while Claire and I got married when she was just 19 and she works part time in our local newsagent – the two have remained very close. When Emily rang to tell Claire that she had just split up from her boyfriend of three years and was feeling very down about it, Claire immediately invited her down to visit us, in the hope it would cheer her up.

Emily arrived on the Friday night, and after a nice dinner and a couple of bottles of wine shared between the three of us, she and Claire sat talking about old times while I sat watching the football on TV. I have always had a soft spot for Emily – she is by far the most attractive of all my wife's friends, with her shoulder-length blonde hair, heart-shaped face and slim yet curvaceous figure – and I hated to see her quite so depressed.

When Claire and I got into bed, I was in the mood for sex, and I ran my hand lightly down her neck to cup one of her big breasts through her nightdress. Claire responded, and soon her nightie was in a heap on the floor and the two of us were lying on top of the duvet, my fingers between her legs and stroking her rapidly moistening sex. She, in return, was wanking my cock to its full seven-inch length, and once she was ready to take it inside me, she straddled me and lowered her pussy on to my rigid shaft. We had completely forgotten about Emily, who was sleeping on the sofa bed in the lounge, as Claire bounced up and down on my cock, sighing and moaning. I have to admit she is pretty noisy when she comes, and as I gave one hard jerk of my hips and my penis spat its load of spunk up into her, she was shrieking like a banshee.

Satisfied, Claire rolled off me, curled up under the duvet and was soon asleep. However, I was finding it hard to drop off as I badly needed to piss. I slipped out of bed and pulled on my dressing gown, then turned on the hall light and padded down the hallway to the bathroom. The lounge in our flat is opposite the bedroom, and as I walked past I noticed the door was slightly ajar, and that the light was still on. I also thought I could hear a faint sobbing sound. Wondering if Emily was all right, I popped my head quietly round the door, and saw the most erotic sight I think I have ever seen. Emily was lying on the sofa bed, the covers pushed back. She was stark naked and it was immediately obvious that she was masturbating. Her left hand was cupping her small, firm tit, her fingers playing with the nipple, while her other hand was working something in and out of her pussy.

I should have gone straight to the bathroom, but I was transfixed by what Emily was doing. She had not shown any sign that she was aware of my presence; her head was hanging over the edge of the sofa bed and her eyes were closed. I realised that what she was thrusting into herself was one of the large candles which we keep on the mantelpiece as decoration. Her hips were bucking as she fed more and more of the candle into her wet cunt. It was such a beautiful thing to watch that I could not help letting out a small groan of pure lust. The noise was enough to bring Emily to her senses and she turned her head to see me silhouetted in the doorway.

She pulled the candle out of herself with an audible sucking sound and made to pull up the bedcovers, but I shook my head. 'Please, carry on,' I urged her. 'You look so horny, I want to watch you come.'

She hesitated for a moment, then beckoned me into the lounge, motioning to me to shut the door firmly behind me. I did as she asked and stood expectantly, my reawakened erection strong enough to tent out the folds of my dressing gown. I was rewarded by the sight of Emily pushing the candle slowly back into her sex, then using both hands to shove it forcefully in and out. She was making little whimpering noises as she moved closer to her climax, then her whole body seemed to convulse as her muscles clamped down hard on the fat waxy taper.

When she had recovered from her shattering orgasm, she told me that the sound of Claire and me fucking had made her feel so horny and frustrated, particularly as she was badly missing the active sex life she had enjoyed with her boyfriend, that the only thing she could do was use the candle to bring herself off. I was so turned on by what I had just watched that I went straight back into the bedroom, woke Claire up and fucked her for a second time. She asked what had got into me, but how could I tell her that it was what had got into Emily that had got me so aroused?

Andy H.,
Portsmouth

My boyfriend Russell and I agree on most things, but rugby is not one of them. Put simply, he loves it and I hate it. I have accepted the fact that he spends most Saturdays watching his team in action, spending a fortune to travel round the country watching them, but when they got into a major European competition and he wanted to go to Toulouse and watch them play there, I put my foot down. A couple of days' holiday in France would have been one thing, but when rugby was involved – no chance! Undeterred, Russell simply said that the match was going to be televised, so he would be able to see it anyway.

Come the evening of the match, Russell settled down in front of the television with a couple of cans of beer and prepared to enjoy himself. I had other plans, however; I was tired of being ignored in favour of fifteen men chasing a stupid ball around a pitch, and I was determined that I would make Russell forget about the rugby one way or another.

I went and had a soak in the tub, applying lots of scented oil to the water to leave my skin fragrant and smooth. Then I dressed in an outfit I had bought especially for the occasion: a black PVC waspie that merely supported my pert little breasts, rather than covering them, a tiny rubber G-string, fishnet stockings and spike-heeled shoes. Over the top, I put a baggy old T-shirt and leggings, then I went into the living room and stood in front of the television, blocking Russell's view of the screen.

Clearly annoyed, he told me to get out of the way. In response, I peeled down the leggings and stepped out of them, then pulled the jumper over my head. Russell's eyes widened in surprise as he realised what I was wearing, and he seemed torn between craning his head to watch what was happening on the TV and keeping his eyes on me to see what I would do next. I pirouetted, giving him the chance to appreciate the way the thong back of the G-string divided my full, round buttocks, and when I turned back to him, I began to gyrate like a stripper, swaying to music I could only hear in my own head and toying with my nipples. The big brown areolae began to crinkle as I got more excited, and I could feel my pussy beginning to twitch and moisten. Russell had forgotten about his precious rugby match as my hand snaked down to play with my pussy. I pulled the G-string tightly into the cleft between my legs, so that my hairy pussy lips bulged out around it, and teased my clit by sawing the little strip of rubber back and forth. The air was heavy with the smell of latex and my sex honey, and Russell's cock was a hard, prominent lump in the jogging bottoms he was wearing.

'Take it off,' he urged. 'I want to see your cunt.'

It always turns me on when he uses crude language, and I eased the G-string down tantalisingly slowly, tormenting him by giving him flashes of my bush before pulling the little rubber garment back into place.

'Take it off now or I'll rip it off you,' he demanded, and so I wriggled it down off my hips, tossing it to the floor and perching on the coffee table directly in front of Russell. I parted my legs widely, so he could see how wet and excited I was, the petals of my sex unfolding like some exotic orchid. He made to touch my pussy, but I slapped his hand away. I hadn't finished the show I was putting on for him by a long way.

There was a bowl of fruit on the coffee table, and I selected the biggest banana I could find. It was slightly under-ripe, and just firm enough for what I was about to do. While Russell watched in fascination, I took the banana and placed it at the entrance to my sex. I gave a little push and it slipped easily into me. I tightened my muscles around it, gripping the banana securely as I began to thrust it in and out. It felt good, and I worked it faster, driving myself towards an orgasm.

Russell has always loved to watch me frig myself, but I know what really turns me on, and I was saving that as the highlight of my performance. I pulled the banana from my cunt; it came free with an audible sucking sound, and was shining with my juices. Then I lay back on the floor. Russell, having realised what I was about to do, groaned with anticipation and freed his massively erect cock from his jogging bottoms. As he knelt between my legs, gently stroking himself, I pushed the end of the banana against my tight anal opening. There was a moment's resistance, then the little ring of muscle gave, and the hard fruit slid all the way into my arse. My bum obscenely plugged with the banana, I began to diddle my clit in earnest while Russell watched me avidly and wanked his own cock. It only took seconds before a shattering orgasm surged through me, and I threw my head back and screamed in pleasure as Russell's come splattered my fishnet-covered thighs.

My little show certainly scored with Russell, so if there are any other rugby widows reading this, they know what to do next time there's a match on.

Anne C.,
London

I TOUCH MYSELF

I know it was a stupid thing to do, but at the time I honestly thought I was on my own. I was working late in the office, laying out a spread for the women's magazine I work for. It's quite a raunchy magazine, it has to be said, full of articles on how to spice up your sex life, and the feature I was designing was all to do with having sex in the bathroom. We had a really beautiful set of black-and-white photographs to illustrate it, featuring a moody-looking bloke stripping out of a white vest and stepping into the shower. My favourite shot featured him standing beneath the spray, holding the rolled-up T-shirt in his fists as though inviting some unseen person to use it to tie his hands together. His leg was positioned so that you could not quite see his cock, just the shadow of his pubic hair, and just looking at that photo was starting to make me feel really horny.

My boyfriend was away on business in the States, and I was missing him – or, more accurately, missing sex with him. The subject matter of the magazine did not help; the last thing I wanted to read about when I was feeling so frustrated was other people having a fantastic time in bed. I would have packed in for the evening and gone home to have a cold shower, but the magazine was running late, and this feature had to be on the editor's desk first thing the following morning, so I carried on. But I couldn't get the photo of that model out of my head. Even as I saved the feature and powered down the computer, I was still thinking about him, imagining how his cock might look when it was erect and almost able to taste the mixture of water and sweat on his glistening skin.

It was too much for me. Sure that I was the only person in the office, the cleaners not being due to arrive for another hour, I did not even bother to go to the toilet – which, in retrospect, would have been a more sensible idea. I simply unfastened my jeans and pulled them, along with my panties, down to my ankles, then sat back in my chair and spread my legs as wide as they would go. I knew before I ran a finger along my crease that I was wet. I almost groaned as I touched my clit, lightly at first, then more firmly. I peeled apart my damp pussy lips, then slipped a finger into my vagina. It felt good: so good, in fact, that a second digit swiftly followed the first. I humped my hips on the seat, my bottom sliding against the smooth black leather, as I frigged myself more strongly. I could hear the squelching noises as my fingers pumped in and out of my cunt, and my breathing was getting faster and more ragged as I moved closer to orgasm.

I was almost oblivious to my surroundings, and although I must have registered the sound of footsteps on one level, it was not until they were almost on top of me that my eyelids finally fluttered open and I realised I had company.

It was Clive, the magazine's advertising manager, and he was looking at me with an almost feral look on his face. I was suddenly aware of what I must look like: naked from the waist down and with my fingers buried in my wet, open pussy. I had no idea if he had been watching me for a while or whether he had literally just burst in on me, but I did know what I had to do next. I pulled my fingers out of my hole and went to pull up my jeans, but Clive stopped me, grabbing hold of my wrist. His grip was surprisingly strong, and for a moment I just stared at him, wondering what was going to happen next.

His words surprised me. 'That looks like fun,' he said. 'Can anyone join in?'

I didn't know what to say. This was not how I had expected him to react.

'You shouldn't be here,' I finally managed to stammer. 'I was just –'

'Yes, I could see what you were just doing, and I want to watch you finish the job,' he replied.

'I can't . . .' I began.

'Oh, yes, you can,' he said, 'but you're going to have to get those out of the way –' He gestured to my bunched-up jeans and panties. Keeping my eyes locked on his, I meekly kicked the offending garments off my legs completely. Try to deny it though I might, something in the way he was treating me was turning me on. There was something in his dark eyes and stubbled chin that reminded me of the model in the photograph I had been lusting over, and I tried to imagine how I would react if he was the one who was ordering me to masturbate for his pleasure.

'Now lift up your top and show me your tits,' Clive said.

I was wearing a tight-fitting white top which must have clearly revealed the outline of my excited nipples, and I pushed it up around my armpits to bare my firm breasts to him.

'Very nice,' he commented, and as I looked down I could see how his erection was pushing at the front of his suit trousers. Almost unconsciously, I let my hand stray over my nipples, the casual touch bringing them to full hardness.

'Now carry on where you left off,' he said.

I groaned as my fingers sank back into the wet depths of my pussy. His cock had looked big where the material of his trousers clung to it, and I wished that was what was pounding into me, and not my own fingers.

'Please,' I murmured. 'I want you to . . .'

'What?' he asked softly, urging me to use the word.

'Fuck me,' I replied, with more passion than I had intended. 'Fuck me with your fingers, then fuck me with your cock.'

It was all the invitation he needed. He ordered me to get on the desk, and I pushed everything that was on the desktop to the floor, clearing enough space so I could lie down. I brought my knees up to my chest, and his fingers slid into my gaping sex. I gasped as he began to wank me hard, using two and then three fingers to stretch me wide. He used the thumb of his other hand to roll my clit, and within moments I was coming, colours dancing behind my closed eyelids as I screamed out my pleasure to the deserted office.

I lay recovering as he quickly stripped off his clothes, and then his body was over mine and his cock was nudging at my cunt, seeking entry. He was even bigger than I had hoped, and that hot column of flesh filled me beautifully. I urged him on as he fucked me, begging him to make me come, my legs locked around his smooth, tanned back. My second orgasm hit me, this one more powerful than the first, and my pussy muscles clutched greedily at his thick shaft, milking his climax from him.

I had to work late a couple more times before my boyfriend got back from his business trip, and strange to relate, Clive found himself putting in some pretty profitable overtime, too.

Louise M.,
London

Waxing Lyrical

HAIR TODAY

It would never have happened if Jilly and I had not had that row. The silly thing is that I can't remember what it was about. Something to do with me not paying her enough attention, I think. Anyway, it was the culmination of a series of rows we had been having. Money was tight as I was on short time, and our sex life was almost non-existent, which gave us plenty of things to fight about. I do recall that she said something to the effect that if she couldn't get sex from me she was going to get it somewhere else, and I said that was fine by me. I thought it was just one of those things that get said in the heat of the moment. I never thought she was serious.

She grabbed her coat, her bag and her keys and said she was off out. I thought she was going for a walk round the block, to clear her head and cool down, and so I simply shrugged and went back to the football match I had been trying to watch. When she hadn't come back an hour later, I started to get worried, but I assumed she'd gone round to a mate's house. I went to bed around midnight, and was woken at four in the morning by Jilly staggering into the bedroom, obviously trying not to make any noise.

I switched the light on, and immediately realised she had been up to something: her tights were laddered, her hair was a mess and her make-up was smeared around her face, and she had a self-satisfied smirk on her face.

'Where have you been till now?' I asked, still half-asleep.

'Doing what I said I'd do,' she replied. 'I told you I'd go out and get sex somewhere else, and I did.'

My initial reaction was one of disbelief, anger and a strange excitement. 'Yeah, right,' I retorted.

'Don't you believe me, Mike?' she said. 'Do you want me to give you the details? Well, I picked him up in the pub round the corner, he was nineteen years old and he had an eight-inch cock that was so thick I could hardly get my mouth round it.'

By now, I was as hard as a rock under the sheets; jealous, hurt, and wanting Jilly to tell me more.

She took off her top and skirt and flung them to the floor. Even in the dim light from the bedside lamp I thought I could see a tell-tale wet patch in the front of her knickers.

'When I left here, all I knew was that I was determined to get laid, and I thought the best place to go was the pub,' Jilly said. 'I saw him drinking at the bar with his mates. He was the best-looking one of the lot. He was big-built, with blond hair cut really short and a big Celtic tattoo running round his biceps. He looked like the sort who'd be up for a quick fuck with no finesse, so I just went up and started giving him the come-on.'

I know what that involves. When Jilly and I first met she did exactly the same thing: came up to me when I was in a crowd of blokes and undid just enough buttons on her blouse that I could see her bra and the tits that were doing their best to burst out of it. I couldn't see how any man could resist her when she was determined to snare him, and it seemed this unknown young stud had not put up too much of a fight.

'He didn't waste any time once he realised I was up for it,' she said. 'Within a few minutes we were snogging at the bar. He had his tongue right down my throat and his hand up my top, mauling my tits through my bra. He had really rough, callused hands, like he worked on a building site or something, and I knew he'd want it hard and fast when we got down to fucking.

'As we kissed, he encouraged me to feel the bulge in his jeans. As soon as I touched it, I realised it was big – a lot bigger than yours, Mike – and the thought of all that cock flesh, combined with the way he was fondling my tits, was getting me really wet. I told him I wanted him now, and he asked if we were going to my place or his. I said it would have to be his, because my inadequate wimp of a husband was sulking at home, and while I wanted him to know a real man had fucked me, I didn't want to give him the satisfaction of watching.'

The gratuitous insults she was throwing at me, coupled with the image she was painting of this uncouth builder groping her so openly in front of all his mates, was fuelling my erection, and I could not resist slipping a hand down under the duvet to wank my stiff length.

'As we were leaving,' Jilly continued, 'one of his friends shouted, "See you later, Donkey." He'd told me his name was Wayne, and so I asked why his mates called him Donkey. Bold as brass, he said it was because they all knew he was hung like one.

'He lived in this really grotty bedsit over a chip shop. When you walked in there, the smell of stale chip fat struck you immediately. He said he was used to it but, to me, it just added to the sleaziness of what I was doing. He told me to strip, just like that, and to lie on the bed with my legs spread while he undressed, so he could look at my cunt while he was doing it.'

Now, sex between Jilly and me might not be all that frequent, but when it happens I always make the effort to spend a long time kissing her, touching her and making sure she's nice and ready for me by the time I enter her. It seemed like foreplay was a foreign concept to her new conquest, but she said she found his crude language and direct approach a turn-on.

'I mean, sometimes you can be too much of a gentleman, Mike,' she said. 'I won't break if you slam your cock into me really hard, you know. Anyway, Donkey said that if I wanted to be wet for him, then I should play with myself. And I did; I lay there on the unmade bed in that smelly little room and frigged my clit while he took his clothes off. When his pants came down, it was obvious his cock was everything I'd been promised and more. It was so long and thick, it makes yours look like a little boy's prick in comparison.

'I was expecting Donkey to just leap on me and start fucking me but, to my surprise, he said, "I want to do something to you that will make sure your husband knows you've been with someone else." And do you know what he did? This.'

As Jilly spoke, she was pulling down her knickers. The sight that greeted me as she did so caused the breath to catch in my throat. When I'd seen her naked earlier that morning, her mound had been crowned with its big, thick bush of black curls. Now, all that had gone, leaving pink, shiny bare skin. This young stud had left his mark by shaving my wife's cunt. My hand moved faster on my cock as I gazed at her.

'He went into his bathroom and came back with a can of shaving foam and a razor. He just swooshed the foam over my pussy, and began to slice away all my pubes. As the lather and hair came away, I could see my naked skin beneath it, all pink and vulnerable. He was pulling my lips around and making sure he got into all the nooks and crannies, and the rough, impersonal way he was touching me was really getting me horny. By the time he'd finished, and my cunt was all smooth and shiny, like a billiard ball, I was just desperate to be fucked, and I pulled him on top of me, guiding his cock to my aching hole. I could really feel the difference between you and him as that big, meaty shaft slid right up into me, and the feeling of his pubes against my newly shaved skin was like nothing I'd known before. I seemed so much more sensitive, and even though he was just concentrating on his own pleasure as he thrust into me, I was soon coming off all over his cock. Then he spunked into me, climbed off and that was it. Not even a word to say if he'd enjoyed it. I felt used and slutty and it was absolutely fantastic.'

By now, my own orgasm seemed inevitable, and I pulled back the duvet to reveal my own erection, shiny with pre-come. Jilly told me she couldn't remember the last time she'd seen it so big and hard, even though she said it was still nothing in comparison to Donkey's massive member. I begged her to fuck me, but she said she was too sore from the pounding Donkey had given her cunt. Instead, she wanked me off until I shot my load, my come arcing into the air to land on my own stomach. The following morning, however, I did get to sample that beautiful shaved pussy. She's agreed to keep it shaved, on condition that I let her go back and sample Donkey's huge cock again. If she does, I'll let you know what happens.

Mike B.,
Liverpool

SHAVE AND PROSPER

When I first started going out with Joey, he told me there were certain things I had to do for him. I always had to wear stockings, I was not allowed to wear knickers unless it was my time of the month, and I had to shave my pussy for him. Now, I have always liked men who act like men, but Joey was different to anyone I had ever met, and I was intrigued by the fact that he was so dominant. He owns and works in the newspaper kiosk at a tube station – I won't mention which one it is for obvious reasons – and when my friends first met him, they thought he was a bit of a wide boy, and told me so quite forcefully. They can't understand why I am still with him, a year after we first met, when we appear to have very little in common, but like I said, the fact that he tells me what to do is a massive turn-on. Plus he really knows how to fuck, unlike some of the 'whip it in, whip it out and wipe it' merchants I have had the misfortune to have sex with. So I comply with his demands, and get a secret thrill every time I walk into the office where I work, knowing my colleagues are oblivious to the fact that my pussy is bare and shaven beneath my neat business suit.

However, Joey is not so discreet about our little arrangement, as I found out recently. I was sitting at home, having a lazy evening with a romantic video and a nice bottle of wine, when Joey came back from the pub. To my surprise, he had somebody with him.

'Caroline, I want you to meet Dennis,' Joey said. 'Dennis and me go back a long way, but he's been out of the country, working in the Gulf. I was telling him all about you, and he was very interested to meet you, so I thought I'd bring him back. You don't mind, do you?'

'Not at all,' I said, although my first impressions of Dennis were not promising. He was small and weaselly looking, with closely cropped dark hair and a scar on his left cheek. He looked like the sort who would not only be able to handle himself in a fight, but who would be responsible for starting that fight in the first place. I wanted to know exactly what Joey had said to him about our relationship, but Joey had disappeared into the kitchen in search of a couple of beers, leaving me alone with his friend.

'So how did you like the Gulf?' I asked Dennis, in an attempt to make conversation.

'Not much,' he replied, sprawling himself in one of the armchairs, his legs widely spread as though drawing attention to his crotch. Despite myself, I could not help but notice that he seemed to have a pretty impressive bulge in his tight jeans. 'The money's good, but there are two things you can't really get out there, and that's booze and women. A mate of mine had his own still, so we coped OK with the first one, but I haven't had a woman in nine months now.'

I wondered why he was telling me that, and thought about changing the subject, but Dennis carried on, 'Joey was saying to me that you're a very obedient girl.'

'Oh, really?' I said. For the first time, I was conscious of the fact that all I was wearing was a white silk dressing gown – as usual, in compliance with Joey's wishes, I had no underwear on.

'Yeah, he says you do what he likes, and what he likes is for you to keep your beaver bald. I've seen some birds who've shaved themselves in a couple of the porn mags I had in the Gulf, but I've never known anyone who did it in real life.'

I realised just where the conversation was heading, and wondered what was taking Joey so long as I said, 'It's no big deal. Joey likes it, so I do it.'

'He also said that he'd like you to show it to me,' Dennis said, and I knew then that I had been set up by my boyfriend. On the rare occasions I have disobeyed him, he has given me a good spanking, and while I find that a turn-on, I knew that if I disobeyed him tonight I would be spanked in front of an audience. I did not say anything; I just looked at Dennis and nodded.

I went to stand in front of him, my fingers fumbling with the tie fastening of my dressing gown. And then it was open, and I was giving Dennis the view he craved of my smooth, naked mound.

'Beautiful,' he said, 'just beautiful.' And he reached out a hand to stroke it. I did not pull away as his callused fingers ran lightly over my soft, bare pussy lips before gently prising them apart. I whimpered softly as he rubbed my cleft, feeling my juices start to flow at his initially unwelcome touch.

I glanced over to see Joey standing in the doorway. 'That's it, babe, be nice to him,' he murmured, and I nodded my assent, widening my stance to give Dennis easier access to my most intimate place.

'I've never licked a shaven fanny,' Dennis said hopefully, and I cast my gaze towards Joey, looking for his reaction. He nodded almost imperceptibly, and I shed the dressing gown entirely. Dennis smiled at the sight of my small, high breasts with their oversized areolae, the flat plane of my stomach and my bare sex below it. Then he dropped to his knees, pressing his lips to my pussy and gently kissing it.

'Part your legs, babe,' Joey urged me. 'Give Dennis what he wants.'

I did as he asked, feeling Dennis's tongue snake out to taste my cunt honey. I moaned; it might have been a long time since Dennis had been with a woman, but he was no novice when it came to licking one out. He seemed to know exactly where to press to give me pleasure, his tongue flickering expertly over my prominent clitoris. The stubble on his cheeks rasped against my delicate flesh, and I caught hold of his head, pulling his mouth harder on to my sex to help bring me to orgasm. I did not care that I had only met this man half an hour ago, or that Joey had put me in this position so he could watch another man lick me; all that mattered was he was about to make me come like a train. I felt my pussy spasming, sweet, warm waves of pleasure flowing through my belly, and held Dennis's head in place until the feeling finally ebbed away.

Dennis asked Joey if he could spend the rest of the night with me, and of course Joey agreed. Needless to say, he had his first experience of fucking a shaven pussy, and I was more than happy to let him slide his eight fat inches of cock flesh into my wet channel. Joey has implied that this will not be a one-off, and I am quite happy with that. Of course, if I told my friends about this they would be horrified, but I know you will understand.

Caroline R.,
South London

The Bare Essentials

WELL BUILT

My mate Davey and I have had some memorable times in the years we have been working together, but the one that sticks in my mind is when we went to do a building job for a bloke in the posh part of town. He had a job in the City which meant he commuted in every day, leaving his wife at home. She was the type who has never done an honest day's work in her life and just lived off his fat salary, and she treated Davey and me the same way she probably treated anyone who came to do any work at that place – like a lower form of life.

It was August, and blisteringly hot, as we started the construction work on the conservatory they wanted. Normally, Davey and I would walk about quite happily stripped to the waist and wearing cut-off denim shorts, but that was not to the liking of Mrs Fortune (or Rosalind, as we were definitely not allowed to call her), and so we sweltered away in T-shirts and jeans while the temperatures climbed into the nineties. Occasionally, she would condescend to bring us a cool drink or ask us if we needed anything, but mostly she would sit around on a sun lounger wearing a tiny bikini, almost as if she wanted us to gawp at her. She seemed to get off on the idea that dirty, common workmen like us could look, but we were not allowed to touch. Mind you, it seemed like her husband was in the same boat as us. If I tell you that her old man was in his fifties while she was a good twenty years younger, I think that will give you some idea of what their marriage was like. We rapidly picked up the impression that although she had a stunning body, with big tits and a luscious arse, her husband very rarely got his hands on it, the poor sod.

As the week went on, and she continued to ignore us, we decided she needed to be brought down a peg or two. She had had a couple of friends round for lunch on the Friday, and the three of them had come and stared at us as we worked away, smoothing the concrete into place on the floor of the conservatory. As they pointed and laughed, Davey was harbouring thoughts about pushing her face into the concrete, but I had a different kind of humiliation in store for her.

A couple of hours later, I got the chance I had been waiting for. Mrs Fortune was lying on the sun lounger, fast asleep, the book she had been reading forgotten on the grass. As usual, she was wearing a polka-dot bikini which consisted of little more than a series of minute triangles of fabric. I took my Stanley knife from the tool kit, and crept over to where she was snoring gently. She did not stir as I caught hold of the thin strip of fabric between the cups of her bikini, and sliced it in two. Then I did the same with the halter fastening of the top before turning my attention to the tie sides of her bikini bottoms. Satisfied with my handiwork, I quietly coughed in her ear. She jerked awake and looked around her.

'What the hell do you think you're doing, you filthy lecher?' she snapped. 'Spying on a defenceless woman when she's asleep.'

'I wasn't exactly spying,' I replied, trying to keep the smirk from my face. When she had sat up, the bikini top had fallen apart, and she did not seem to realise that I could now see her naked tits with their plump pink nipples.

'What are you staring at?' she asked. 'Just go and get on with your work. I'm going to go and run myself a bath and I don't want to be disturbed. Honestly, I should ring my husband and tell him to sack the pair of you.'

'Yeah, you do that, love,' I said. She rose to her feet in fury, obviously about to say something, then stopped as she felt the scraps of material that had once been her bikini bottom slithering down her legs.

'What the hell . . .?' she exclaimed, glancing down her body. Her hands flew to cover her nipples and pussy, but not before I had got a good look at her cunt. I could not fail to notice that it was considerably darker than the ash-blonde hair on her head.

She turned and made a dash for the house, but that was when I realised Davey had played our trump card. He was sitting on the doorstep, waving the key to the back door and grinning his head off. Mrs Fortune looked rapidly from one to the other of us, weighing up the situation and quickly coming to the realisation that Davey and I had the upper hand.

'What are you going to do to me?' she asked anxiously, obviously afraid that we might hurt her. Of course, that was not our intention, but there was no harm in letting her get a little worried.

'Actually, it's what you're going to do to us,' I replied. 'We're sick of the fact that you treat us like something you've scraped off the heel of your shoe, and we're tired of the way you flaunt your body all the time, trying to turn us on.'

'I never . . .' she began, but I had spoken the truth, and she knew it.

'So what you're going to do, Rosalind, is apologise for your rudeness and your snobby ways, but you're going to do it by giving me and Davey a nice blowjob each.'

'You can't expect me to do that,' she said anxiously. 'I mean, my husband doesn't expect me to . . .' Her voice trailed away as she realised just what she was telling us. As I said before, the poor sod.

There was the sound of a zip coming down, and when Rosalind and I looked round, it was to see Davey holding his cock and giving it a few firm rubs to bring it to full erection. I've seen Davey in the football club showers before, so what he was holding was no surprise to me, but Rosalind's mouth was hanging open as she took in the sight of almost nine inches of hard, pulsating flesh – with amazement, lust, fear or a combination of the three I couldn't tell.

'Come on, wrap those luscious lips of yours round this,' Davey said, with the cocksureness of someone who knows when the scales are tipped in his favour.

Rosalind glanced at me in mute appeal, but as far as I was concerned, she deserved everything that was coming to her, and I wanted to savour it. A push in the small of her back sent her to her knees in front of Davey, and when he put the head of his cock to her lips she merely gave a little gasp and took it in her mouth. For the next ten minutes or so, she sucked on that huge, solid column of flesh, her lips stretched almost to tearing point around its bulbous helmet. I could not resist taking my own cock and wanking it lazily as I watched Rosalind's dyed blonde head bobbing up and down frantically. At last, Davey announced that he was coming, and pulled out of Rosalind's mouth to spray her face and hair with jet after jet of viscous spunk. She used her fingers to wipe the sticky stuff off her skin as best she could.

Now it was my turn, and I was more keen to sample Rosalind's cunt than her mouth. However, I had one more humiliation planned for her first. I told her to lie down and spread her legs for me. Her eyes widened as I picked up the Stanley knife once more and took one of the mousy curls that covered her mound.

'Don't worry,' I told her, 'I just like to get a better view of what I'm getting into.' I used the knife to hack the curl away. Working quickly, I reduced the forest of hair to nothing more than messy and uneven stubble. As I did, I took every opportunity to dip my fingers into the growing pool of juice at the entrance to her cunt. She tried, unsuccessfully, to stifle a moan as I touched her clit almost absent-mindedly; I was determined that by the time I had finished this tight-arsed bitch would be begging me to fuck her.

At last, I threw the knife to the ground and pulled my jeans and underpants down and off. Pushing Rosalind's legs even further apart, I positioned myself between them and thrust up into her cunt. While I can't match up to Davey in the size department, I know what to do with what I have got, and she was soon whimpering and writhing beneath me as I ground my pelvis hard against hers. Her hot, tight channel clutched convulsively at my cock and I knew she was coming. The spasms were fierce enough to trigger my own orgasm, and I shot my load deep inside her, what I can only describe as the climax of a very good afternoon's work.

Needless to say, Rosalind was as nice as pie towards us for the couple of days that remained until we finished the job. But it just goes to show you should never treat people as though they are beneath you, because the tables might get turned and you might end up beneath them.

Baz D.,
Hounslow

When my sister asked me to go along and see her boyfriend's new band, to say I was not looking forward to it would be an understatement. Alex has always fancied grungy types who write music for bedwetters and aren't my idea of a good time. However, she finally persuaded me, so I decided to dress for the occasion in a tiny denim miniskirt, black bra top and fishnet tights. When we arrived at the pub where the band were playing, my heart sank. The place was dingy, with black-painted walls and a carpet your feet seemed to stick to as you walked, and crappy metal was blasting out from the jukebox at ear-splitting volume.

The band were setting up their equipment on the stage, and Alex went to talk to her boyfriend, Chaz, while I went to get us a couple of bottles of beer from the bar. On my return, I couldn't help but notice that the drummer was actually very good-looking. He had floppy black hair and a dusting of stubble on his cleft chin, and the sleeveless vest he wore revealed an intricate Celtic tattoo circling his muscular biceps. At least he would be a pleasant distraction if the music turned out to be as uninspired as I expected it to be, I thought.

When the band struck up, a group of about three dozen people gathered at the front of the low stage, Alex among them. I stood at the back, and kept my eyes fixed on the cute drummer. Thankfully, their set only lasted about thirty minutes, before the main band came on. Alex and Chaz came over to find me, and I was pleased to see the drummer had come with them.

'This is Mick,' Alex said, before turning to order drinks.

Mick put his arm round my waist and whispered in my ear, 'I want to fuck you. Now.'

'Sure,' I said, a sudden pulse beating rapidly between my legs at his unsubtle approach, 'but where?'

'Outside,' he said, and ushered me quickly over to the fire exit. Pushing the bar, he led me out into a little alleyway that ran behind the pub. Boxes of rubbish were piled up against the wall, and the air stank of urine and rotting food. It was the last place I would have chosen under any other circumstances, but something about Mick's approach, and the scent of sweat on his brawny body, was getting me very horny. We began to kiss, and he pushed my bra top up to expose my breasts. He pinched my nipples roughly, while I tangled my hands in the damp tendrils of hair at the nape of his neck. His hand moved between my legs, rubbing my pussy through my knickers. His fingers edged under the gusset, slicking the oily wetness they found there over my clit.

I was panting heavily as his mouth closed over my nipple, his teeth nipping the delicate bud and his stubbled cheek rasping my flesh. In one swift movement, he yanked my knickers down to my knees. I pulled them the rest of the way down while he unzipped his flies and pulled his cock out of his pants. I could hear music thudding in the club behind us, and the sound of raised voices, and it excited me to think that we were so close to so many people who were completely oblivious to what we were about to do.

He hoisted me up, his hands underneath my bum, and I lowered myself on to his hard dick. He pressed me hard against the wall, and my legs locked around his back, my knickers dangling from one ankle. I felt like a total slut as he fucked me hard and fast in that sordid, smelly little back alley, and when he came inside me I almost screamed with the intensity of the pleasure I was experiencing.

When we got back to the bar, Alex said nothing about where I might have been, but I'm sure she must have noticed my messy hair, smeared make-up and the look of sheer satisfaction on my face. What she could not have noticed was that Mick had my lacy white knickers in his pocket as a souvenir. He might not be the greatest drummer I've ever seen, but he was certainly one of the greatest fucks I've ever had.

Kim T.,
Brighton

GENTLEMEN TAKE POLAROIDS

When my best mate, Nick, started going out with Sonia, I was gutted, to say the least. I had fancied her since the first time I had seen her walking across the college campus, but as she and Nick were studying on the same English course and I was doing photography, it was no surprise that he got there first. However, I soon realised things between them were not exactly rosy: over a couple of pints in the union bar he confided in me that Sonia would not let him fuck her. She would go so far, until his hard-on was practically threatening to burst out of his boxers, but at the last minute she would always pull out of having sex. Not only that, but she had told him she wondered why he hung around with me, because I was so rough and uncouth. When Nick told me that, I decided to teach her a lesson.

I got my chance when I was handed an assignment to produce a portfolio of portraits which featured the female form. I got Nick to ask Sonia if she would pose for me and, eventually, she said she would, though I got the distinct impression she was not at all happy about doing so, and had only said yes to keep Nick sweet. If she had known what she was letting herself in for when she turned up at my rented flat the following Saturday, I doubt she would have ever agreed.

I had placed a white bedsheet on the living room floor, set up my lights to cast artful shadows and put a high, three-legged wooden stool in front of the plain white wall. She took one look around the general squalor that passed for the rest of my flat, and wrinkled her snub nose. I could tell she thought the whole situation, me included, was distinctly beneath her.

I asked her to kick off her shoes and position herself on the stool. She was wearing a simple white cotton shirt and a pair of faded jeans, and with her long, dark hair falling over one eye, she looked stunning. She had the kind of bone structure which would make it difficult for anyone to take a bad photograph of her, and as I quickly loosed off a few black-and-white shots, encouraging her to move for me, she gradually began to relax into what she was doing.

Suddenly, I said to her, 'Right, I want you to take your shirt off.'

She looked at me with surprise. 'Whatever for?' she demanded.

'Didn't I tell you?' I said. 'Part of the exercise is that we have to take some shots that show the texture of skin. And I can hardly do that if you keep your shirt on, can I?'

She did not look at all happy, but did as I asked her. Beneath the shirt, her small breasts were cupped in an expensive-looking white bra. I did not tell her that before long I intended to have that off, too.

I moved in close and took some photographs of her from behind as she obediently raised her hair to display the nape of her neck. The pose was undoubtedly sensuous, showing her smooth, creamy skin and the sinuous curve of her back. If I had liked her more than I did, the chemistry between us would have shown through in my work; as it was, I knew these shots would be nothing more than a technical exercise.

'And now the jeans, please,' I said. 'I want to capture the muscle definition in your legs,' I added quickly, not giving her a chance to object.

Grumbling, she undid the fly on her jeans and slipped them down off her legs. I could not help but notice she was wearing the skimpiest of white lace G-strings, which left her taut buttocks almost completely bare. If she dressed like this for Nick's benefit, no wonder he was left frustrated every time she pulled her clothes back on and went home.

I got her to cross and uncross her legs. Not only did this enable me to take the photos I had told her I wanted, it also gave me good glimpses of the way her dark pubic hair curled out of the edges of her G-string.

'Is that it?' she said, after a while.

I shook my head. 'No, we've only really started. You see, I want some shots with your bra off, now.'

'Oh, no,' she said. 'No way.'

'Is that what you say to Nick, when he asks you to take your bra off?' I asked.

'What are you talking about?' she retorted.

'He's told me about you,' I replied, my tone stern. 'He tells me what a little tease you are. Well, I'm not going to let you tease me. I know exactly what I want from you, and I'm going to get it. Take it off.'

At that moment, she would have been quite within her rights to snatch up her clothes, dress and go home. The fact that, instead, she reached behind her and unfastened the catch of her bra told me everything about how things stood between us. She pulled the straps off her shoulders and let the garment fall to the floor. She had small, perky breasts, beautifully shaped, with dark nipples surrounded by big, reddish areolae.

'Put your hands on your head,' I told her, and she did, letting me watch the way her little breasts lifted and tightened as she moved. My cock was stirring in my jeans, betraying my excitement at the situation, and I hoped she would not notice it and realise what effect her almost naked body was having on me. I moved nearer to her, breathing in the subtle scent of her perfume and her freshly washed hair, and reached out to brazenly pinch one of her nipples, wanting to stiffen it for the close-up shots I intended to take. My touch had the desired effect, and though Sonia quickly pulled her body away from further contact, she could not prevent a little moan escaping from her lips.

'And now your panties,' I told her. 'A couple of nude shots will be the finishing touch for my assignment.'

She kept her legs tightly together as she wriggled the flimsy G-string down off her hips, trying to prevent me from getting even the merest glimpse of her bush. When her last item of clothing lay discarded on the floor, she looked at me nervously, as if afraid of what I might ask her to do next. My response was to take a couple of shots as she sat stiffly on the stool, but at last I said, 'It's no good. You're not giving me what I want. Just like you never give Nick what he wants.'

'Nick should be more patient,' she snapped.

'Well, maybe Nick has time to be patient, but I don't,' I retorted. 'I have to develop these photos tonight to complete the assessment in time, so no more of this coy virgin act. You're going to give me the poses I need.'

'And if I refuse?' she asked, but I sensed her resistance had been broken and I could make her do anything. I could not help noticing that her nipples were still hard and her breathing was slightly ragged, as though on some level she could not consciously acknowledge she was actually getting turned on by submitting to me.

I was completely in control now, and Sonia knew it. When I told her to get down off the stool and crawl across the floor to me, she did so without complaint. The sight of her on all fours, with her tits swaying slightly and her hair falling down over her face, had me hard as a rock in my jeans as I took shot after shot. Then I had her lie on the floor, looking up at me and cupping her breasts as though offering them to the camera – and to me. For the final few shots, I told her to bend over the stool and spread her legs wide apart. This was the most explicit pose I had asked her to adopt, and she must have known that, as I stood behind her, my camera lens was focused on the cleft between her legs, the lips of her pussy glistening unmistakably with her juices, yet she said nothing.

'Spread your lips for me,' I ordered, and she did so obediently, expecting the sound of the camera shutter clicking as I took shots of her wet, open sex. However, what she heard instead was my zip coming down, and she glanced round over her shoulder.

'Please . . .' she murmured, her eyes wide at the sight of my erection rearing up, demanding release.

'You would have let me photograph your cunt, wouldn't you, you little slut?' I said, coming up behind her and pressing the swollen head of my cock to her moist entrance. 'Even though you had no idea who might see those photos. I should have shown them to Nick, let him see what he was missing.'

Sonia only groaned as I pressed home, my glans lodging snugly between the walls of her vagina. She was unbelievably tight and hot, and as I moved within her I knew I would not be able to last long. I pumped into her hard and fast, relishing her little gasps as she got used to the feel of my thick cock opening her up. Within a couple of minutes, my buttocks clenched and I gave a groan as I felt the spunk rising up from my balls and flooding her velvet sheath.

'What about me?' Sonia moaned, as I pulled out of her. 'I need to come.'

'Well, you know what to do, don't you?' I replied, and pushed her hand firmly between her legs. Realising she could only have an orgasm if she gave herself one, she began to frig herself desperately, and I watched as she brought herself to a panting, squealing climax.

Job done, I threw her clothes at her, thanking her for her co-operation as she dressed hurriedly. Nick has no idea what happened that afternoon, but since then, he says, Sonia has never refused him sex. The photographs I was able to submit for my assignment got me a pretty decent grade, but I only wish I could show people the ones which showed the hidden side of stuck-up Sonia.

Paul K.,
Birkenhead

YOU'VE BEEN FRAMED

I'm not the first person to have sex with someone after an office party, and I certainly won't be the last.

However, I don't know if anyone else will have had their antics immortalised the way I did.

It all happened last Christmas. The firm had hired a suite in a plush hotel in town for the annual party, and everyone in our department had a couple of drinks in the office before getting ready in the loos. The party itself was much like most works functions – the food was uninspiring, the managing director made a speech full of so-called jokes that nobody laughed at and then the dancing started to an Abba tribute band. I had got talking to a bloke from the marketing department who had only been with the firm for a couple of months. His name was Ian, and I couldn't work out why I had never noticed him before, because he was seriously cute. He was a little shorter than my own five foot ten and had short, dark hair and soulful brown eyes. The more we talked, the more I found myself wondering what he would be like in bed. Images flashed through my mind of the two of us tangled together in crumpled white sheets, sweat dripping from our bodies as his cock drove into me. He must have been thinking along the same lines as me, because he suddenly suggested that we leave and find somewhere a little more private.

I didn't need asking twice. We drained our drinks and headed for the underground car park. I think Ian intended to drive us back to his place, but once we got there, in the dark, cool, petrol-scented atmosphere, I suddenly found myself getting too horny to wait any longer. I pressed him up against one of the concrete pillars and began to kiss him hard, pressing my body against his. He pushed my tight skirt up round my waist, and was delighted to discover that I wasn't wearing any panties beneath it. Immediately, he dropped to his knees and began to lick my cunt. I could feel his hot breath on the entrance to my vagina as his tongue circled my clit, and I caught tight hold of his hair so that he couldn't pull his head away until I had come. When I finally released my grip on him, my body shuddering with the last little shocks of my climax, his nose and mouth were glistening with my juices.

Still with my skirt hoisted high and my blonde triangle on display, framed by my suspender straps and the tops of my stockings, I found myself being pushed by Ian so that I was bending over the bonnet of a Mercedes. I caught sight of my own reflection in the darkened windscreen, my hair falling from the elegant French pleat I had arranged it in and my eyes glazed with pleasure, as I heard Ian unzipping his trousers. The next thing I felt was the blunt head of his cock nudging at the entrance to my sex. It was big, and I almost squealed with pleasure as I felt it thrusting into me, stretching me wide.

Ian fucked me rapidly, pushing me so hard against the car that I was sure I would dent the bodywork. The metal was cool against my stomach, sending a thrill of pleasure through me as I strove to keep my grip on the bonnet. All too soon, Ian was groaning, his body tensing as his cock gave a powerful jerk and his come jetted inside me.

It was only once we had pulled apart and made ourselves look respectable again that we realised there was a closed-circuit camera high on the wall above us, and it must have been trained on us all the time we were fucking. I don't know whether the security guard was watching us at the time, or whether he saw our inadvertent exhibition when he wound through the tape, but I only hope he enjoyed it as much as we did.

Julie M.,
Swindon

All the other girls told me when I joined the firm that the bosses could be very generous with their Christmas bonuses – as long as you were prepared to meet their demands. I wondered what they meant by this, but I did not think too much about it, particularly as the boss in my old job would not have known a bonus if it had slapped him in the face.

I found out exactly what was involved during the last week of November, when we were told that each of us would be seeing the bosses individually to determine the size of our bonus. There are five girls in the department I work for, and as the newest member of staff, I was the last one to be seen, on the Friday night.

The company is run by two brothers, both in their early sixties. You have to admire them for having built it up from nothing, but they have a reputation among their competitors for being old-fashioned in their ways. For instance, they like female staff members to wear skirts, rather than trousers, although as my legs are my best feature, I did not have a problem with that particular requirement.

I was still nervous as I waited to see them. None of the other girls in the department would tell me exactly what the interview entailed, and I could not help but wonder if they were hiding something from me. I soon found out, as I knocked on the door and went into the office, with its beautiful wood panelling and thick carpet the colour of blackberries. The two Smith brothers were sitting together behind the desk. They smiled benevolently at me and asked me to sit down, but that air of good humour soon vanished as they outlined what was required of me.

'The system we run here is one of a kind, we admit that,' the older Mr Smith said. He was the better-looking of the two, having retained a full head of white hair where his brother's had receded quite badly. 'We firmly believe in rewarding success and punishing failure.'

I must have looked startled at the word 'punishing', because the younger Mr Smith chipped in, 'Don't worry, Julie, you haven't failed. In fact, we are very pleased with how well you have performed since you arrived here, and the only question we need to answer is how large a bonus we shall be giving you. You can help us to determine that by removing your jacket and blouse.'

I thought they were joking at first, and stared at them blankly. The older Mr Smith said quite sternly, 'Come now, Julie, it's not much to ask, is it?'

I supposed he had a point; after all, to sit in front of these two old men in my bra was not so difficult. After all, I would have shown them more if I had been sitting on the beach in my bikini, so I shrugged off my navy blue jacket and placed it over the back of the chair. My white blouse followed it, the brothers' expressions becoming more interested with every button I undid.

'There, that wasn't so painful, was it?' asked the older Mr Smith. I glanced down briefly at my breasts, cradled in the plain white cotton bra, and shook my head briefly.

'So I take it you won't object if we ask you to remove your skirt and tights – or are they stockings?' his brother said quickly, with what I detected was a hopeful note in his voice.

'They're tights,' I replied, then paused for a long, long moment before adding, 'and no, I won't object.' I know I should really have called a halt to proceedings at that point, but I was being driven by other considerations. While money is not exactly a problem for me and my husband, a bigger bonus would enable us to have a more comfortable Christmas.

I stood up, and unfastened my skirt before removing it and adding it to the growing pile of clothing on the chair. When I took off my sensible tan tights, I was surprised that the younger Mr Smith demanded that I hand them to him. He sniffed appreciatively at the gusset, before opening a drawer in the desk and slipping them inside. I thought I got a brief flash of a stocking, and something white and lacy before he shut it again, but I could not be sure.

'Very nice,' the older Mr Smith said. 'How do you keep your body in such good trim, Julie? Do you go to the gym, like some of the other girls, or do you burn off the calories fucking your husband?'

I did not know how to respond to such an intimate question, and tried to stammer an answer. I felt like a rabbit trapped in headlights, and realised for the first time that I might be in a situation I could not easily get out of.

This was proved by the older Mr Smith's next words. 'Your bra, Julie. Take that off for us, please.'

If I did this, there was no going back. I might have to answer other rude questions, or show them even more of my body. I wished one of the other girls had given me some advice, and that I could have asked them how far they had gone to please our lecherous bosses. But I was on my own, and I could only do what my instincts told me. I did not want to do what they asked, but the alternative might be worse. They had talked about punishment. They might not award me the bonus I had already earned. They might sack me. Or they might have meant punishment of a physical kind. I could feel tears welling in my eyes as I reached behind me and unfastened the bra.

When I dropped it on the desk in front of them, there was silence for a moment. I knew they were both staring at my breasts, and wished I knew what they were thinking. I have always thought they are too small, though my husband, Keith, loves them.

At last, the younger Mr Smith said, 'Very nice. Little ones are more sensitive, aren't they, Julie? Do you find that? When your husband pinches them, does the feeling travel to your cunt?'

The shock of this kindly looking, white-haired gentleman using such a crude word was like a physical blow, but there was no denying the truth of his question. When Keith plays with my tits I do feel it in my cunt, and he can take me to the brink of orgasm just by nibbling my nipples. I just nodded dumbly, and hoped he would take that as an answer.

'Prove it to me, Julie,' he said. 'Pinch your nipples for me.'

Too dazed to object, I did as he asked, feeling a surge of pure sensation arrowing down to my pussy as I gripped my nipples between thumb and forefinger. I could not prevent a little moan from escaping my lips, and when I looked up, the brothers were watching me with rapt, feral expressions.

'You realise the bonus will go up extensively if you take off your knickers,' the older Mr Smith said. Of course I did; I would have been stupid not to. Everything that had happened until now had been leading up to the moment when I stood before them naked.

I gave an involuntary little sob as I pulled down my panties. I had been a virgin when I married, and no one but my husband had ever seen me like this. I was shamefully aware that if the brothers asked to see the panties they would find them wet and infer, correctly, that on some hidden level I was turned on by what was being done to me.

The two old men looked at each other, and then at me, holding my panties in front of my sex like an ineffectual little shield. 'Would you mind, Julie?' the younger Mr Smith said, holding out his hands to take them from me. Though my reluctance must have been obvious to both of them, I meekly handed them over.

This time, he sniffed them extensively, as though savouring the bouquet of a fine wine. I waited for whatever personal and humiliating comment he might choose to make, but nothing was forthcoming, and I began to relax, thinking that this was the end and that I could dress and leave with my bonus payment secure.

His next words shocked me back to full awareness. 'There's just one last thing,' he said. 'Part of your annual bonus is performance-related. Did the other girls not tell you?'

Of course not. They must have known how I would react at the thought of giving my body to these two lechers, for that was what was being implied. I wondered how many of them had agreed to the proposal, spurred on as I had been by greed for more money. I could hardly stand the thought of those gnarled, liver-spotted hands pawing my body, and their wizened old cocks entering my cunt, and yet somehow I found myself saying, 'They didn't, but it's not a problem.'

'Good girl,' the older Mr Smith said, advancing round the desk towards me. He was unzipping his fly as he came, and as he brought his penis out into the light I could see that it was only partially erect, hanging limply between his fingers. 'Suck it for me,' he urged, and I sank to my knees on that deep-pile carpet and obediently took the head between my lips.

It seemed to take ages for the thing to begin to grow under my ministrations, and all the while I sucked it, I was aware of his brother, standing beside us, wanking his own puny member to full hardness. Neither cock could have been more than five inches long, and in other circumstances I might have compared them to my husband's big, fat prick and laughed, but this was no laughing matter. The fact the two of them had remained fully clothed just emphasised my total nudity, and I felt vulnerable and completely at their mercy.

When the older Mr Smith was at last erect, he made me bend over the big wooden desk and spread my legs wide. I felt his brother's elderly fingers reach between my legs, slicking the wetness they found there over the head of my clit. He rubbed me until I was on the brink of orgasm and then, cruelly, he pulled his hand away. While he stood, licking my juices from his fingers, his brother's cock pressed at the entrance to my cunt. I groaned as he eased himself home and began to thrust, feeling the zip on his trousers rasping the delicate flesh of my pussy. He was swift and brutal in his fucking, despite his advanced age, and within a couple of minutes I felt him jerk once, hard, and squirt his come deep inside me.

He pulled out, only for his brother to take his place. As I was fucked for the second time, the older Mr Smith merely wiped his subsiding manhood with a tissue and readjusted his clothing. By now, I was desperate with need, and I found myself begging the younger Mr Smith to make me come. I no longer cared that these men were using me with disdain and, in fact, the thought was only adding to the fire which burned in my belly. His answer was to push me harder against the desk, so that my pubic bone was rubbing along the polished wood. That extra stimulation was just enough to push me over the edge, and

I cried out as I came, my pussy spasming around my boss's stubby cock. As the younger Mr Smith climaxed, too, I knew that I had well and truly earned my bonus. They kept my underwear, of course.

A new girl started in the office a couple of weeks ago, fresh from getting her A-level results. She is blonde and quite pretty, and I know the two Mr Smiths will love conducting her bonus interview. When she asks me what it involves, I will say nothing and let her find out the hard way, just like I did.

Julie M.,
Manchester

PASSING THE TEST

In all my years of teaching women's studies at university, Jo was the most difficult and disruptive student I had ever had to deal with. In tutorial sessions, she constantly tried to dismiss my arguments and undermine my position in front of the other members of the group. Her attitude was that, at the age of twenty, she had been everywhere, done everything and had an opinion on it all – an opinion which always conflicted with mine. Eventually, I asked her how she had come to think the way she did, and why she was so certain that my ideas were incorrect. She told me she had taken a year out before coming to university to earn enough money to pay her way, but things had not turned out the way she had expected and she had spent six months working as a prostitute. She did not regret a moment of it, she said; it had taught her a lot about the behaviour of men and the attitudes of society towards women who earn their living in this way, and as a result she had much more experience of life than someone like me who had spent all their life teaching, shut away from the real world. I told her all it had done was make her cynical and cocky, and that was when she laid down the challenge: if I spent a night on the streets, selling my body the way she had, I would soon learn everything she said was true.

I was completely taken aback at this, and I should have declined her offer. But she had thrown down the gauntlet in front of the rest of the tutorial group, and I did not want to lose face before them. I told her it was nothing I could not handle, and that she was to name the time and place.

Thus it was that the following Friday night I found myself going round to the house where she lived, close to the city's red-light district. Jo had told me she would take me out on the streets she had once walked, and she would supply me with one of her old outfits. She was sure there was nothing in my wardrobe which would suit the part, and she was right: my one indulgence is buying expensive clothes for work, and I could not see any prostitute walking the streets in a neat little skirt suit. I turned up in a tracksuit, with my hair scraped back and wearing no make-up, ready for my transformation at Jo's hands. When I saw what she had laid out on the bed ready for me, I could hardly believe it: there was a white, see-through blouse in cheap nylon, a black lycra miniskirt which looked no wider than a belt, red fishnet stockings, a red suspender belt and black stiletto-heeled mules. I could not see a bra or panties, but assumed I would be wearing my own. I was wrong.

'Right, take all your clothes off – and I mean all your clothes,' Jo said. Away from the lecture theatre, she had become even more domineering, and I shivered as she stood there with her arms folded, casually watching me undress. I have a better figure than anyone who has seen me in my work clothes might guess, and Jo's expression was one of grudging approval as I stood before her naked.

'OK,' she said, 'get dressed and then I'll do your make-up,' she said.

'But ...' I replied hesitantly. 'But there's no underwear there.'

'Look, love, men aren't going to want to waste time pulling your knickers down. They just want to be straight in and straight out,' Jo told me crudely. 'So no knickers, and no bra, because they won't want anything to get in the way when they're groping your big tits.'

I shuddered inwardly at the images her words were creating in my mind. I had told Jo nothing about my sex life, but if the truth be known I had not had a boyfriend for the past couple of years, having been too wrapped up in my work to meet anyone suitable, and the relationships I had had before had been loving and tender. Words like 'grope' and 'tits' had never passed the lips of anyone I had had sex with, and I wondered again just what I was letting myself in for.

When I had finished dressing, I looked at myself in the mirror. Jo's figure is much more slender than my own, and the blouse gaped slightly, straining to cover my braless tits. The skirt, too, was stretched across my bum, and the hem was so short that it barely covered my pussy. The straps of my suspenders and the tops of my stockings were clearly visible beneath it, and the mules made me stand awkwardly, teetering on the high, spindly heels. Anyone who saw me standing on the street dressed like that would have no doubt what my intentions were.

Jo seemed satisfied, though, and she completed the effect by pulling my long, brown hair out of its band

and tousling it between her fingers till it looked like I had just got out of bed. Then she applied make-up, much more thickly and in darker colours than I would ever have used. By the time she had finished I looked – and felt – cheap and sluttish, and much younger than my thirty years.

'Excellent,' she said. 'Just two final touches.' She took a packet of condoms from her bedside table and handed them to me. 'I know you're not stupid, so you've probably brought your own supplies. You just might be getting through a few more of them than you expect.' I did not like the cruel smile that flashed across her face.

'And what's the last thing?' I asked.

'This –' she said, and reached between my legs as I sat at her dressing table. Her fingers brushed my sex lips, and I could not hide my gasp of surprise and arousal. I could not remember the last time any hand other than my own had touched me there, and to my shame, instead of pushing her away, I found myself parting my legs, offering her easier access.

'God, you're just like a bitch on heat,' she sneered, continuing to stroke me until my juices were flowing freely and I was making little mewling noises. I knew she was doing this to humiliate me, but I was too far gone to care. I threw my head back and hooked my legs over the arms of the chair, opening myself fully for her. She licked the middle finger of her free hand and slowly, deliberately, inserted it into the tight pucker of my anus. Feeling that unexpected and, for me, entirely new penetration, I lost it. I howled out my orgasm while Jo laughed at me.

'The punters like a girl who doesn't fake it,' she commented. 'They'll also like the fact you're already juicy for them. Now come on, let's go. Time is money, after all.'

She let me put my coat on before we left the house, and then we walked down to the place where, she claimed, she used to stand herself. 'You won't get any trouble from the other girls,' she said. 'If you do, tell them you're Candy. That's the name I used to use with the punters. After all, we don't look too different.'

Remembering my reflection in her bedroom mirror, my face and body still flushed with the aftermath of my orgasm, I had to admit she had a point. Perhaps that was another reason why we clashed: deep down, we were really not so dissimilar.

'I'll be back for you in three hours,' Jo told me. 'Don't do anything I wouldn't.' Then she took the coat from me.

I stood there, feeling exposed and vulnerable. I could see a couple of girls further down the street, smoking cigarettes and chatting. They glanced over in my direction, but seemed more interested in the car which pulled up in front of them a couple of moments later. The smaller of the two, a peroxide blonde, stuck her head in the car window and conducted some brief negotiations which concluded with her jumping into the passenger seat.

I was concentrating so hard on that little tableau, I was barely aware of a car coming to a halt and a voice asking me something. 'Sorry?' I said.

'I said, how much?'

I did what the blonde had done and went close to the car window. Jo had told me what to say. 'Ten for hand relief, twenty for oral, twenty-five for straight sex.'

'How much to come between those big tits of yours?' he asked.

Jo had not prepared me for that little line, so I quoted him the same price as for oral sex. He agreed without question, and I climbed into the car, hoping the girl standing near me had seen what was happening and would remember what the guy was driving. As he took me round the block to a quiet bit of land that had once been a factory, I studied him. Mid-forties, stubble on his chin, a little on the podgy side, but not too bad. Certainly not as repulsive as I had feared.

He parked up behind the remains of a brick wall, and unfastened his seat belt. I had no idea how to work the mechanics of what he wanted from me, but after thinking about it for a moment, I told him to come round to the passenger side and drop his trousers. I opened the car door and turned in my seat so my feet were on the ground. He was standing in front of me with his cock in his hand, wanking it to its full six inches. I unbuttoned my blouse and opened it wide; he had already seen my nipples through the thin nylon, but now I was holding my breasts, cupping them together and presenting them to him. He slid his erection up into the warm, soft tunnel I had formed between my breasts and jerked his hips rapidly back and forth. It only took moments before he was groaning and his semen was dribbling out of his cockhead. I took a tissue from a box on the car's parcel shelf and quickly wiped him clean. He zipped himself up, counted the money into my hand and drove me back to where he had found me.

For my first time, that was not too bad, I thought. Things changed when my second punter accosted me. He was younger than the first, but rough-looking, with clothes crusted with dirt from a day's work on a building site, and smelling strongly of alcohol. I thought about telling him I was finishing for the night, but then how would I look to Jo if I ran away at the first unwanted advance, so I quoted him my prices. Needless to say, he wanted straight sex. He was on foot, so we went into the nearest alleyway and he dropped his trousers. When he put his hand up my skirt and realised I had no knickers on, an evil leer spread across his face.

'I've got a real loose one here, eh, darling?' he muttered. I said nothing, but concentrated on rolling the condom on to his cock. I had a shock when I saw the size of it: it must have been eight inches long and very thick around, and I wondered how my pussy would cope with something that size after being out of practice so long.

He thrust up into me without ceremony as I tottered on my high heels. He smelled of ground-in dirt and body odour, and I was clinging on to him, trying not to breathe too deeply as his big, hard hands pulled open my blouse and mauled my breasts. I was being stretched wider than I ever had been, and my body was responding, my juices easing the passage of his latex-clad cock. His hips jerked and his member seemed to grow even bigger inside me in the moments before he came, and despite myself I was having an orgasm, too. He didn't even bother to thank me; he just tucked his wilting penis back into his clothes, chucked the money at me and wandered off, leaving me slightly disorientated from the strength of my climax.

I must have had another six or seven clients before Jo came to collect me. A couple simply wanted hand relief, which was easy, but I found myself sucking off an enormously fat man, and then, for what turned out to be the finale of the evening, I was taken by a young black man. He had stripped me of everything but my stockings and heels, and his hands were all over my body, pinching my nipples and tugging at my pubic hair. There was a moment when he briefly pulled out of my pussy and his erection bumped against the entrance to my arse. For a moment I thought he was going to fuck me there. However, he simply ripped the condom off his cock and masturbated himself till he came, splattering my bum cheeks and back with his pearly seed. Then he wiped himself on my clothes before he left me to dress.

That was how Jo found me standing on the street, stinking of spunk, my breasts bruised from brutal treatment and my pussy swollen and sore. And yet I had over a hundred pounds to show for what I had done, and I felt the satisfaction of having passed a test in Jo's eyes.

After that night, we both respected the other a little more, though she never became my favourite pupil. And she let me keep that cheap, tarty outfit as a souvenir; what she doesn't know is that I occasionally put it on and go walking the streets – not for money, but for the thrill of quick, rough sex with men I would never contemplate fucking under any other circumstance.

Adele T.,
Nottingham

Wet and Wild

BARELY HOLDING ON

I was already late back from lunch when the lift broke down. I had been out for a couple of drinks with a few of the other girls in the department to celebrate a birthday, and we had lost track of the time. At first, when the lift ground to a halt between floors, I was slightly annoyed, but as time went on I began to get more anxious, as my bladder was becoming uncomfortably full.

There was only one other person in the lift with me, a bloke called James from the accounts department. I didn't know him very well, but though he was fairly good-looking in a blond, languid sort of way, he had a reputation in the company for being arrogant and self-centred. He'd pressed the alarm, to alert the security staff to the fact that we were trapped in the lift, but neither of us had any way of knowing how long we might be stuck there. The overhead lights had failed, and only the dim glow of the emergency lighting enabled us to see each other. He didn't seem the type to make small talk, so I just leant against the wall and prayed that we would start moving again within the next few minutes.

As time dragged on, I was getting really desperate to pee. I was jiggling slightly from foot to foot, and squeezing my thighs tightly together to try to hold on that little bit longer. I was becoming convinced that if we didn't get out of the lift soon, I was going to wet myself where I stood.

James had obviously noticed that I was in some distress, and he glanced over at me, a sneering smile on his face. 'Are you OK there?' he asked.

'Yes, I'm fine,' I told him, which was far from the truth, as I had just felt a little spurt of pee dribble into my knickers.

'It's just that you look like you could really use the toilet,' he said.

'It's OK, I can hold it,' I said through gritted teeth, certain that I was about to embarrass myself by pissing my knickers in front of him.

'Are you sure?' he asked, coming to stand beside me. He put a hand on my belly, which was bulging somewhat thanks to my swollen bladder, and pressed firmly. I moaned, clenching my thigh and pussy muscles in an attempt to stop myself letting go.

'Lift your skirt up,' he said. 'You're going to piss yourself, and I want to watch you do it.'

'I can't,' I whimpered, although I was desperate to end the discomfort I was in.

He pressed harder on my stomach, and the trickle in my knickers became a gush. By now, I would do anything to spare myself further humiliation, and the cruel, strangely seductive smile on his face told me he knew it. I raised my tight black skirt up around my waist. Looking down, I could see even in the half-light that the white nylon knickers I was wearing were going transparent where my pee had soaked them. My thick, dark bush was visible beneath, matted with liquid.

As James massaged my belly with firm, circular motions, I gave in and let my piss stream out in a golden torrent that ran down my stocking-clad legs to the floor of the lift. The relief was so overpowering it was almost sexual. The need to come hit me like a tidal wave and, oblivious to everything but the urgent ache in my pussy, I started to rub my clit through my pee-stained knickers.

James unzipped his fly, freeing his long, hard cock. He pulled down my knickers in one swift motion and thrust hard up into me, his entry aided by the mix of piss and love juice that lubricated my cunt. Suddenly we were fucking, with my back pressed up hard against the wall of the lift and him banging into me like there was no tomorrow. It only took a few strokes before we were both coming, him first and me moments after, as his hot spunk jetted into me.

By the time the lift started moving again, a couple of minutes later, we had both straightened our clothing and were acting as if nothing had happened. If anyone noticed the tell-tale puddle of pee on the floor, nothing was ever said, and the whole thing has been a secret between me and James – until now.

Ellen K.,
Ipswich

A WET AFTERNOON

When I split up from my husband, my best friend, Shirley, was very sympathetic. We spent a lot of time together, shopping and going out for long lunches, and in truth we got closer than we had been at any time since Dominic and I got married. Though I knew the pain of the marriage break-up would take a long time to abate, with Shirley's help I was starting to get on with my life again.

One gloriously sunny July, we decided to drive down to Brighton for the day. We had a great time, shopping in the antiques shops in the Lanes and sunbathing on the beach. We also went to a nice restaurant and had a long lunch, drinking a bottle of wine and plenty of water between us. Everything was fine until we got held up in traffic on the way home. By now, all that liquid was starting to have an effect on me, and I confessed to Shirley that I was dying for a pee. 'I have to go soon, or I think I'll pee myself,' I said.

'If the upholstery in this car wasn't so expensive, I'd say you went ahead and did it,' she replied without batting an eyelid. I stared at her, unable to believe what she had just suggested. 'You mean you've never deliberately wet yourself?' she said, registering my shocked expression. 'I do it in public all the time. It's a fantastic feeling, almost as good as having an orgasm.'

All this talk was just making me even more agitated, and I found myself clutching at my crotch through my trousers. Shirley, seeing my obvious distress, pulled into the nearest lay-by, stopped the engine and encouraged me to make a dash for the bushes. I did so, with Shirley in hot pursuit. I found a convenient spot, and expected her to look for somewhere else, to preserve the modesty of both of us. To my surprise, however, she followed me and, while I was struggling with the zip on my trousers, she just lifted her skirt out of the way and began to pee. The sight of the spreading dark patch on her red satin knickers and the rivulets of piss that streamed down her bare legs was bizarrely erotic. I still don't know why I did what I did next, but part of me reasoned that there was no shame in following her example. Giving up the battle with my zip, I simply let go and felt warm pee flooding my knickers and soaking into the heavy cotton fabric of my trousers. Shirley was right; after holding it in for so long, there was something almost orgasmic about releasing that golden stream, and I found myself groaning aloud with the relief of the moment.

I was groaning again within seconds, as I felt Shirley's hand reach between my legs and massage the now-sodden material that adhered to my crotch, pushing the seam of my trousers so that it rubbed against my clit. The fact that this was my best friend handling me in such a crude and exciting way was making me unexpectedly horny, and while she continued her manipulations, she slipped her free hand into her wet panties and frigged herself with abandon. Suddenly, I felt myself coming and, as my knees buckled with the force of my climax, Shirley smiled and rubbed her sex harder. I collapsed on the grass and watched the beautiful sight of my friend playing with herself. I could see the saturated, skin-tight satin clinging to her hand as it moved faster and faster, and it was obvious that she was slipping a couple of fingers into her pussy every now and again, before returning to concentrate on her clit. At last, she threw her head back and cried that she was coming, before her fingers finally slowed and she pulled her skirt back down.

We drove the rest of the way home in excited silence, with plastic bags on the front seats of Shirley's car to protect them from our pee-soaked clothing. Since then, I've wet myself in the privacy of my own home a few times but, unlike Shirley, I haven't yet had the courage to do it in a public place. If I do, I'll be sure to let you know.

Helen K.,
Surbiton

My girlfriend, who is eighteen, and I were out shopping a couple of Saturdays ago. It was a hot day, and Allie had been swigging from a big bottle of mineral water as we walked round the shops. Suddenly, she told me that she needed to use the loo. We were in a large department store at the time, so she went to find the ladies' toilets, only to discover that they were out of order. Allie said it didn't matter, as she could hold on until we got home. We went in two or three more shops, none of which had a toilet, and by this time it was getting obvious that Allie needed to go quite badly. She was jogging from foot to foot, or standing cross-legged, obviously trying to lessen the pressure on her bladder. During the bus ride home, which took nearly twice as long as it should have due to roadworks holding up the traffic, she kept her legs tightly crossed and fidgeted, having again dismissed the suggestion that she should look for a loo before we got on the bus. By now, part of me was beginning to hope that she would lose the struggle to hold on to her bladder and would wet herself where she was sitting. The thought of that was exciting enough to get my cock twitching in my underpants.

When we finally got home, she said, 'That's it, I have to go to the loo. I just can't wait any longer.' However, I did my best to persuade her to hang on just a little longer. I confessed to her that I was incredibly turned on by the obvious predicament she was in, and that one of my long-standing fantasies was to fuck a girl who was desperately in need of a piss. She looked a bit shocked at this, but I sensed that deep down the thought was turning her on, too.

We hurried up to the bedroom, where Allie pulled the duvet off the bed and put a couple of towels down to soak up the flow. Then we both undressed so we were naked from the waist down, and the two of us got on the bed. We were soon sharing deep, sloppy kisses while I cupped her firm tits through her T-shirt. I moved my hand down so I could feel her tummy, which was swollen and bloated with her need to pee. At the feel of this gentle pressure on her suffering bladder, she groaned, and I saw a little gush of pee spurt out on to the towel beneath her.

Thrusting a hand between her thighs, I began to stroke her clit, which was sticking out stiffly from its protective hood, indicating just how aroused she was. As I continued to massage her tummy and her clit at the same time, I could see she was torn between her excitement and the humiliation she would feel at wetting herself while I played with her.

By now, my cock was begging for its own relief, but I resisted the growing temptation to wank it. I wanted to come in Allie's hot, tight cunt, and I knew the moment was approaching when she would finally give in and let me enter her. By now, her pee was a steady trickle that she was no longer making any attempt to contain, and her eyes were closed as she moved closer to her orgasm.

At last, she finally let go and began to wet herself. Her pee streamed over my hand, the warm flow getting me so excited that I just pushed Allie's legs wide apart, thrust my cock into her incredibly moist pussy and fucked her while the last of her piss dribbled on to my balls.

John P.,
Guildford

THE WAITING GAME

My partner Josh and I have experimented a lot sexually since we first met, and there is not much we haven't tried. One of our particular favourites is watersports, and there's a game we have played a few times which turns us on incredibly because we can do it without anyone else knowing what we are up to.

If we are going out for the evening, I will wear my sexiest underwear. Not only does this make me feel good, but it is the ideal preparation for what is to come. I will wear a black satin corset, which Josh will lace very tightly indeed for me. By the time he has finished, my waist is much narrower than normal, and my already very large breasts are emphasised even further. Then I will fasten suspenders to the straps which hang down from the corset, and wear my favourite floor-length red velvet dress over the top. I never wear any knickers on nights like these.

Then the fun begins. Josh will make sure that before I have left the house, I have drunk an entire bottle of sparkling mineral water, and for the rest of the evening, wherever we are, he will keep providing me with more drinks at regular intervals. Of course, you can imagine the effect all this liquid begins to have, and soon I am becoming anxious to use the toilet. However, as I well know, that is most definitely not allowed.

The tight corset is very restrictive, and it causes an extra pressure on my bladder which is very unwelcome. If we have gone to see a play or a concert, I find it almost impossible to sit still in my seat, and this becomes more of an ordeal as the evening progresses. If we are at a dinner party or a works social function, it is easier for me to get up and walk about, though I am sure I must draw attention to myself as I try to cross my legs discreetly to fight the overwhelming urge to pee. By the end of the evening, I am finding it almost impossible to hold on any longer. Josh can see exactly how much discomfort I am in as I bite my lip in the back of the taxi, and press my hand between my legs. I am always afraid that one day I will actually disgrace myself and let go in the taxi, but so far this has not happened.

When we get home, my first instinct is to rush to the toilet, but that is not how this game ends. Josh takes me into the bathroom; by now, I am taking the tiniest of steps because I know that any more strenuous movement will cause my pee to start leaking out. He helps me out of my dress, but not the corset or the stockings. Then he tells me to stand in the bath. Just climbing into the bath is torture, and on a couple of occasions I have started to wet myself in the process.

Josh looks at me as I stand there, with a cruel smile on his face. The very prominent bulge in his trousers tells me how much he is turned on by seeing me in this state. I beg him to finally let me pee, but he has one last trick up his sleeve. He tells me I can't do it until I have made myself come. My clitoris is feeling particularly sensitive by now, and my bladder is swollen and distended, like a grapefruit, and as I reach between my legs and begin to finger myself the additional stimulation is too much. Unable to stop myself, I begin to pee, the golden liquid trickling down over my hand as I rub at my pussy like a woman possessed. By the time I have finished, my thighs and the tops of my stockings are shining with a mixture of urine and my love juices, and tears of humiliation are shining in my eyes. Josh has been stripping off as he watches me, and he will bend me over and enter me roughly from behind, fucking me with rapid strokes. Just before he comes, he will pull out and spray his semen over my bum cheeks, letting it slide down to mix with my own fluids. At last I can take off the corset.

As I said, no one has ever worked out what Josh and I are doing, and why I look so flushed and excited when I'm out for the evening. Perhaps if they read this letter, it will make everything clear to them.

Mary S.,
London

PISS PARTY

Since my wife and I moved to Germany to live and work, we have discovered a whole new side to our sexuality that we never knew existed. People are far more open about sex here than they are in Britain, and once they discover that you have a particular kink, they are only too happy to help you indulge.

Like a lot of couples who have been married for a while, Pam and I had tried a few things to try to recapture the excitement of our early days together. She had dressed in sexy underwear and rubber, I had spanked her on occasions, and we had even tried making love outdoors on the lawn on hot summer evenings, knowing that there was a chance our neighbours might see what we were doing. However, none of these really gave us the added spice we were looking for, and it was when we began to experiment with watersports that we really found our niche. Pam has a mildly submissive side to her nature, but she doesn't like pain, which is why being spanked did very little for her. It was only one evening when, in a moment of drunken bravado, I ordered her to strip off and lie down in the bath, then pissed on her that she began to get very excited. By the time I had soaked her body head to foot in a hot, golden stream of urine, she was more turned on than I could remember, and the fuck that followed was mindblowing.

I have made some good friends at work, and I happened to mention to one of them, Dietmar, that Pam and I had discovered a love for pissing games. He told me that this was one of his own personal turn-ons, and that he had once been to what he called a 'piss party', where like-minded people got together to play all sorts of wet games. I mentioned this to Pam, and she suggested that we should host such a party, and invite Dietmar and a couple of other men to join in.

Needless to say, Dietmar was delighted to accept our invitation, and the following Saturday, he arrived at our house at seven o'clock prompt, along with two friends, Matthias and Jens. Pam had provided drinks and nibbles – with the emphasis, of course, being on the drinks – and we sat in our lounge, chatting and listening to music while we men downed glass after glass of lager. The knowledge of what was to come added a strong edge of sexual tension to our conversation, and I found myself getting hard at the thought of these strangers pissing on Pam's lovely body.

At last, it was time to go upstairs. Pam feigned a reluctance to take things further, encouraging me to grab her by the arm and haul her forcefully upstairs. I knew this was her submissive streak coming out; the more she protested, the more excited she would be getting as I asserted my dominance over her.

In the bathroom, I ordered her to take off the beaded cocktail dress she was wearing. What little she had on beneath it could not have been more provocative: her bra and matching panties were of sheer black nylon, and did nothing to conceal her pink nipples and luxuriant blonde pubic bush. Lace-topped hold-up stockings completed the outfit. As she loosed her hair from its clip to let it tumble over her shoulders, we four men quickly undressed, revealing four cocks in varying stages of erectness in tribute to my wife's beauty.

She got into the bath without undressing further, and lay down. I looked at our guests, inviting one of them to go first. Instead, the three stepped into the bath together, and positioned themselves around Pam's body – Dietmar at her head, Jens by her midriff and Matthias at her feet. Then, as if at some signal they had prearranged between them, they began to piss. Three powerful jets of liquid hit Pam simultaneously, gushing over her face and down her body, soaking the flimsy underwear she wore and sending it almost transparent. Pam lay back, eyes half-closed and mouth open, lost in her own private world, and when Dietmar directed his stream between her red-glossed lips, she did not even flinch, but drank it down with relish.

At last, the three of them finished, and looked to me to conclude proceedings. I asked them to strip her completely, and they complied eagerly, rolling down her sodden stockings and peeling off her bra and knickers. I told Pam to open her legs wide, and as she did we could all clearly see that her cunt was not only wet with piss but with the glistening evidence of her arousal. I straddled her supine body and she moaned in anticipation, begging me to piss in her face and over her big tits and pussy. I let fly, aiming a torrent of piss directly at her exposed sex and playing it over her swollen clit. She writhed in the bath, pulling at her own nipples as she revelled in the sheer erotic degradation I was putting her through.

I have never seen Pam so aroused as she was that night, and my three German friends were amply rewarded by her for our pissing prowess – but that's a story for another time.

Martin S.,
Hamburg

My two fetishes are PVC and peeing. I'd like to tell you about the ways in which I have combined the two.

I first discovered these were my turn-ons when I went to university. Until then, I had been very sheltered. I was no virgin – I lost that on my sixteenth birthday to a boy I'd been seeing for a year – but I'd found sex to be a disappointing experience, and I couldn't see why people made so much fuss about it. Then I met Howard, who was in his final year and knew a hell of a lot more about sex than I did.

It was Howard who first took me to a fetish clothing shop in West London, because he said he wanted me to dress up for sex. I had tried wearing the limited amount of sexy underwear that I had, which consisted of stockings, suspenders and a little lacy G-string, and while it excited him, he clearly wanted to see me in something more suited to his fantasies.

I don't know what I was expecting when we went shopping, but I'll never forget the moment I stepped through the door of that place. It looked innocuous on the outside, like a light industrial unit, but the smell of the rubber will stay with me as long as I live. As I ran my hand tentatively over a little black rubber dress, I couldn't believe that people could get pleasure from wrapping themselves in the cold, clammy fabric. However, Howard had something slightly different in mind for me. He picked out a peephole bra in red PVC, matching crotchless knickers, and a shiny black PVC mac which I could have worn out in the street without anyone turning a hair. I didn't realise at the time that was exactly what he intended me to do.

I stepped into the little cubicle, pulled the curtain and stripped off. The bra and knickers looked like they had been made for me, and while they looked sleazy, combined with the black hold-up stockings I was wearing, they did not look cheap, as a skimpy nylon set from a more usual sex shop would have done. I put the mac on over the top and did a twirl, delighting in my new reflection. When Howard saw me, he liked the outfit as much as I did. When I went to take it off before we paid for it, he shook his head. 'Keep it on, you're going home like that,' he said. I stared at him, open-mouthed, as the shop assistant cheerfully bundled the clothes I had been wearing into a carrier bag. I wondered what sort of game Howard was playing, and knew that I had no choice but to go along with it.

We stepped out into the sunshine, me looking somewhat overdressed in the shiny black mac and wondering what people would say if they knew how little I had on underneath it. It was a warm day, and I was soon sweating beneath the heavy PVC. The lining was also stimulating my exposed nipples, and I found myself beginning to get strangely turned on.

As we took the tube back to the university, Howard was taking the opportunity to fondle my barely clad bum through the mac. He pressed up against me so that I could feel the hefty bulge in his jeans and know that he, too, was turned on by the situation. I wondered for a moment whether he was going to order me to open the mac and flash my nipples and lightly furred mound at our fellow commuters. My cunt moistened as I realised how much I would enjoy being made to do that.

However, the only thing he had on his mind was sex, as was proved the moment we stepped into his study-bedroom. His hands went up underneath the hem of my mac, searching out my slippery, sweaty pussy. The smell of PVC, perspiration and my musky arousal was heavy in the small room as his fingers parted the lips of my quim, seeking out my clitoris. I groaned, and stroked my own breasts through the mac, feeling my nipples harden as they rubbed against the thick material.

That was when I became aware of another sensation, as Howard's clever fingers stroked me towards a climax. Suddenly, I didn't just want to come, I wanted to pee as well. I pulled away from him, telling him I needed the toilet.

'No, you don't,' he replied, 'not when you have the mac. Take it off, Karren.'

I did as he asked, unbuttoning it and spreading it on the floor beneath us at his request. By now, my need to pee was becoming unbearably urgent, and I wondered whether he expected me to dash down the corridor to the bathroom. The dormitory block he lived in was single-sex, and I wondered how the other residents would react if they saw me heading for the loo in my revealing PVC underwear, my hard, pink nipples and wet pussy clearly on display. I wriggled in Howard's grasp and told him that if he didn't let go of me soon I was going to wet myself.

'Then do it,' he said. 'Wet yourself.'

I couldn't even protest, as his hand began to rub my stomach, putting a pressure on my bladder that I was unable to fight. I groaned as I felt the first drops of urine leak out of me to spatter on my shiny new mac. And then the floodgates opened and I was wetting myself without thought of the consequences, feeling the relief as my bladder emptied couple with my mounting sexual excitement. Howard held me as my body shook with the spasms of orgasm and the pee ran in streams down my stocking-clad legs and on to the mac beneath us. By the time I'd finished, there was a large pool of urine on the shiny PVC, and

Howard's erection was threatening to burst the zip of his jeans.

He pushed me down so I was lying in the pool of my own making, and then we had hot, frantic sex on the pee-soaked mac, Howard's cock bigger and harder than I ever remembered it as it thrust up into my wet cunt. The smell of PVC coupled with my urine was almost overpowering, but it simply spurred me on to another bone-jarring orgasm.

That was my initiation into the world of PVC clothing and watersports. Howard and I are still together, and my fetish wardrobe has grown extensively. Sometimes I wear it out of the house, but I prefer it when we stay in and get it all wet and sticky with a mixture of my love juices, Howard's come and our piss.

Karren L.,
Watford

BAD GIRL

The relationship I have with my boyfriend Aiden may seem strange to some people, but to us it's perfectly normal. Basically, I get off on behaving like a naughty girl and putting myself into situations where I have to be punished for it. Aiden can always tell when I'm in the mood for this type of fun because I dress up in a flirty little floral dress and white ankle socks, tie my blonde hair in bunches and act more giggly and silly than usual. It's an act that's guaranteed to annoy the hell out of other people, and I'm sure if they saw us at the end of the evening, me over Aiden's lap with my pants down while he spanks my bare bum, they would think it was nothing more than I deserved.

We've also discovered that wet games turn us on, too. This first started by accident. We were at an all-day rock concert a couple of years ago, and we had managed to get a really good position to see the headline act. However, they were delayed due to some technical problem, and as time went on I was really starting to need the toilet. I was reluctant to go for two reasons. If you have ever been forced to use the portable loos at an event like this, you will know they rapidly become the most disgusting, smelly places on earth, and are to be avoided at all costs if possible. But I also knew that if I left my place at Aiden's side, in this packed crowd it would be impossible to find my way back to him. So I stayed where I was, with the inevitable consequences. My bladder became so full it was painful, and I knew I was losing the struggle to hold on to my pee. In the end, I just couldn't stop myself; I let go a trickle of piss that rapidly became a flood. I was pressed up tight against Aiden and he had his arms around me, and I heard him give a little murmur as he felt the hot liquid seeping through my skirt and wetting his jeans. His reaction changed from disbelief to something very different, as I suddenly became aware of his cock hardening rapidly and pressing into my back through all the layers of clothing. I still can't quite believe what I did next: in that swaying, excited crowd, I dropped to my knees, unzipped Aiden's fly and rapidly sucked him off, breathing in the scent of my own pee where it had soaked his jeans. It was such a dangerous and reckless thing to do, but I was really turned on as I sucked on his hard, pulsing shaft. The situation must have got Aiden pretty excited, too, as it was only moments before his spunk was squirting down my throat. It was so dark that I don't think anyone around us was aware of a thing, as Aiden tucked his cock back into his pants and we turned our attention back to the band on stage, each of us with a massive grin on our faces.

After that night, I started putting myself in situations where I might have no other choice but to piss myself, and when Aiden saw me greedily downing pint after pint of fruit squash, he knew he would be in for some wet fun later in the evening. It always ended with me having my piss-soaked knickers pulled down so I could be given a thorough spanking, and it got both of us in the mood for some hot, sweaty sex.

It was only very recently that other people became aware of the bizarre games we play. It was an unseasonably hot Saturday night in September, and Aiden and I had arranged to go out with a few mates of his for a drink. It was such a nice evening that we travelled out to a country pub we know, Aiden tugging occasionally on my pigtails as he drove and me retaliating by stroking the growing bulge in his trousers.

When we got there, we discovered that Aiden's friends were already sitting at one of the big wooden tables out in the garden. We joined them, and I found myself sitting on Aiden's knee, guzzling orange squash and flirting with all the men there in a way which was guaranteed to get up the noses of their girlfriends.

After an hour or so, with a couple of pints of liquid inside me, I realised I needed to use the loo pretty badly. I could have made my way through the packed pub to the ladies', but Aiden had already realised I was in the mood to play games, so I doubt if he was too surprised when I put my arms round his neck, stuck my tongue in his ear cheekily and then whispered, 'I'm going to pee.'

'Go ahead,' he replied with a smile, and I did. I relaxed my bladder and felt my pee flow out powerfully over his lap, soaking the back of my dress and seeping into the cloth of his trousers.

'That was careless of me, wasn't it?' I giggled, and then stopped, realising that the girl who was sitting next to me, Judy, was staring at us, clearly having noticed that something odd was happening.

'Is everything OK, Patricia?' she asked.

'I'm afraid you've had a little accident, haven't you, love?' Aiden said. I wondered what he was playing at as he urged me to stand up, then rising to his feet so Judy could see the damp patch on his lap.

'Yes, Patricia's been a very bad girl,' he continued. 'It's a shame, because she knows how to behave in public and she just chooses not to. And when you act like that, you deserve everything you get, don't you, love?'

I glanced at him, fearful of the turn the situation was taking and yet excited by it. I knew in that moment that Aiden was intending to smack my bum in front of all his mates. For all my bravado, I did not know whether I could go through with something like that, but Aiden soon made it clear that I had no choice.

He turned round so that he was facing away from the table, giving him room to manoeuvre, then he roughly hauled me over his lap as I squealed and tried to pull out of his strong grip.

'Would anyone object if I gave this little brat a spanking?' he asked, as he put a hand in the small of my back to hold me in place. There was no dissension; I had done quite enough tonight to convince everyone sitting around that pub table that I was spoilt and annoying and worthy of any punishment which came my way. While the others sat and watched, Aiden peeled my damp dress away from my bottom and folded it back on itself. Then he took hold of my virginal white cotton pants and made to pull them down.

'Is that really necessary?' one of the other girls, Tina, asked.

'Oh, yes,' Aiden replied, and I am sure his sentiment was being echoed by all the men sitting around the table, though I was too ashamed to raise my head and check their expressions. Aiden had threatened to smack me in public – just as a joke, I had thought at the time – but now it seemed he was deadly serious.

There was complete silence from everyone as Aiden tugged down my soaking pants to just below the crease where my bottom met my thighs. I knew that the people sitting behind me, Judy and her husband, Jim, would be looking straight at my pale, naked bottom, and that when I started to thrash around on Aiden's knees – as I always did when I was being spanked – that view would widen to include my matted pubic hair and the wet, crimson flesh of my cleft. As that thought began to sink in, I felt Aiden's palm land squarely across my cheeks. I yelped and wriggled, but could not get off my boyfriend's lap.

The first couple of slaps were, in truth, little more than taps. I knew he could – and would – hit me much harder than that. It was the fact I was being spanked in public, my bare bottom exposed to anyone who might pass by our table, that was causing the real pain. I was totally humiliated, and at the same time more turned on than I could ever remember. I was sure that if Judy or Jim looked closely, they would see little drops of love juice glistening on my sex lips.

Aiden spanked me thoroughly, alternating the slaps between my bum cheeks and gradually increasing the severity. Soon it seemed like my entire rear end was on fire, and I was sobbing and pleading with him to stop. But he had no intention of doing that, not when all his friends were so clearly enjoying the spectacle I was presenting. Finally, he seemed to take pity on my blotchy, aching backside and stopped, leaving me to pull my own pants up and wipe the tears from my eyes as though nothing out of the ordinary had happened.

So all Aiden's friends saw me get a very public punishment. What they did not see was what happened when we got home. Aiden fucked me from behind as I stood at the bottom of the bed, hanging on to the bedstead, naked but for my ankle socks. Every thrust of his groin reawakened the throbbing in my bottom, but the orgasm at the end was worth it.

Patricia J.,
Tunbridge Wells

The Eyes have It

THE BIGGER THE BETTER

For as long as I can remember, I have always been turned on by the idea of being fucked by a man with a very big cock. When I met my husband, Mike, he was perfect in every respect – except one. He was kind, intelligent, very good-looking and had a good job as the boss of his own software company, but when I first saw him naked, I had something of a disappointment. Mike's cock was a little over five inches in length, but it was also very thin. Somehow, I had always hoped that the man I married would have the beast I had always longed for.

Despite that, we had a very good sex life. Mike knew exactly what to do with his fingers and tongue to make sure I had as many orgasms as I wanted, but I couldn't quite forget my fantasy of being filled with a good eight inches or more of solid cock flesh.

One night, we started talking about our fantasies, and that was when I admitted to Mike that I wanted to be fucked by a really well-endowed man. To my surprise, he replied that he had guessed he was not satisfying me the way I would have liked, and he was happy for me to go ahead and find a lover who had a much bigger penis than he did – on the grounds that he could be there to watch. I had not expected that, but after thinking it over, I agreed to the arrangement.

For a while, I had been buying a top-shelf magazine that was aimed at women. Although the pictures only showed the male models in their flaccid state, it was obvious that when they were erect they would be very big indeed, and I would often masturbate while fantasising about being fucked by the men in the magazine. There was also a contact section, and a couple of the men there claimed to be much larger than average, so Mike and I went ahead and wrote to them. A week or so later, we had a reply from a man called Gary, who turned out to live only a few miles down the road from us. It seemed like too good an opportunity to pass up, so we arranged to meet him in a pub halfway between our respective towns. If we all liked each other, then we would go back to our house and take things from there.

Gary wasn't at all what I was expecting; I was so used to the handsome studs in the photo sets I wanked over that I was taken aback by the small, skinny guy who met us in the pub. He couldn't have been more than five foot six tall, and he had mousy hair and freckly skin. However, he turned out to be very funny and incredibly good company, and as we relaxed over a couple of drinks, I found myself warming to him more and more. When Mike went to the bar to get another round in, I told Gary that I liked him, but that it was important for me to find out if what he had said in his advert about being bigger than average was true before we took things any further. In reply, he just took my hand and placed it on his crotch. I couldn't believe what I felt: the bulge in his jeans was so big that I could barely cover it with my hand. He smiled, and asked if I needed any more proof. I told him I didn't, and downed my glass of wine in record time.

Gary had travelled in on the train, so Mike and I drove him back to our house. I sat on the back seat with Gary, and while Mike drove, we took the opportunity to get to know each other a little better. Soon we were kissing, our tongues exploring each other's mouth, while Gary caressed my small, firm breasts through my dress. I don't usually bother wearing a bra, and Gary's fingers were soon teasing my nipple to hardness. In return, I reached down and stroked his cock through the fabric of his jeans. Big as it was, it seemed to grow even more as I touched it, straining against his zip. Unable to restrain myself, I undid his fly and reached in to bring out his dick. I could see Mike watching in the rear-view mirror as I got my first view of Gary's cock. It was a beauty: it must have been nearly ten inches long, and so thick my fingers could only just close around it. My pussy was getting damp as I thought how it would feel to have that enormous column of flesh inside me.

By the time the car finally pulled up in our drive, my dress was rucked up round my thighs and Gary was fingering my pussy through the gusset of my G-string, while I was running my hand up and down his erection. I would have quite happily let him fuck me then and there, but Mike ushered us into the house.

We went straight up to the bedroom, and Gary quickly stripped me of my dress. All I wore was my G-string and hold-up stockings, and I stood, rolling my nipples between my fingers and thumbs as I watched Gary undress. Mike, too, was removing his trousers and underpants, but when Gary saw this, he immediately stopped him.

'Oh, no, mate,' he said. 'We agreed that you could watch, not that you could join in. Sit over there.'

Cowed by Gary's sudden dominance, but also excited by it, as the erection tenting out the front of his shirt proved, Mike did as he was told. I watched as Gary used the belt from Mike's trousers and his own to strap my husband's legs to the chair. However, he left Mike's arms free so that he would be able to stroke his cock as he watched.

I got on my knees in front of Gary, and crammed as much of his cock as I could into my mouth. I ran my tongue over the big, purplish head, tasting the drops of pre-come that were already oozing from its little eye.

After a while, I lay back on the bed, and Gary eased my G-string down. Naked as Gary was, the contrast between his small, slight body and huge cock was even more pronounced, and I was growing even wetter in anticipation. Out of the corner of my eye, I could see Mike already wanking himself at the sight of my widely spread legs and open pussy. His erection, though so much smaller than Gary's, seemed longer and harder than I had ever seen it, and I could tell how excited he was at the thought of my fantasy coming true.

Gary mounted me, and positioned his cock at the entrance to my wet channel. For the first time, I began to fear that I might not be able to fit him inside me, but as he pushed forward and the tip of his massive member slipped into my cunt, I knew my fears were unfounded. Tantalisingly slowly, he inched into me, until I was full to the hilt of warm, solid flesh. The thought that I had taken so much cock was enough to have me coming on the spot, my pussy muscles spasming around Gary's girth.

For the next twenty minutes, he fucked me like I'd never been fucked before in my life. I was screaming in pleasure, my legs wrapped around his skinny back as he pumped steadily in and out of me. The sight was too much for Mike, who came within moments of Gary first entering me, his spunk arcing up into the air. When Gary finally climaxed, it was like a geyser gushing inside me, and I came again as I felt him flooding me with his come.

Mike and I are so glad we answered Gary's advert. Next time we see him, Mike is going to be allowed to join in, but only to lick my cunt and Gary's cock clean after my massively endowed lover has fucked me.

Lisa K.,
St Albans

A SIMPLE PLAN

Looking back, I have to say that what I am about to tell you was the most exciting sexual experience of my life, but at the time I thought it was going to be one of the worst.

My boyfriend Eddie and I had gone to a party that was being thrown by a friend of a friend. We turned up just as the pubs were closing, to find no more than half a dozen people there. I didn't know anyone there except Eddie, and I soon found myself very bored as my boyfriend was whisked off by the bloke whose house it was to play some stupid computer game, leaving me to my own devices. I was sitting in the kitchen, nursing a glass of some lethally alcoholic punch, when a really good-looking guy started talking to me. His name was Ivano, and he was of Italian extraction, with short, gelled-back dark hair and the sort of stubble on his chin that suggested he probably had to shave twice a day. Everything about him seemed virile and masculine, and it was obvious that he was blatantly chatting me up. I knew I shouldn't be responding to him, with Eddie zapping aliens in the next room, but he was so charming and sexy, and when he suggested we go into the bedroom where we could talk more privately, I found myself following him.

To be honest, we didn't talk much once we got in the darkened bedroom. Ivano just pushed me down forcefully on to the bed and started kissing my lips with aggressive little nips that rapidly made them sore. I don't usually get off on being treated so roughly, but there was something about the illicitness of the situation and Ivano's lack of finesse that was really making me horny. I knew that we would be fucking very soon, and the thought of Eddie downstairs, oblivious to the situation, was making my juices flow freely with excitement.

I lay back as Ivano pushed my top up to bare my breasts in their black see-through bra. He bit at my nipples through the thin nylon, and I wanted him to pull the cups away so he could bruise my flesh with his sharp white teeth. I could feel the length of his erection pressing against my stomach as he pinned me firmly to the bed with his body, and though it was not particularly big, certainly no bigger than Eddie's, it seemed solid and meaty.

He reached up under my skirt and pulled my knickers down, almost ripping them to shreds in his haste to get them off. Then he pushed my legs apart widely, staring down at my rudely exposed pussy. A fierce pulse was beating between my legs as I waited for the moment when he would penetrate me. He unzipped his trousers and pushed them down around his knees. When he pulled his cock free from his briefs, I gasped. It was so thick I knew it was really going to stretch me as he fed it into me.

He positioned the blunt, circumcised head at the entrance to my sex and pushed home, hard. I cried out as he shoved it up into me, knowing the sound would be muffled by the thumping of music from the sound system in the living room. We were lying on a pile of coats, and I could feel the harsh teeth of a zip fastener digging into my bum as he pushed me along the bed with every thrust. I clung to him desperately, my lubrication beginning to ease the passage of his incredibly fat shaft as my body reacted to the sheer brutality of his fucking. It felt good; no, it felt better than good, and I wondered why Eddie had never thought to take me in this way.

And then the door opened, and Eddie stood silhouetted in the light that spilt in from the hallway. I tried to struggle out of Ivano's embrace, wondering how I could talk my way out of the situation and knowing that there was no way Eddie could have misinterpreted the sight of Ivano's olive-skinned buttocks pumping between my widely parted legs.

I couldn't believe it when he spoke. Instead of the anger and outrage I was expecting, he just said, 'That's it, fuck the little tart till she squeals.'

'Wh-what?' I exclaimed, not quite sure what was happening.

'Don't you know?' Eddie said. 'Ivano's a good mate of mine, we work together. I've always wanted to see you being fucked by someone else, and this seemed as good a time as any. I suggested to him you might be up for some fun tonight, and I was right.'

I stared at him, realising this was all a set-up, but the indignation I felt at being used in this way was being replaced by the hunger in my pussy to reach the climax I had been so close to when Eddie had thrown the door open. Ivano seemed quite happy to carry on where he had left off, and as Eddie stepped into the room and took up a position at the side of the bed where he could see everything that was going on, Ivano began to thrust hard into me again.

'Not like that, mate,' Eddie told his friend, 'I want to see you shafting her from behind. She loves it doggy-fashion.'

This was true, partly because I love the extra depth Eddie can get when he's fucking me in that position, but with Ivano's massive girth I knew I would feel every thrust as I had never felt it before. Ivano urged me on to my hands and knees, and then pulled my skirt off so I was naked from the waist down. I groaned as his cock slid into my gaping pussy, my eyes locking with Eddie's as Ivano really began to slam into me hard and fast.

Eddie had loosed his cock from his flies, and now he spat on his fingers before beginning to shuffle them along the length of his shaft, pumping his own cock in time to Ivano's thrusts.

'Play with your clit,' Eddie urged me, and I reached obediently under myself, my fingers settling on the little bud. The skin of my pussy was stretched almost painfully taut around Ivano's dick, making it even more sensitive as I rubbed frantically at my clitoris. I could tell that Eddie was loving the sight of me frigging myself as I was impaled on his friend's cock, and my fingers gripped hard at the bedcovers as my orgasm washed over me. Within moments, Ivano was coming, too, his seed spurting into my clasping vagina. Eddie sighed, and surrendered to his own climax, his come arcing into the air to splatter across my cheek. I wiped it from my face and licked every drop from my fingers.

Eddie and I left the party about half an hour later, and spent most of the rest of the night fucking as we relived the excitement of what we had just done. I've told him that I will happily let him watch me with another man again, but next time I want to be warned about it beforehand.

Chloe R.,
Newcastle

CAN YOU HANDLE IT?

The most humiliating night of my life – and the most exciting – was the one I watched my husband fuck another woman in front of me. We have played all kinds of sex games during our seven years together, but the ones which turn us on the most are the ones where he takes control and makes me do whatever he wants. So when he got a set of wrist cuffs out one Friday evening, I was not too surprised. I thought we were in for a nice, sexy session of bondage, with Tom forcing me to submit to him while I pretended I did not want to. How wrong I was!

He took me into the living room and ordered me to strip. We have big French windows which lead out into the garden, and I had to stand in front of them as I took my clothes off. It was highly unlikely that anyone in the neighbouring house would see what I was doing, but the thought that they might was a highly exciting one. We have a sturdy old beam running the length of the ceiling, and Tom looped a long piece of chain over a hook in the beam, before joining the chain to the cuffs and cuffing my wrists in place, my hands above my head. I was hardly in the most dignified of positions, but Tom likes to secure me like that because it raises and tautens my large breasts. I was all ready for him to take his belt to my naked bottom when, instead, I had the shock of my life.

The doorbell rang and he went to answer it. I strained my ears and caught the sound of a female voice. I had no idea who might be calling at this time of night, and I began to panic slightly as I heard footsteps coming nearer. Any minute now, someone was going to enter the living room and find me, naked, chained up and completely helpless.

I struggled, but there was no way I could free myself. My eyes widened as the door opened and in stepped Tom with his secretary, Gina. I had met her at his last office Christmas party, and I knew she was very much Tom's type, a petite redhead, but he had never done or said anything to suggest that there was anything going on between them. However, from the way she regarded me as I hung there, without the slightest expression of shock or disgust in her eyes, it was obvious she knew everything about what went on between Tom and me.

'So it is true,' she said, as she walked round me, inspecting my body from every angle. 'She does let you use her.'

'Oh, yes,' Tom replied, 'and so far, she's never objected, whatever I've asked her to do. I make her play with herself or lick my arsehole or wear nipple clamps, and she loves it all. I haven't found her limits yet, but I think I might tonight. You see, Sarah,' he said, finally turning his attention to me, 'Gina's fancied me since she first started working for me, and I have to say the feeling is mutual. But I've never laid a finger on her – until tonight. I want you to watch as I fuck her. I don't think you'll be able to do it without asking me to stop.'

I was sure what he was saying was true, every word of it. Whatever Tom and I had done, we had always been completely faithful to each other, and I did not think I could bear the sight of him touching and caressing Gina's shapely body. It did not seem I was going to have the choice, though, as Tom put his arms round his secretary and began to take her clothes off. Soon, she was down to nothing but a black basque that made the most of her small, round breasts, a tiny pair of matching panties and hold-up stockings. I could barely stifle a pang of envy as my husband freed Gina's tits from the basque and began to roll her big, brown nipples between his fingers and thumbs. I wanted it to be my tits that Tom was caressing, my nipples that he was bending to take between his lips and suckle. I had to admit, however, that I was also starting to get turned on by what he was doing to her, and I found myself willing him to go further. I wanted him to take off her panties and bare her pussy, and I wanted to know how she would react as he played with her wet quim. Would he lick her first, or would he just push her to the floor and fuck her?

Tom glanced over to me for a moment before hooking his thumbs into the waistband of her panties, as if gauging my reaction. I think he was expecting me to look distressed and beg him to stop, but I realised we had engaged in some kind of battle of wills, and I was determined not to give him the satisfaction of seeing me broken by what he was doing. Gina's panties came down slowly, to reveal the flame red bush of hair that crowned her neat little pussy. My own mound is always kept shaven, on Tom's instructions, and I had seen Gina looking at my long, fleshy sex lips as she had scrutinised my naked body.

Tom bent Gina over one of the arms of the settee and spread her legs widely, giving me a good view of her pussy, pouched between her legs, and the dark pucker of her anus. I watched enviously as he began to finger her, causing her to moan extravagantly as his thumb slipped into her arsehole while his fingers stretched her cunt wide. I sensed that he was getting her tight anal passage ready for something much bigger than his thumb, and I shivered at the thought of watching him pleasure her in that dark and deviant way. My own pussy was pulsing, making me aware of how much it wanted to be filled, and I whimpered with longing and envy. Tom has a good eight inches of cock flesh and, unlike a lot of men who are well hung, he knows exactly what to do with it. The prim-looking Gina was in for the fuck of her life, and all I could do was hang in my bonds, a frustrated spectator.

Tom asked Gina to play with her own clit while he stripped off. The fact that I was staring greedily at her busily working fingers did not seem to deter her, and I suspected she was putting a performance on especially on my behalf.

Tom's rigid erection was jutting out proudly from his groin, and he gave it a few rubs to spread its own lubrication along its length. Gina glanced over her shoulder, gasping as she registered just how big Tom's cock was. Like me, she seemed to have realised that it was destined for her anal hole, and for a moment I thought she would be the one to call a halt to what was happening. Instead, she wriggled her rump, as if inviting Tom to enter her.

'Shall I?' Tom asked me abruptly. 'Could you bear the sight of me fucking Gina's tight little arse, Sarah? All you have to do is tell me to stop.'

'No,' I replied in a voice that did not sound like my own. 'I want you to fuck her.'

And then I want you to fuck me, I wanted to add, but knew I could not. All I could do was watch in silence as he pressed his wet, raw-looking knob to the entrance of Gina's anus. She bit her lip, fighting against the pain as he began to ease himself home. I found I was holding my breath, entranced by the erotic spectacle unfolding in front of me.

Once Gina's arse was completely full of my husband's cock flesh, he began to thrust gently. I felt so envious, watching him give her the fucking I craved so badly. And yet it was a beautiful sight; Gina's pert little bottom pushing back at Tom's groin as he increased the tempo. One hand had reached underneath her and she was frigging herself with abandon. Gina was making little mewling noises as she headed towards orgasm, and Tom was grunting and gasping. The room was full of the sounds and scents of sex, and I could smell my own arousal, strong and musky. At last, Gina was coming, throwing her head back as a rosy flush suffused her little tits. The contractions of her anal passage around Tom's cock must have been enough to trigger his orgasm, and he pulled out to send a jet of spunk arcing across Gina's white bum cheeks.

They collapsed together, the sight of Tom's arms around Gina as he whispered endearments in her ear sending another pang of jealousy through me.

Tom unfastened the chain that fastened me to the beam, and I thought my turn had come. However, he simply ordered me to lick his cock clean of the spunk that had dribbled down it, ignoring my pleas to be fucked. I was able to taste traces of Gina on his wilting erection, and wondered what other degradations he might put me through. He took pity on me, however, and decided I had suffered enough. My reward for watching him take Gina up the arse without complaining was to have his pretty secretary kneel between my legs and lap at my pussy with her pointed little tongue until I came.

Since that night, Gina has joined Tom and I for more sex sessions. Tom is encouraging her to take the dominant role with me, and I must say I am beginning to enjoy having a mistress as well as a master.

Sarah T.,
Wrexham

I WATCHED HIM DO IT

When my husband Brian confessed his most secret fantasy to me, I must admit I was shocked. He told me that it was somewhat out of the ordinary, and so I expected him to say he wanted me to dress up in rubber and act as his personal slut, or that he wanted me to tie him up and then use a dildo on him. Instead, he admitted that what turned him on most was the thought of having sex with another man – preferably his best friend, Michael. He went on to say that when the two had been at university together, they had once masturbated in front of each other at the end of a drunken evening, but they had never taken the situation any further. Since that night, he had often fantasised that their hands had been on the other's cock, rather than their own, and those fantasies had progressed to the stage where he imagined fucking Michael.

After thinking about this for a while, I ended up telling him I would be happy to help him set the situation up, but on one proviso. I wanted to watch what happened. Both men are very good-looking – Brian is over six foot tall and blond, with high cheekbones and pale blue eyes, while Michael is slightly shorter and dark-haired, with the physique of an athlete. Just thinking about the two of them naked together and exploring the other's body was enough to turn me on, and though many women would no doubt be worried about letting their partner explore his bisexual side, I knew I could trust my husband implicitly to take all the right precautions.

We invited Michael down to stay for the weekend. He has a very pressurised job on a local newspaper, and he jumped at the chance to take some time away from the office and visit our quiet country town. Brian and I kept quiet about our ulterior motives, but we had planned exactly how the attempted seduction of my husband's best friend was to take place.

Michael was sleeping in our spare room, and on the Saturday afternoon, I made the excuse that I was going into town to shop. What I actually did was park the car a couple of hundred yards from the house, quietly creep back and hide myself in the wardrobe in Michael's room while he and Brian were out in the garden, chatting. Brian brought Michael up to the spare room on the pretext of showing him the view from the window, and I watched through the slightly open wardrobe door as Brian quietly turned the subject of the conversation to sex. They had been sharing a bottle of wine in the garden, and Michael was relaxed enough to let his guard down completely.

'Do you remember that night at Durham when we wanked in front of each other?' Brian asked, his tone a mixture of amusement and nostalgia.

'Yeah,' Michael said. 'I can't believe we did that now. We must have been so drunk.'

'But did you enjoy it?' Brian asked. 'I did. I enjoyed it so much I could happily do it again right now.'

'Are you serious?' Michael said.

'Why not?' My husband was at his most persuasive. 'After all, Jenny won't be back for ages, and I'm really feeling horny.'

For a moment, I thought Michael would reject the offer out of hand, but then he surprised me by saying, 'OK, why not?'

'Why don't we take our clothes off and get really comfortable?' Brian suggested. To emphasise his words, he began pulling his T-shirt out of his jeans, to reveal his chest with its sprinkling of blond hair. Within moments, he had stripped naked and was reclining on the bed, stroking his cock. Michael, much to my joy, followed suit – and I had a very pleasant surprise when he pulled down his boxer shorts. While Brian is not exactly lacking in the penis department, what Michael had hanging between his legs must have been a good five inches long in its flaccid state, and I could only dream about how big it might get once it was erect.

I watched, scarcely daring to breathe as Michael, now naked as well, joined my husband on the bed. There was a bottle of hand cream on the bedside cabinet, and Brian tossed it to Michael, encouraging him to spread some along the length of his shaft to aid him in his masturbation. Their eyes were locked on each other as they began to wank in earnest; Brian rubbing his cock in the pattern of long and slow strokes that had become familiar to me over the years while Michael's movements were more abrupt, helping his cock to harden rapidly.

What happened next will stay with me for the rest of my life. As Michael continued to wank himself, Brian reached out and gently cupped his friend's balls with his free hand. I expected Michael to pull away, or leap off the bed, offended, but he did not. Instead, he reclined back slightly and let Brian continue. When Brian suggested that Michael reciprocate, he seemed only too glad to do so, and soon each was playing with the other's cock and balls. The sight was so exciting that I found my own hand straying down to rub my crotch through my clothing.

As if from a long way away, I suddenly heard Brian saying to Michael, 'I want you to suck me.' I gazed out of the crack in the wardrobe door to see Michael's dark head bending as his lips parted to take my husband's erection in his mouth. I could hear the soft slurping as Michael sucked, and I could only imagine what tricks his tongue might be working on the wet, plum head of Brian's cock. By now, my fingers were inside my panties, slithering in the moisture that was flowing from my cunt. I was loving the spectacle of one man giving the other such a tender blowjob, but I knew that Brian's ultimate aim was to fuck Michael, and I was desperate to see it happen.

Brian pulled his dick out of his friend's mouth and encouraged him to lie face down on the bed. He took more of the hand cream and used it to lubricate Michael's arsehole. I watched the play of expressions on Michael's face as my husband toyed with his anal ring and then slipped a finger inside, and knew in that moment that nothing had ever penetrated this man's arse before.

The moment had come, and Brian took a condom from the bedside table, unwrapped it and slid it down over his straining erection. He straddled his friend, and I had a wonderful view as the tip of his latex-clad cock disappeared into the dark crevice between Michael's bum cheeks. Inch by inch, more of his length slid home, and then they were fucking, Brian's buttocks clenching as he thrust up into Michael's arse. Both men were groaning and gasping in pleasure as the bedsprings creaked like fury beneath their weight. My fingers were a blur as they rubbed my clit, and I bit the fleshy part of my other hand to keep from making a sound as I moved towards orgasm.

Brian's movements had speeded up, and I knew it could only be seconds before he came. Suddenly, he groaned and gave a couple of final hard thrusts. I closed my eyes and surrendered to my own climax, and, when I opened them again, Brian had pulled out of Michael's arse and was wanking his friend off in an effort to help him reach his own orgasm.

When Michael had come, with a guttural cry, he and Brian hugged each other. Afterwards, they showered, though of course I wasn't present to witness the sight of them soaping each other down, much as I would have liked to. By the time they had finished, I was downstairs, pretending I had just come back from my supposed shopping expedition. When I asked them if they had got up to anything in my absence, Michael said, 'Oh, just boys' stuff.' He has no idea that I know everything about what happened that afternoon, and the only way he will find out is if he reads this.

Jenny L.,
Lymington

MEET THE GANG

My wife Maureen once confessed to me that her deepest fantasy was to take part in a gang-bang. She said she was incredibly turned on by the thought of being used by at least four men, but she could not see a way of making this fantasy into reality, as it was hardly the sort of thing we could ask our close friends to join in, and she did not like the idea of using contact magazines.

Then I got a job as the head waiter in a restaurant which had a high turnover of casual staff. As we live in a university town, there are always lots of students looking for part-time work to supplement their grants, and when I mentioned this to Maureen it planted the seeds of an idea in her head. We're both in our late thirties, and the thought of being fucked by a group of fit young men aged about nineteen or twenty really appealed to her, so she asked me to suggest it to the ones I thought most likely to go for it.

I felt a bit stupid trying to recruit other men to have sex with my wife. At first, they thought I was joking, or some kind of inadequate wimp who could not satisfy a woman, but when they realised I was serious, and that I was giving them carte blanche to do whatever they wanted to her, I soon found four who agreed.

So it was that, one Friday night after the restaurant shut, I found myself taking Billy, Rod, Alan and Paul back to our flat, where Maureen was waiting. Maureen had dressed for the part in the most sluttish outfit she possesses. She was wearing a see-through cream blouse over a black uplift bra, a short, tight black miniskirt, stockings, suspenders and stiletto-heeled court shoes. She was wearing a lot more make-up than she normally would, and her blonde hair looked tousled and tangled, as though she had just got out of bed. As she still has a great figure and just oozes sex when she is dressed this way, I could not see any of the lads failing to get turned on by her. She had laid on drinks and nibbles, and as she went round with a tray, introducing herself to everyone, I was gratified to see that Billy, who was rapidly becoming the natural ringleader of the group, was not shy in fondling her bum as she passed.

Once they were all sorted with glasses of beer and something to eat, I slipped a tape into the video recorder to enhance the mood. It was one I had picked up on a trip to Amsterdam, and it is one of Maureen's favourites. It features a woman being fucked by three men at the same time, and in the scene that was playing, she was squatting over a big black guy, sliding up and down on his massively erect cock, while one of his colleagues was energetically shafting her arsehole. Rod and Alan were watching the action on the TV screen open-mouthed, but Billy and Paul seemed to have taken it as a cue to go into action. Paul started kissing Maureen and groping her tits through her clothes, while Billy was running his hands up and down her thighs, pushing her skirt up until her stocking tops were clearly visible. Paul was quickly unbuttoning Maureen's blouse as their tongues battled together, and Billy was gently easing my wife's legs apart. As he did, the other lads and I were treated to the superb sight of Maureen's quim revealed through the split in the pair of black crotchless knickers she was wearing. I had never seen those knickers before, and I suspected she had bought them specifically for this evening.

Once Maureen's blouse was off, Paul turned his attention to her bra, not taking it off but simply pulling her big breasts free from the cups. She looked magnificently cheap sitting there with clothes in disarray and her tits and pussy on display; I could see Rod stroking his cock through his trousers, and my own erection was straining to be let free from my pants. I had not expected to be quite so turned on by the sight of these relative strangers mauling my wife, but now it was happening, I could not stop myself from getting my cock out and wanking as I watched.

Billy had undone Maureen's skirt and encouraged her to wriggle out of it, and now she was sitting on the settee between the two men in nothing but her tarty underwear. Paul was suckling one of her nipples while his fingers twisted the other, and Billy's hand was moving between Maureen's legs. I had turned the volume right down on the video, so instead of the moaning of the actress as she came, we could hear the wet, squelching sound as Billy's fingers explored the juicy folds of my wife's pussy.

'I want you to suck me off, you dirty slut,' Paul told my wife. I had let the lads know that using the crudest of language gets Maureen really horny, and it was obvious from the way she hurried to free his manhood from his trousers that his words were having the desired effect. Erect, Paul's cock was no bigger than my own five and a half inches, but it looked very thick, with a bulbous head that my wife's lips were struggling to wrap themselves around.

Meanwhile, Billy had stripped off completely. He, too, had an average-sized member, which he was bringing to full hardness with a few swift rubs. He urged Maureen on to all fours so that she could keep on sucking Paul while he guided his cockhead through the slit in her knickers into her expectant pussy. It was beautiful to see Maureen taking a cock in both ends at the same time, and so clearly enjoying every minute of it. Her vivid red lipstick was smearing across her face and leaving a ring around Paul's shaft, and with every thrust from Billy, her mouth was being pushed further on to the cock in her mouth, until she was taking all its length, her nose brushing his wiry pubic hair.

Rod and I were openly jacking ourselves off as we watched what was happening in front of us, but Alan had kept his cock firmly in his trousers. 'Come on, don't be shy. Show us what you've got,' I urged him, but as he unzipped his trousers and dropped them and his boxer shorts down to his knees, my words died in my throat. Quite simply, Alan had the biggest cock I had ever seen – it must have been ten inches long, and as thick round as my forearm. The thought of my wife taking something that size inside her made me feel sick with envy, but I could not stop rubbing my own erection as I stared at it.

With a groan, Paul announced that he was coming. Normally, Maureen will not swallow my come, but Paul was holding her firmly by the hair, forcing her to take every drop down her throat. This was the rough treatment my wife had craved, and I could see she was loving it. Billy followed a couple of moments later, his thrusting movements speeding up and his balls slapping against Maureen's arse before he gave a jerk and exploded inside her.

Rod almost shoved Billy out of the way in his haste to take his turn. Billy simply moved round to Maureen's head and presented his wilting cock to her mouth, ordering her to suck it clean. She licked the mixture of his spunk and her pussy juice off his shaft with obvious relish, as Rod slipped six rigid inches of cock flesh inside her. I carried on wanking as I watched Rod fuck Maureen without any finesse at all. His hands were gripping her hips and he was banging into her ferociously. By now, I was very close to coming, and I went to stand in front of my wife, who was thrusting hard back on to Rod's cock, her eyes closed in ecstasy. My come arced out of my love-eye, the first jet landing in Maureen's hair and the second and third splattering on her cheek and lips, making her look like the sex-hungry slut she was tonight.

Rod groaned and came, and I waited for Alan to take his place, but Billy had other ideas. He was already hard again, and he ordered Maureen to take his cock between her tits. She knelt up obediently and removed her bra, pushing her breasts together around Billy's cock. As it slid back and forth in her cleavage, I positioned myself underneath her so I could lap at her freshly fucked pussy. I had never tasted another man's spunk before, but I licked it from Maureen's cunt without complaint.

Billy lasted longer this time, but at last I heard him give a groan as his spunk oozed out on to my wife's tits.

'While you're down there, mate,' I heard him say, as I continued to tongue Maureen's pussy, 'lick her arsehole, too. We're going to have her in every hole before we leave.'

His words caused my cock, which had been slowly growing as I licked my wife out, to spring back to full hardness. And when Billy dragged Alan over by the arm, I realised just whose cock would be going up my wife's forbidden passage.

'He's never done a woman up the arse before,' Billy announced, 'but he's going to love it, aren't you, mate?'

As he urged Alan to lie on the floor, Maureen got a look at the lad's dick for the first time, and her eyes widened in fear and amazement. I, too, was unsure how she would get something that size into her tight anal hole, but Rod had spotted the pat of butter which Maureen had placed on the table to accompany the crackers and cheese she had been serving. Alan smothered his shaft with some of the butter, while Paul spread the rest around and into my wife's anus. Egged on by his mates, he slipped a finger inside her, then a second.

'See if you can get your fist inside her,' Billy suggested. 'That'll get her used to Alan's donkey dick.'

There was complete silence in the room; it seemed like we were all holding our breath as Paul slowly worked a third finger into Maureen's arse. She seemed to be in some discomfort at first, but as she grew used to the penetration she began to relax, and soon he was able to push a fourth finger into her. I was eager to see his whole fist disappear into her hole, but Alan had overcome any nerves he had been feeling, and was now eager to fuck my wife's arse.

Almost reverentially, Rod and Billy helped position Maureen over Alan's skyward-pointing erection, and slowly lowered her till she was impaled on the tip of his cock. Then they let go, and allowed gravity to pull her down until her anal passage was packed with hot, solid flesh. She was still wearing the slutty crotchless knickers and her stockings, which were by now laddered, and the streaks of dried come on her tits and face added to her well-fucked, used appearance. I have never been so turned on as I was watching her shift herself up and down on Alan's member. The other lads were wanking themselves furiously, and one by one they came, decorating her sweating body with strings of spunk. Finally, Alan announced that he, too, was coming, and Maureen screamed with pleasure as his cock shot its load inside her.

Again, I had the task of licking her clean, spunk running out of her widely stretched arsehole and into my mouth. It was the perfect finish to a perfect evening, and one that Maureen is as eager to repeat as I am.

Eric T.,
Birmingham

TAKE MY WIFE

When I met Stan, I thought he was so different from the other men I had been out with. He was kind and attentive and he paid me lots of compliments. It was only after we got married that I realised he was actually a bit of a wimp. His big problem was that he would never stand up for himself, no matter how badly he was being treated.

Our next-door neighbour, Del, was soon quick to realise how he could take advantage of Stan. He was living on his own following a divorce and was hardly the most pleasant man we had ever met, always playing his stereo too loud and letting his big Rottweiler dog foul the pavement outside our house. The worst part was he was always borrowing things from us, which he would never return, and Stan would never go round to ask for them back, no matter how much I pressed him on the subject. At first, it was just little things, like the lawn mower and a couple of sun loungers, which was annoying, particularly as the grass in the back garden grew longer and longer. Stan just said that he hated gardening and let it go, but then one night Del came knocking at our door with the strangest request of all.

Stan went to answer the door, as I had just got out of the bath. I stood at the top of the stairs, listening to the conversation, and could not believe what I heard.

'My TV has broken down,' Del said, and I thought he was going to follow this statement up with a request to borrow our colour portable, which I knew we would never see again. Instead, he said, 'But there's nothing on tonight I wanted to watch, so I thought I'd make my own entertainment. I wondered if I could borrow your wife to keep me company.'

I expected Stan to shut the door in Del's face, like any sensible man would have done. But my spineless husband merely said, 'I'm sure she'd love to come round and spend some time with you. I'll just see where she's got to. Louise, where are you?'

Now, he knew damn well I had been having a bath, but I came to the top of the stairs, clutching a towel around me and with another one wrapped round my wet hair, as though I had not heard a word of what had been said.

'I'm here, Stan . . . Oh, hello, Del,' I said sweetly.

'Del came round to see if you wanted to pop round for the evening. His telly's broken.' Stan seemed to be treating this as though it was a perfectly reasonable request, and I did not need to feign my astonishment.

'But, Stan, I've just got out of the bath and I was going to get an early night,' I said, desperate for my husband to stand up to our odious neighbour.

'But Del *is* our neighbour,' Stan replied. 'Maybe you should for a while.'

We should show him the door, I thought, but I knew Stan was going to accede to Del's ridiculous request, so I just said, 'I'll go and put some clothes on.'

'Oh, don't worry about that,' Del chipped in. 'You're perfect just as you are.'

I looked to Stan for some support, but he merely grinned and said, 'Off you go, and don't be too late back.'

What could I do? I patted as much water out of my hair as I could with the towel, and then I came downstairs. I slipped on a pair of shoes, glaring mutinously at Stan, who was merely shifting nervously from foot to foot, as he often did in Del's presence.

'Come with me,' Del said, ushering me out of the house, and I scurried after him, not wanting anyone to see me as I followed him next door.

Once we were inside his front door, I glared at him. 'What do you think you're playing at?' I said.

'I just wanted to spend some time with you,' he said. 'It's a while since I had a woman around the place.'

That much was obvious: the living room was a mess, with an overflowing ashtray on the coffee table, clothes flung over the back of the settee and dirty plates on the floor. The place smelt of dog and burnt food, and I immediately wanted to be anywhere other than where I was now.

Del went and sat on the settee. 'Come and sit down, Louise. I'm not going to hurt you,' he said.

There was nothing else I could do, so I went and sat next to him. Physically, Del is everything Stan isn't. He is over six foot tall, with big muscles from doing a labouring job, and has a thick head of dark hair where my husband's is fair and starting to recede. I could not help but be conscious of his masculinity; he had said he wanted to make his own entertainment and I shivered as I wondered what his idea of entertainment might be.

I did not have long to find out. Del poured us both a glass of whisky, and we sat side by side sipping it for a while. Then he put his hand on my thigh, on the bare skin just below the edge of the towel.

'Don't you think it's getting a little warm in here?' he said.

I shook my head. 'I'm fine.'

'Well, I say it's too warm, and you'd be so much cooler if you took that towel off.' His tone of voice made it clear that this was an order rather than a request. I thought of Stan sitting at home in ignorance, and though I will admit I was more than a little frightened of Del, it had been such a long time since Stan had even thought of asking me to strip for him that the thought of displaying myself was strangely exciting. My fingers fumbled with the knot I had tied in the towel, and I let it fall free, baring my body to Del's gaze.

I have always been a little self-conscious that my breasts are not as big as some men like, but Del was staring at them with undisguised approval. 'Very pretty,' he said. 'They should just fit in my hands nicely. But I'm more interested in seeing what's between your legs. Spread them for me.'

I swallowed hard, feeling a pulse begin to beat in my pussy. I heard the dog barking in the kitchen, and wondered if Stan had had second thoughts about leaving me alone with Del and come round to collect me. But the doorbell did not ring and Del was gazing at me expectantly. I took a deep breath and eased my legs apart a little way.

'More than that. I want to see everything,' Del said. Slowly, I pulled my feet up on to the seat of the settee and let my knees fall apart. I knew he would be able to see every detail of my hair-fringed pussy lips and the slick, pink flesh beneath them, and I glanced at the crotch of his trousers, where a solid-looking bulge was beginning to reveal itself. Something about the fact that I was displaying myself so rudely to a man I did not even like was turning me on, and I was aware that my sex was starting to swell and grow moist.

'Lovely,' Del said, with real admiration in his voice. 'Now touch yourself. I want to see you frigging that sweet little pussy of yours.'

Too dazed to disobey, I let my hand slip down between my legs and rest on my mound. My fingers teased the petals of my sex apart, searching for my clitoris. When my index finger landed on it and began to rub, Del gave a groan of satisfaction.

'If only that wimp of a husband of yours could see you now,' he murmured, 'playing with yourself because another man's told you to.'

'I don't care,' I replied, my fingers never stilling in their busy movements. 'Stan doesn't like me to do this. He thinks his cock is enough for me, but it isn't.' I don't know why I was telling Del this, but it was true: not only did Stan have a penis which was barely five inches long when erect, he also had no idea how to use it. A few swift humps in and out of my cunt and he was usually done. I had put up with it for a long time, but I could not pretend that it truly satisfied me.

'Well, I like to watch you diddling yourself,' Del said. 'I'd like it more if you'd got three fingers up your cunt and the fingers of your other hand up your arsehole, though.'

I groaned at his words. My anal rosebud was strictly off-limits as far as Stan and I were concerned, and here was my boorish neighbour telling me he wanted to see me frigging it. I slipped a finger into my pussy; my muscles clamped greedily around it, welcoming the intrusion, and I knew I was wet and ready enough to take more. As Del continued to watch me, by now openly rubbing his crotch through his trousers, I eased a second and then a third finger into myself, stretching the walls of my channel wider than Stan's stubby little penis ever did.

'Your arse. Finger your arse,' Del grunted, and I shook my head. 'Do it, or it'll be my cock that goes up there, dry.'

The threat was enough. My juices were trickling down the length of my crease, and I scooped some up with my finger, using it to circle the rim of my forbidden entrance. I can't deny that it felt good, the sheer filthiness of what I was doing adding to my excitement, and when that finger breached the tight ring of muscle it encountered only a brief resistance before slipping fully into my arse. Now I was wanking myself like a woman possessed, thrusting in and out of both holes simultaneously, my bum bouncing on the cushions of the settee as I panted and moaned.

I had completely forgotten that Del was watching me, and it was only when he grabbed hold of the hand that was fingering my pussy that I was pulled back to awareness. He had pulled off his jeans and underpants, and his cock was standing up stiffly beneath the hem of his grubby T-shirt. He used his strength to flip me over, so that I was kneeling up. Though it was much bigger than my husband's, it slipped into my juiced-up cunt without difficulty, and I hung on to the back of the settee like grim death as he began to pound into me hard and fast, his big balls slapping against my bum cheeks. The springs of the settee were creaking and complaining, setting up an answering howl from Del's dog in the kitchen, and with the desperate wailing noises I was making as I moved closer to climax I felt sure that Stan would hear us and come round to investigate. But he didn't, and the next thing I felt was Del tensing behind me as he prepared to shoot his come into me. I increased my grip on the settee as my cunt was flooded with his hot spunk, my own orgasm following rapidly behind his. Then he pulled out of me and wiped his cock on the towel I had been wearing before using it to dab the traces of our fucking from my pussy. The rough touch of the towelling on my sensitised clit was enough to make me come again, and I could hear Del laughing as he watched my body bucking desperately.

'Well, that was better than the telly,' he said with a nasty chuckle. 'Now go home and tell your husband I'll probably want to borrow you again tomorrow night.'

What I actually told Stan was every detail of what happened, just as I have told it to you. And, to my surprise, Stan lay in bed wanking himself off as he listened to my story. It turns out that he has always got off on the thought of me being fucked by another man, and he has told me that Del can borrow me any time he likes, on two conditions: firstly, I tell Stan everything that happens and secondly, I let Stan fuck my arse. As I type this, I am waiting for Del to ring on the doorbell. I will let you know what happens.

Louise M.,
Derby

NEXUS NEW BOOKS

To be published in April 2005

CONCEIT AND CONSEQUENCE
Aishling Morgan

Conceit and Consequence follows Lucy Truscott and her three female cousins through a series of romantic entanglements – some more bizarre than others – with spankings and other assorted humiliations inflicted on the girls by the bossy Lucy on the way. Smuggling, swashbuckling and sodomy mix in a plot that's tighter than Mr D'Arcy's breaches.

£6.99 0 352 33965 9

NO PAIN, NO GAIN
James Barron

No Pain, No Gain is a collection of short stories united around their narrator's search for satisfaction through sexual submission. The pseudonymous author, a film-industry insider, has spent his own life questing after strong and beautiful women who will dominate him - sometimes for money, but mostly for love. Inspired by the results of his search, *No Pain, No Gain* turns the usual male memoir of sexual conquests upside-down and inside-out.

£6.99 0 352 33966 7

PLAYTHING

Penny Birch

This classic book in the Penny Birch series features bad girl Penny's dirtiest antics yet. After going a whole month without doing anything naughty, she is desperate to be even more filthy, despite her imminent departure to Brittany where she is instructed to set up a university field course. Once there, her academic responsibilities get pushed aside for more delieiously rude indulgences. This time, however, she will encounter a French voyeur called Tom, whose penchant for dirty fun will shock even Penny and her playmates.

£6.99 0 352 33967 5

If you would like more information about Nexus titles, please visit our website at www.nexus-books.co.uk, or send a stamped addressed envelope to:

Nexus, Thames Wharf Studios,
Rainville Road, London W6 9HA

NEXUS BACKLIST

This information is correct at time of printing. For up-to-date information, please visit our website at www.nexus-books.co.uk

All books are priced at £6.99 unless another price is given.

THE ACADEMY	Arabella Knight 0 352 33806 7	□
ANGEL £5.99	Lindsay Gordon 0 352 33590 4	□
THE ANIMAL HOUSE	Cat Scarlett 0 352 33877 6	□
THE ART OF CORRECTION	Tara Black 0 352 33895 4	□
AT THE END OF HER TETHER	G. C. Scott 0 352 33857 1	□
BAD PENNY £5.99	Penny Birch 0 352 33661 7	□
BARE BEHIND	Penny Birch 0 352 33721 4	□
BELLE SUBMISSION	Yolanda Celbridge 0 352 33728 1	□
BENCH-MARKS	Tara Black 0 352 33797 4	□
BROUGHT TO HEEL £5.99	Arabella Knight 0 352 33508 4	□
CAGED! £5.99	Yolanda Celbridge 0 352 33650 1	□
CHERRI CHASTISED	Yolanda Celbridge 0 352 33707 9	□
COMPANY OF SLAVES	Christina Shelly 0 352 33887 3	□
CONFESSIONS OF AN ENGLISH SLAVE	Yolanda Celbridge 0 352 33861 X	□
CORPORATION OF CANES	Lindsay Gordon 0 352 33745 1	□

CRUEL SHADOW	Aishling Morgan 0 352 33886 5	☐
DANCE OF SUBMISSION £5.99	Lisette Ashton 0 352 33450 9	☐
DEMONIC CONGRESS	Aishling Morgan 0 352 33762 1	☐
DISCIPLINE OF THE PRIVATE HOUSE	Esme Ombreux 0 352 33709 5	☐
DISCIPLINED SKIN £5.99	Wendy Swanscombe 0 352 33541 6	☐
DISPLAYS OF EXPERIENCE £5.99	Lucy Golden 0 352 33505 X	☐
AN EDUCATION IN THE PRIVATE HOUSE £5.99	Esme Ombreux 0 352 33525 4	☐
EMMA ENSLAVED	Hilary James 0 352 33883 0	☐
EROTICON 1 £5.99	Various 0 352 33593 9	☐
EMMA'S HUMILIATION	Hilary James 0 352 33910 1	☐
EMMA'S SECRET DIARIES	Hilary James 0 352 33888 1	☐
EMMA'S SECRET WORLD	Hilary James 0 352 33879 2	☐
EMMA'S SUBMISSION	Hilary James 0 352 33906 3	☐
THE GOVERNESS ABROAD	Yolanda Celbridge 0 352 33735 4	☐
GROOMING LUCY £5.99	Yvonne Marshall 0 352 33529 7	☐
HOT PURSUIT	Lisette Ashton 0 352 32878 4	☐
IMPERIAL LACE	Aishling Morgan 0 352 33856 3	☐
IN FOR A PENNY £5.99	Penny Birch 0 352 33449 5	☐
THE INDIGNITIES OF ISABELLE	Penny Birch writing as Cruella 0 352 33696 X	☐

INNOCENT	Aishling Morgan 0 352 33699 4	□
THE INSTITUTE	Maria del Rey 0 352 33??? ?	□
JULIA C	Laura Bowen 0 352 33852 0	□
NON-FICTION: LESBIAN SEX SECRETS FOR MEN	Jamie Goddard and Kurt Brungard 0 352 33724 9	□
LESSONS IN OBEDIENCE	Lucy Golden 0 352 33892 X	□
LETTERS TO CHLOE £5.99	Stephan Gerrard 0 352 33632 3	□
LOVE-CHATTEL OF TORMUNIL	Aran Ashe 0 352 33779 6	□
THE MASTER OF CASTLELEIGH £5.99	Jacqueline Bellevois 0 352 33644 7	□
MISS RATTAN'S LESSON	Yolanda Celbridge 0 352 33791 5	□
NEW EROTICA 6	Various 0 352 33751 6	□
NURSES ENSLAVED £5.99	Yolanda Celbridge 0 352 33601 3	□
NURSE'S ORDERS	Penny Birch 0 352 33739 7	□
THE OBEDIENT ALICE	Adriana Arden 0 352 33826 1	□
ONE WEEK IN THE PRIVATE HOUSE	Esme Ombreux 0 352 33706 0	□
ORIGINAL SINS	Lisette Ashton 0 352 33804 0	□
THE PALACE OF PLEASURES	Christobel Coleridge 0 352 33801 6	□
PALE PLEASURES	Wendy Swanscombe 0 352 33702 8	□
PARADISE BAY £5.99	Maria del Rey 0 352 33645 5	□
PEACH	Penny Birch 0 352 33790 7	□

PEACHES AND CREAM	Aishling Morgan 0 352 33672 2	☐
PENNY IN HARNESS £5.99	Penny Birch 0 352 33651 X	☐
PENNY PIECES £5.99	Penny Birch 0 352 33631 5	☐
PET TRAINING IN THE PRIVATE HOUSE £5.99	Esme Ombreux 0 352 33655 2	☐
THE PLAYER	Cat Scarlett 0 352 33894 6	☐
THE PLEASURE PRINCIPLE	Maria del Rey 0 352 33482 7	☐
PRINCESS	Aishling Morgan 0 352 33871 7	☐
PRIVATE MEMOIRS OF A KENTISH HEADMISTRESS	Yolanda Celbridge 0 352 33763 X	☐
PRIZE OF PAIN	Wendy Swanscombe 0 352 33890 3	☐
THE PRIESTESS	Jacqueline Bellevois 0 352 33905 5	☐
THE PUNISHMENT CLUB	Jacqueline Masterson 0 352 33862 8	☐
PURITY £5.99	Aishling Morgan 0 352 33510 6	☐
REGIME	Penny Birch 0 352 33666 8	☐
SATAN'S SLUT	Penny Birch 0 352 33720 6	☐
THE SCHOOLING OF STELLA	Yolanda Celbridge 0 352 33803 2	☐
SEE-THROUGH £5.99	Lindsay Gordon 0 352 33656 0	☐
SERVING TIME	Sarah Veitch 0 352 33509 2	☐
SILKEN SLAVERY	Christina Shelley 0 352 33708 7	☐
SLAVE ACTS	Jennifer Jane Pope 0 352 33665 X	☐
SLAVE GENESIS £5.99	Jennifer Jane Pope 0 352 33503 3	☐

SLAVE-MINES OF TORMUNIL	Aran Ashe 0 352 33695 1	☐
SLAVE REVELATIONS £5.99	Jennifer Jane Pope 0 352 33627 7	☐
THE SMARTING OF SELINA	Yolanda Celbridge 0 352 33872 5	☐
SOLDIER GIRLS £5.99	Yolanda Celbridge 0 352 33586 6	☐
STRAPPING SUZETTE £5.99	Yolanda Celbridge 0 352 33783 4	☐
STRIPING KAYLA	Yvonne Marshall 0 352 33881 4	☐
THE SUBMISSION GALLERY £5.99	Lindsay Gordon 0 352 33370 7	☐
THE SUBMISSION OF STELLA	Yolanda Celbridge 0 352 33854 7	☐
THE TAMING OF TRUDI	Yolanda Celbridge 0 352 33673 0	☐
TEASING CHARLOTTE	Yvonne Marshall 0 352 33681 1	☐
TEMPER TANTRUMS £5.99	Penny Birch 0 352 33647 1	☐
TICKLE TORTURE	Penny Birch 0 352 33904 7	☐
THE TRAINING GROUNDS	Sarah Veitch 0 352 33526 2	☐
THE TRAINING OF AN ENGLISH GENTLEMAN	Yolanda Celbridge 0 352 33858 X	☐
UNIFORM DOLL	Penny Birch 0 352 33698 6	☐
VELVET SKIN £5.99	Aishling Morgan 0 352 33660 9	☐
WENCHES, WITCHES AND STRUMPETS	Aishling Morgan 0 352 33733 8	☐
WHEN SHE WAS BAD	Penny Birch 0 352 33859 8	☐
WHIP HAND	G. C. Scott 0 352 33694 3	☐
WHIPPING GIRL	Aishling Morgan 0 352 33789 3	☐

- - - - - - ✂ -

Please send me the books I have ticked above.

Name ....

Address ....

....

....

.... Post code ....

Send to: **Virgin Books Cash Sales, Thames Wharf Studios, Rainville Road, London W6 9HA**

US customers: for prices and details of how to order books for delivery by mail, call 1-800-343-4499.

Please enclose a cheque or postal order, made payable to **Nexus Books Ltd**, to the value of the books you have ordered plus postage and packing costs as follows:

UK and BFPO – £1.00 for the first book, 50p for each subsequent book.

Overseas (including Republic of Ireland) – £2.00 for the first book, £1.00 for each subsequent book.

If you would prefer to pay by VISA, ACCESS/MASTERCARD, AMEX, DINERS CLUB or SWITCH, please write your card number and expiry date here:

....

Please allow up to 28 days for delivery.

Signature ....

Our privacy policy

We will not disclose information you supply us to any other parties. We will not disclose any information which identifies you personally to any person without your express consent.

From time to time we may send out information about Nexus books and special offers. Please tick here if you do *not* wish to receive Nexus information. □

- - - - - - ✂ -